Adelais Selwyn

Adelais Selwyn

Lulu

This is a work of fiction. Names, characters, businesses, places, events and incidents are either the products of the author's imagination or used in a fictitious manner. Any resemblance to actual persons, living or dead, or actual events is purely coincidental.

First published 2014

www.eadric.co.uk

ISBN 978-1-291-73159-0

Contents

Preface 9

1. 1010, Leaving 11
2. 1010, Fate 17
3. 2010, School Sucks 21
4. 2010, Night Terrors 27
5. 2010, Science Shock 29
6. 2010, Red Report 35
7. 2010, Birthday Drinks 39
8. 1010, Cursed 45
9. 2010, Date Night 49
10. 1010, Brom 53
11. 1011, Burh Burns 57
12. 2010, The End 63
13. 1011, First Flight 67
14. 2010, Alone 71
15. 2010, Despair 75
16. 1011, Family 77
17. 2010, Visitor 81
18. 1011, Travelling 83
19. 2010, Truth 89
20. 2010, Test 95
21. 2010, Results 99
22. 1012, Trojan 103
23. 2010 A Fellow Beast 109

24. 1012, Trouble Ahead 113
25. 2010, St Michaels 121
26. 1012, The Monk 127
27. 2010, Hunting 135
28. 1012, Base Camp 139
29. 2010, Training Begins 145
30. 1012, The List 151
31. 1012, Borin and Fendrel 157
32. 2010, Smug 163
33. 1012, Althalos of Carhampton 167
34. 2010, Complicated 171
35. 1012, The Royal Court 175
36. 1012, The Tale of Sadon 181
37. 2010, My True Nature 185
38. 1013, Portland 189
39. 2010, Fatal Flight 195
40. 1013, Separate Ways 197
41. 1013, Canterbury 201
42. 2010, Lost 207
43. 1013, Surprise Guest 213
44. 1013, Broms Trip 217
45. 1013, The Reveal 221
46. 2010, Decision 229
47. 1013, Winter Training 231

48. 1013, Plans 233
49. 1013, The Vikings are Coming 239
50. 2010, Family History 245
51. 1013, Final Battle 249
52. 2010, Knowledge 255
53. 1013, They're Here 259
54. 2010, Crossing the Line 265
55. 1013, Tilsted 277
56. 1013, No Rest for the Wicked 285
57. 2010, Eadric 289
58. 1030, Descendant 291

The Monks List

1. Alric (the afraid) – *The Royal Court / Corfe Castle*
2. Tybalt – *The Burh of Wareham*
3. Ulric – *The Burh of Wareham*
4. Forthwind – *The Burh of Wareham*
5. Sadon – *Swanage*
6. Terrowin – *Portland*
7. Eadric – *The Burh of Shaftesbury*
8. Brom – *The Burh of Shaftesbury*
9. Rowan – *The Burh of Shaftesbury*
10. Borin – *Exeter*
11. Fendrel – *Exeter*
12. Althalos – *Carhampton*
13. Hadrian – *Gloucester*
14. John – *Worcester*
15. Henry – *Chester*
16. Frederick – *Canterbury*
17. Walter – *Canterbury*
18. Leofrick – *Chertsey*
19. Lief – *Selsey*
20. Barda – *Selsey*
21. Thomas – *St Michaels*

1. Wareham
2. Swanage
3. Portland
4. Shaftesbury
5. Exeter
6. Carhampton
7. Gloucester
8. Worcester
9. Chester
10. Canterbury
11. Chertsey
12. Selsey
13. St Michaels
Scotland
Ireland
Irish Sea
Danelaw
Wales
Wessex
English Channel
9
8
7
6
4
11
5
3
1
2
12
10
13

www.eadric.co.uk

Eadric
2010

I don't recall what happened that first night. When I came around the sky above me appeared darker than it had done before as if the light of each star that had previously shone so vividly had been snuffed out in an instant, gone. A sinister chill tore through the air unusual for the season and an unnatural silence hung like fog; a dense, suffocating lack of sound that caused my mind to scream, filling the void it created. The world had changed. It had been torn and twisted, shattered beyond repair. I knew it without question for I could feel it within every inch of my being although at the time I knew not what the change had been.

She lay on the ground some distance away. As my mind registered my surroundings I became aware of her presence and I knew at once, even from this distance, that she was dead. The wound in her chest made me gag, choking on the sick sensation as bile rose from the pit of my stomach. I had never seen so much blood; it flowed out around her body, running out as if searching for a new host having abandoned its previous occupant. My eyes flicked from one part of her body to another and I was dimly aware that a small part of my brain was cataloguing every detail, the mud matted into her long blonde hair, the position of her body, twisted and torn, the broken rib visible through the wound, the blood stained trainer no longer attached to her foot. As the images overloaded my senses I felt my knees hit the hard ground below me although I did not register any pain. My mind spun trying to piece together the events leading up to this, trying in vain to make sense of the scene but I just came up blank, no answer was forthcoming as to what had happened here.

The sound of sirens wailed out in the distance, drawing closer with every moment. The remains of my car were visible to my right but it was going nowhere, torn apart as if it had been made of paper. Panic gripped me; a primal desire to flee rose inside. I looked once again to the body of the girl I had known and cared for, my body convulsed violently in response, repulsed by the scene. The horror of it all crashed in waves against my consciousness, each wave bringing a new bout of nausea to the pit of my stomach.

Growing up I had always known I was different. I had always felt different. Constantly I'd questioned myself; my life, my motives and my desires. I'd searched for answers to feelings that had not yet formulated into questions and had known not the questions to the answers I believed I had already gleamed. I did not know where it was that I'd fitted in, only that this life, the day to day ordinary life that I'd lived was not it. This life was merely a façade; a mask that had hidden what I'd known was inside buried deep within my soul. I could feel it, the truth of what I am. Every minute of every day it had been a constant reminder that my days beneath the mask were numbered. I don't know what I had thought of it as back then, before, but I'd never expected what came next.

1
1010
Leaving

If I had known then the fate that awaited me and my fellow men, I would never have left my wife, my son and the home that we had built together.

In those days men dreamt of undertaking epic quests, risking life and limb for great wealth, glory, or the most sought after prize of all, the secret to eternal life, the fountain of youth, immortality. I'd never dreamt of riches or wanted bard's to write tales of my valour, but fate had a different idea. In my time I have faced death head on and won, seen more years than any man deserves and have died more than once. I too now search for the secret of life, but my search is not with the intention to prolong. I wish to end it.

The England of 1010 was raw, dangerous. Famine and death were mans daily companion as they worked long, gruelling days in the field to hold starvation at bay for themselves and their families. It was a time of Gods and Demons. Heaven and Hell. Life and Death.

My name is Eadric; and this is my tale.

1010 was a time of great historical change in England but the workers in the fields would have seen little of this. I had been a farmer in our small community, as were most people at the time. The burh in which I grew up was little more than a collection of huts in which we worked, lived and on the rare occasion played. The community consisted of a few families that had resided within this burh for generations; they were both our closest friends and our family. We had among us little by the way of home comforts and the village as a whole had contained only the basics that were needed for survival. The main attraction that I recall had been a large water mill that had modernised our daily lives, fed by the steady current from a passing stream the mill had allowed us to effectively grind grain for bread. The days had been spent tending the fields, the evenings prepping and storing food to ensure we had enough to see ourselves and the live-stock through the rapidly approaching winter. The horses had been a fundamental part of life for us, used to plough the fields in preparation for the next crop, collect the harvest and pull the carts to bring supplies from neighbouring villages. I still look fondly on the work I had done with our horses in those days, it was satisfying, honest work.

At the time the lord of Wessex, Alric the Afraid, had recently become King of England after the tragic and somewhat suspicious death of his brother Osric. The country was under constant threat from the Norsemen and the Danes, who ravaged the land, demanding or stealing silver from every village in their path. In the year 1005 a famine had swept across England after a spell of horrific weather had devastated crops across the land. For many years we had lived in fear of Gods wrath as the ever real threat of starvation loomed in the back of our minds.

These were dark days for many, but for me they were the happiest of my very long life.

I had married my wife Jolecia many years earlier, at the age of fifteen. This may seem odd to the modern world but life in those days was short, boys became men far younger and were expected to pull their weight from the moment they could walk. Jolecia and I had grown up in the same village, this was the way of life back then, she had been my ray of sunshine during what were otherwise very dark times. Jolecia would prepare the food, tend the stores and take care of me when I returned from the hard days labour, working the fields. She also gave me the greatest gift a man could ask, a son and heir.

The day Arthur, my son, had been born was both the happiest and the saddest day of my life, at least one of the saddest. I was eighteen by this time and the day had been an incredible affair, the feeling of holding my son in my arms for the first time made me happier than I had ever known. A warm glow filled my being; I couldn't believe the Gods had gifted me with such a beautiful boy. However, that night after I had prayed to the Gods for the birth of my son and a safe harvest I thought, really thought, probably for the first time in my life, of the future. More accurately I thought of the future that my child would face. Famine had devastated the land, men had turned to monsters through desperation and fear and the thought of bringing a child into this world caused a deep sorrow to flood my heart and soul. A grief like nothing I had ever felt before hit me like a stampeding bull. The weight of the world strained heavily across my shoulders as I dropped to the floor from the burden. That night I made a promise to my son as I held him in my arms. I pledged that I would fight to the ends of the Earth for him, that no harm would befall him and that I'd take on the Gods themselves to keep him safe. This was to be a promise I couldn't keep.

Later that month whilst tending to the crops, news spread to the village. A passing traveller stopped for supplies on his way to London, travelling ahead of the King himself. The traveller spoke of a band of warriors that marched east, advancing into London to meet our Viking foe on the banks of the river Thames. The King himself was riding at the forefront of the army, recruiting men as they passed. The traveller requested that our town's folk join the troop, suggesting that we should march forward with the King to fight for our country and defend the right for our families to live on English soil. The English had lived in fear of these Viking savages for longer than we cared to remember and many of the men were keen to fight back; but the country at the time had been suspicious of the new King. He was not held in high regard and people were not keen to follow him into battle. I sat within our humble little cabin that evening watching my newborn son sleep, the promise I had made rang clear in my mind and I knew then what it was that I had to do.
A little under a week later the King's troop arrived. A gathering of a few hundred men and boys had marched by our Burh, the King himself entering, with a few of his strongest fighters, intending to rally more troops. He gave an inspiring speech of heroic deeds, of fighting for King and country, but we'd known they were just words and very few of the men were willing to follow. We had seen the troops that had already been recruited as they'd passed by and they

were not much to behold; Children mostly, kids with sticks that believed in tales of heroism and dreamed of killing Viking savages.

The King had stood before us waiting for men to step forward. I looked to my wife who held my son in her arms and Jolecia had looked into my eyes, a look I will never forget, pleading me to stay. I remember her grabbing my arm as I took the first step forward and I remember the words she spoke as I took the second step.

"How can you protect your son if you are not here?" She had asked her eyes welling, her voice trembling as she spoke.

"That is why I must go; if they make it this far it will be too late." I'd replied as I took another step from the crowd and approached the King.

"I will join." I had declared to the King directly before falling into step behind the other soldiers. Only two other men joined willingly, Rowan and Brom. Like me, both men had families to protect and had no intention of waiting for the Vikings to kick in the door before they did something about it. The King had also recruited other men from the village by simply selecting the biggest and the strongest and marching them from the village at sword point.

We left our home to begin the long walk onto London and onto an unknown fate.

My heart broke that day, having to leave Jolecia and Arthur, but I knew I'd had no choice and so I held onto that strength of belief deep inside. I thought of them often as we travelled, we'd marched for many days and nights with little supplies and even less rest as the King had insisted that time was scarce. We mostly rested just long enough for the King to rally more troops from the various villages as we passed. For Rowan, Brom and I this was the furthest we'd ever travelled from home. Once a month someone from our settlement would travel to London for supplies. We would trade our wares with the men of the sea who would bring goods from exotic places, as well as stories from the outside world. But of the three of us none had ever made the trip.

As we travelled the weather had begun to turn as the weeks passed through into winter. The days grew shorter, the weather was bleak and the going got tougher; but eventually we had made it to the river Thames; to London. London was a busy place when compared to the village I had come from. I remember looking on with wonder at the sprawling market places that lined the river and the huge boats that transported goods and traders around the world. Of course this was nothing compared to the London of today, but to us it was another world altogether.

We'd spent maybe two weeks in London training by day, resting by night; all the time waiting, anticipating the impending attack. We had grown almost comfortable in those weeks; training had instilled a new confidence within the troops, while mead and tales of battle filled the evenings, playing on the dreams of the naive, myself included. The first snow began to fall the day that they arrived; I remember it as if it were yesterday. The news of the approaching horde of ships entering the mouth of the Thames estuary had travelled along the river, horses racing back to London carrying with them the latest information. Our troop lined the bank of the river, a few hundred men, armed with our inferior weaponry and awaiting the arrival of our enemy with a zeal that would soon be wiped from our faces. Our brave but seriously misguided King before us, sat proudly astride his steed.

The first Viking longboat came into view an hour later. The sight of it was terrifying and sent a murmur of fear along the assembled army before a second boat came into view and then a third. Ten minutes later the Thames was full. Viking longboats obscured the view, each boat carrying at least forty men. As the first boats rammed the shores hundreds of giant Viking men leapt from their boats and charged. It was a massacre. These weren't everyday working men like us just here to protect our land, these men were warriors, years spent rowing the oceans, fighting their way across various lands had made these men animals, barbarians. Each and every one of them was an oxen compared to our flock of sheep, their massive forms swinging giant stone hammers as if they were mere sticks. The expression on their faces scared me to the very core. These men didn't hesitate, the devil glinted in their eyes as they swung lethal axes towards our men, their grins widening with every kill. I don't think we killed a single one of their number.

Our brave King turned at the sight of these barbarians and fled, earning his name, Alric the Afraid.

It was to be a moment I would always regret but as I stood with Rowan and Brom, each of us looking to the other as the Viking horde ploughed their way closer killing every man and child in their path. We shared a single thought and we too turned and ran. This was a moment of self preservation of which I am not proud, it is also I fear why God decided to punish us that day in the way he did.

We didn't make it far. After running through the markets of London we had stopped to regain our bearings when we were captured by another group of Vikings. This second group must have landed further up the river, circling round to attack from behind. These men weren't just skilled fighters; they also planned and thought strategically.

We had been so unprepared for this battle it was unreal, kids playing at war. In the distance we could see the Viking horde plundering the town, burning the remains to the ground as they went. Later that morning we were taken back to what remained of London by our captors where we were thrown together into a large group. All that remained from our pathetic army. This group also included the King himself.

Each man looked sheepishly at the other knowing that they had each either deserted and been caught, or surrendered to the enemy, for no man still fighting would have been left standing. We'd stood huddled together awaiting our fate and we knew then that the country was doomed; we could not win against such a bloodthirsty foe.

2
1010
Fate

After some time under watch a sudden silence swept over the previously raucous guards surrounding our rag tag band of 'want to be' warriors. I knew the moment had come, that our fate had been decided and that the most likely outcome was death. To this day I do not know why they had not killed us upon our capture but whatever the reason they spared us at the time I was grateful. Now I'm not so sure. The Vikings that surrounded us were now all business, they stood visibly taller. As a huge Viking approached our group, he appeared different to the other warriors, bigger, stronger and visibly scarred from years of battle. This had to be their leader, their chieftain, this was the man that had organised their ranks and meticulously planned their assault. The chieftain approached our King. The man held a better grasp of the English language than I would have expected. He spoke with a gravely, course tone, in a broken form of English that only accentuated the menace in his voice. I could not hear the details of the exchange that had entailed, but our King looked noticeably dejected, his shoulders sagging as they spoke. I guess that he was taunting Alric, describing our intended fate in gory detail and after a moment the chieftain laughed mockingly, his laughter filling the air around us and sending chills down my spine. As the laughter died away a second, smaller man approached our band and the mood in the surrounding Vikings changed again.

The second man was also noticeably different to the main horde of Vikings. Smaller than the other warriors, clearly not a fighter and he carried no weapon. The warriors all wore thick woollen skins and leather decorated with skulls and bones intended to intimidate their enemy and it worked. This newcomer however wore a simple hooded tunic, dressed more in keeping with our own culture than theirs; only his tunic had various leather pouches around the belt each containing

God only knew what. This man looked like a man of magic, a Warlock. Many stories of Norse sorcery had travelled around the villages and were the source of great fear among our people, although none had ever seen a Viking Warlock, until now.

The Vikings chieftain had listened respectfully as the Warlock spoke into his ear and then, after a moment's deliberation, nodded his agreement to whatever had been discussed. I remember the feeling of dread that washed over me as I watched malice gleam in his eyes. Another minute of conversation passed before the warriors turned and marched us from the town. And that was that; each of us had been bound together to form a chain, in a similar manner to that of slaves before being marched out of London and into the dense woodland that surrounded it. The Warlock walked silently but confidently at the front of the pack ahead of the huge scarred commander who led the Vikings with the prisoners in tow. There had been maybe twenty of us captured that day. All that remained of hundreds of men and all of us cowards. Each of us trudged begrudgingly onwards, our heads bowed by the weight of our shame, our cowardice. After some time whispers had begun to spread through our group, concerns growing from fear of death to outright panic at the unknown. Brom had tried to ask me where I'd thought we were being taken, I assume trying to formulate a plan, but he was quickly silenced by a large, brutish fist as it slammed into the side of his face. A heavy thud resounded around us as blood spilled from the side of his mouth. To Broms credit a lesser man would have crumbled under such a blow but Brom held his ground although silenced. He may have withstood the first blow but he was not looking for a second.

The day turned to evening as we walked deeper into the surrounding woodland, the shadows of daylight had grown darker and more menacing as they were engulfed by the night. I worked at the ropes that bound my hands, desperately trying to free them as we staggered onward, despair growing ever deeper with every passing moment. I remember feeling the binding tear at my wrists as my skin was lacerated by the bonds. Occasionally the Warlock would stop and pick a few leaves from a shrub or bush, adding them into one pouch or another around his waist. Eventually we had come to a stop in a haunting, moon lit clearing. Over the years I have often pondered why the sorcerer had picked this spot, but to this day I have no idea if it held any significance. It could have been the time of day, its distance from London or just that the location was convenient. I would never know, but at that moment, for whatever reason, the Warlock had turned stopping the group. The warriors had surrounded us in an expert manner, perfected through years of practice and I knew in that moment that this was the end of the line.

As we stood at the centre of this circle of barbarians the Warlock began to chant. The words, spoken in a language I did not know, filled the small clearing in which we stood. Panic rose from the silent, previously unspoken, fear that we all felt to outright cries of terror among our assembled rabble of cowards as the old tales of Viking sorcery and curses now filled our heads. The smell of urine became prevalent as fear got the better of the younger, naive men I was bound with and the gentle sobs of regret emanated from a particularly young man barely out of childhood beside me; the sound was heartbreaking to hear.

I watched from the front of the assembled crowd. I had managed to work my binds loose, now enough to allow my hands to be free if required. As far as I knew in that moment I was the only person who had escaped their binds, but I had not disclosed this fact to my fellow captives for fear of death from the surrounding Viking warriors if they knew. As I listened to the enchanting, rhythmic mantra that was now emanating loudly from the Warlock I knew I had to act before his spell was complete. I discreetly observed my surroundings, taking in the woodland now shrouded in the foreboding darkness of the evening, our captors surrounding us and the expression on their faces as they leered with anticipation. They knew what was coming and were looking forward to it. My eyes panned back to the Warlock before me. The chanting was rising in volume clearly getting to its climatic conclusion. Excitement boiled inside each of the warriors as they too sensed the end approaching and began to howl in pace to the chant as they stood guard around us.

I knew the moment to act was upon me, the shame of my previous cowardice echoed tauntingly in my mind. I wouldn't again allow myself to sink so low. I thought of my son, of his future; the future he'd have under the Vikings rule. This was it, now or never. And with that I pulled my hands from the ropes that bound them and attacked.

A lot happened as I leapt towards the Warlock. I'd had no plan in mind other than to stop him and his insane chanting. The instant I moved the highly trained Viking warriors that surrounded us acted. From the corner of my eye I saw the glint of metal as axes and swords were unsheathed; a sight I would never forget. In that moment I saw the Warlock as he turned towards me, his spell almost, but not quite, finished. The Vikings face contained an oddly perplexed expression for just a moment, a fleeting look of surprise before his mouth turned upwards into a wicked grin. The Viking horde hit the assembled crowd of English men, forcing them to the ground. Yells of pain rose up from the group at the same moment that I barrelled into the Warlock, his hands still raised…

…then the air around us exploded.

3
2010
School Sucks

It was a cold day in October and whilst it wasn't raining it might as well have been. The grey nothingness that passes for weather around here had settled in for the day and my mood had aligned accordingly. We'd been back at school for a month or so and it sucked as much this year as it had every other that I could remember. I entered the school gates, as I did every morning, safe in the knowledge that this day would hold nothing more exciting than the greatly drawn out anticipation that I always felt for the final bell of the day. The one that meant it was over.

I hated school. School meant spending time with people I didn't like, whilst having to learn about subjects that didn't interest me. It was a sentence for a crime I hadn't committed. I turned up every day, did my time and left again at the earliest possible opportunity; hopefully with as little excitement as possible. On a good day I would go fairly unnoticed, keeping myself to myself, my head down. On a bad day; well, a bad day was when I got noticed.

"Oi! James, wait up."

Damn. It was going to be a bad day. I turned to see William Blake running up the path behind me; I hadn't slept well last night and this was all I needed. I guess you could say Will was the local bully, only he didn't take your lunch money or want you to do his home work. No, Will just tormented people because he was bored. In my mind this was the worst kind of bully, you couldn't just hand over your money and they'd be on their way; no they lingered, thriving on your discomfort and fear, the more you squirmed under their scrutiny, the more they scrutinized and for what? Because without it the two minute walk up the path would what? Not be interesting enough? I didn't understand the seemingly pointless humiliation that they regularly inflicted upon me. But I figured that if I did, it would probably mean that I was one of them, after all to truly understand someone and their intentions, you have to walk a mile in their shoes. Or so they say.

"Hey, lames, I mean James. Where you heading?"

"To the form room." I answered, choosing, as I always did, to ignore his apparently accidental slip of the tongue.

"So James, Craig here tells me that you fancy a girl in our English class, is that right?"

This was of course crap; it was exactly the sort of thing Will did. He'd ask you awkward questions with no basis of fact just to watch you squirm trying to answer them. The worst part was that you knew that any answer given would only escalate the situation. I considered the question for a moment, looking for a simple answer that would not offend him but would also not lead to further questioning. I just settled for.

"No Will, I don't."

"Did you hear that Craig?" Will now said turning to his right hand goon of a friend. Craig was bigger than Will but didn't posses the cognitive capabilities that would enable him to rapidly form a witty response. So instead he just grunted a general acknowledgement and Will continued regardless.

"James here is calling you a liar."

My heart sank. Craig may be thicker than the average brick but it didn't take him much thought to slam me into the wall; which he did. I picked myself up from the floor. I could half hear Will and Craig laughing as they walked away. Their job here was finished as their attention was diverted by a passing group of girls who had also begun laughing at my defeat. Damn I hated school.

My name is James Tyler. I'm aware that it sounds a lot like James Taylor. People have told me far too many times and just to save any future attempts at bad puns, I don't have Carolina on my mind and the sun doesn't shine whether she's here or not. I hate my name, which I let my parents know regularly.

Life is pretty quiet in my town. Longton has little to offer the world, I mean, how many famous people have ever come out of Longton? It's a mid sized town, close enough to London to pale by comparison whilst being far enough away to prevent its inhabitants from actually being able to claim being Londoners. So the Longton locals, live, work and play within the same few streets that comprise the entirety of its town. I live in a small village outside of Longton called Tinley. It's nice enough in a retirement village sort of way. It's peaceful and trouble free, which in turn means its boring. I'm seventeen years old but at times I feel eighty. I go to school like everybody else, studying for my A levels. I'm not particularly bright or funny. I'm not bad at sports, but I don't win either. Generally I am just very average, whilst also fearing that I'm going insane.

I had always believed that crazy people would be blissfully unaware that they were nuts, but I'm not. I know full well that I'm a few cards short of a complete pack. My calm, impassive exterior masks the insane concoction of thoughts and emotions that crash around the inside of my mind. I often wonder if the thoughts are even my own. The primal urges that I fight to contain are so out of character when compared to the scared little boy that otherwise occupies the space between my ears.

My day didn't really get a lot better once I got to class. I sat in Science, first period just after registration, only to be hit by a flying rubber in the back of the head. It hadn't been aimed at me, but these things had a way of finding me. The class had been incredibly dull, although for once it wasn't the subject that bored me. I actually quite liked Science but my teacher had a monotone voice that could put the most studious pupil into a concentration coma. The rest of the morning continued in much the same manner, one class followed another and by lunch time I honestly couldn't remember what classes I'd had. I sat now on a wall outside my form room with the two guys that were the closest thing I had to friends. Our friendship had been born out of a natural aversion to people in general, thrown together because no one can spend their whole time alone in school, not without getting bullied, a lot, as well as a reputation for being a serial killer or the likes. So the three of us had sort of drifted together for safety reasons initially; bullies tended to pick on the weak, single stragglers so groups tended to blend into the background.

Steve and Ben were in many ways a lot like me, shy, clumsy and socially inept; so the three of us got on well, all things considered. Steve was currently sat beside me playing a game on his phone whilst Ben sat the other side reading a book, something Sci-Fi based. This suited me. We would often go whole lunch times barely saying a word to each other, which is why it made me jump when Steve suddenly hit me in the arm. This was Steve's way of subtly getting my attention, hitting me in the arm, in turn causing me to jump and prompting me to curse him in the process. Like I said, it was subtle. I looked up in time to see Rebecca laughing at my over reaction and suddenly it dawned on me why Steve had been trying to get my attention. Rebecca had been approaching and was now passing by; smiling at me.

Rebecca Arlington was the object of my infatuation, an attractive girl from my art class. Rebecca was beautiful, not in your typical sort of a way; no, she had a more natural beauty. I didn't like the clichéd 'popular girls.' The cheer leader types tended to be vain; too much attention will do that to a person. Rebecca was shy and avoided the social hierarchy of school life, preferring instead to spend her time in a quiet corner of the art room. I returned the favour and hit Steve in the arm as I settled back down, my face bright red as the humiliation rose into my cheeks.

The bell rang, signalling the end of lunch so I walked into the form room to grab my bag before heading over to the art room. I had a free period for the final class of the day, so I'd decided to catch up on my art assignment. This was no big surprise; I spent all my spare time in the art block. As A level students we each had our own desk space assigned in the art studio. It was a sort of safe haven from the rest of the school. Art wasn't considered cool so the bullies tended to avoid the place. Rebecca was there as she often was. She, like me, seemed to be more at ease in the gentle seclusion of the art room. Rebecca was working on some large scale paintings, abstract stuff, I honestly didn't know what they were meant to be, but they were pretty good all the same. I had been working on a couple of pieces of my own, derelict buildings were my subject matter and I used a variety of available materials painted, glued or smeared onto the eight by four foot canvas. I did a single smaller piece last year depicting a farm track that lead up to a couple of buildings in the distance and at the end of term the local town mayor had come to see our school exhibition. The mayor had stood in front of my piece and had said, 'I can actually smell the shit coming from this picture,' before catching himself, turning red and trying desperately to back track. Apparently he'd been referring to the realism of the painting; either way I thought it was ace. I liked my art to provoke a strong reaction, that's the point of art. Needless to say my other classes suffered considerably as my time was mostly spent in the art room. Art was the only redeeming feature of what was otherwise my own personal hell.

4
2010
Night Terrors

That night I sat on the windowsill of my parents mid sized detached house, in the centre of our 'retirement village'. I lit up a cigarette, inhaling deeply before blowing the smoke out into the cold night air. I didn't really smoke a lot but there was something about this spot as my feet rested upon the roof of the garage below my bedroom window. I just enjoyed sitting out here at night, letting my thoughts wonder, pondering the stars above that make me feel so insignificant by comparison. The cigarette gave the sitting outside a purpose, but it wasn't really necessary. As I sat there, the time being somewhere around midnight, my thoughts turned to the prospect of trying to sleep. I didn't sleep much, my mind tended to run away with itself when left to its own devises. When I shut my eyes at night to sleep my mind began to play scenarios through my head, replaying a variety of things, all seemingly intentionally designed to scare me, to play on my fears and prevent me from sleeping. The sleep I did get was fragmented; I spent most evenings tossing and turning, drifting in and out of consciousness or waking up in the middle of the night, drowning in my own sweat.

Night terrors haunted me most evenings. It was as if I was bullying myself as if my own mind was punishing me, I just didn't know what for. As I sat on the ledge I threw the butt of the cigarette over into the neighbour's garden, exhaling the last pull from my lungs. I knew it was ridiculous that I couldn't sleep. When awake the issues seemed trivial. I knew that they were nonsense but whilst asleep they seemed so real. I once saw a shrink who said it was a form of depression; apparently I need to find what was wrong in my life, to fix it and put my mind to rest, only I genuinely didn't know what was causing it. Depression is a vicious circle; it's often accentuated by a lack of rest, exhaustion and in turn prevents you from sleeping. Some days were better than others, some days I didn't think too much about the terrors that lurked in my mind, other days I felt as if I hadn't woken up at all. Those days the terrors stayed with me after I had awoken. They lingered at the back of my mind throughout the day, not an image as such, more of a feeling of wrongness that spun me out, disrupting my daily routine.

That night I dreamt of fire. It coursed through my veins burning every inch of my skin. An ever lasting burn that never ebbed or faded, forcing its way into every coherent thought, filling my mind with fear and pain. I awoke, I think. My eyes opened at least. The burning sensation was slowly fading from my mind but my body was still as of yet unresponsive. I tried moving my hand but it didn't seem to react, an eerie silence filled my brain as if my ears weren't yet registering anything. Then suddenly my body caught up. The surrounding noise of the night flooded my brain, extinguishing the remaining flames within my mind as my hand jolted upward.

I rolled over switching on the light beside my bed before throwing back the covers and trying to turn away from the sweat patch that was now soaked into the bed sheet. I knew that I wouldn't sleep again now so I picked up a book, opened it up to a random page and began to read, anything to divert my mind from that nightmare.

5
2010
Science Shock

Another week passed by much the same as any other. Most days were spent awkwardly avoiding the pitfalls of social conduct during the daily routine of a school day whilst failing to sleep for more than an hour or two at any one time during the nights. It was getting to the end of October and the typical cold weather, infamous across Britain, was beginning to rear its ugly head once again. It was early Monday morning and I was sat with Steven and Ben on the wall outside class before it started. Steve was currently giving me and Ben a running commentary of the film he'd seen the previous night, I hadn't caught the name of it, but it didn't sound like my sort of thing. Apparently it was some sort of low budget horror movie, I lost interest at that point, I didn't need any further horror to fuel my mind and prevent me sleeping; it was quite capable of that on its own. As he talked on someone caught the corner of my eye and a feeling of unease washed over me as if I was being watched, a predatory sense that momentarily caught me off guard. I turned to look around me but there was no one there.

"So are you doing anything for your birthday James?" Steve called to me, pulling my thoughts back to the present.

"What? No. I don't think so. Why?"

"Dun no, it's just that it's your eighteenth, sort of a big one."

"What date is it today anyway? I'd forgotten that it was coming up."

"It's the twenty first today, so your birthday's Saturday isn't it?"

"Yeah it must be." I replied. I'd forgotten all about my birthday. I'd never really celebrated it in the past and I wasn't about to start now. "I'm not planning on doing anything to be honest. I guess I should have a beer or something, isn't that what your meant to do on your eighteenth? Get off your face?"

"Dun no," Steve replied. "I guess so, but you're the only one who's old enough to drink, me n Ben'll have to watch." Steve said, laughing to himself at the thought.

"Yeah, scrap that then." I replied turning to walk into class.

Our first class was a double science lesson with Mr Singh. He was a smart man and a good teacher, which was one of the reasons I chosen to stay on to study science at A level, however I'd had even less than the usual amount of sleep the last few nights and didn't know if I was going to be able to prevent my head from hitting the table if I dozed off. I considered skipping the class but decided against it as I'd skipped a couple of last weeks lessons and was already behind. As I entered the class I looked over to the desk at which I normally sat and instantly I knew I'd made the wrong decision by not dodging this class whilst I had the chance. Craig was sat at my desk and had a look on his face that suggested he was up to no good whilst still managing to maintain the usual senseless expression he always wore. A mischievous stupidity covered his face that told me all I needed to know. Whatever he was planning was guaranteed to both amuse him, like a child with a new toy and humiliate me.

Mr Singh hadn't yet arrived so I quickly scanned the room looking for another seat, preferably one as far away from my usual spot as possible. As I scrutinized the room the first thing I noticed was Rebecca sat at the back in the middle watching me with a concerned look; the second was that there were no other available seats in the room except at my usual desk, where Craig now sat. I sighed deeply as the realisation hit that Craig was undoubtedly up to no good and that I was going to have to approach the spare seat beside him eventually. I wondered briefly what was holding up the teacher knowing that he should be here any second and then I realized what a cowardly thought that was before looking once again towards the anxiety on Rebecca's face. As the moments ticked by, each second resounding clearly within my mind, I realised that I was going to have to move soon for fear of looking like a scarred little girl in front of the class; in front of Rebecca. I began to approach the spare seat. At least Craig was alone; this would be a lot worse if William was with him. Thankfully Craig doesn't have the ability to comc up with anything clever on his own; he probably just intends to punch me or pull away the chair. The more I thought about it, each step carrying me closer to finding out, the more it began to dawn on me that William should be here? This was one of his classes.

I reached the table and looked into Craig's face as he sat grinning stupidly at me, unable to suppress his excitement; he was almost visibly bouncing in his seat. I put my bag under the table, taking out my books as I did so and then sat in the seat. Nothing happened. A few seconds passed and still nothing. Had I imagined the look on Craig's face? Had the expression just been his standard look of stupidity? Maybe I really was paranoid. I was certainly in need of some sleep.

And then suddenly I felt it, something being forced over my head, something thick, scratchy, but soft at the same time. What was it? Who? And then sound filled my ears as the class burst out into fits of laughter.

My mind sharpened.

I could hear the din of the class all laughing at full volume, but simultaneously I could also make out each individual voice. Craig's deep baritone boomed in my ear before the all too familiar sound of Williams laughter came into focus. He had been here after all; hiding, waiting. I felt embarrassment, humiliation and anger all flooding my senses. A new found rage swept through my body, my senses heightening as adrenaline coursed through my veins.

I raised my hands to the item now firmly wedged over my head and taking grip of either side of it I pulled at it, without thinking. The foam item tore into two pieces as my vision sharpened, focusing. There, now stood directly in front of me was William, his head tipped back as his laughter echoed out around me. Impulse took over as something inside me snapped. Maybe it was the years of bullying; maybe it was the lack of sleep, whatever it was I was angry. With the fairly rigid foam items in hand I took a step towards William. I saw the look on his face change rapidly as he saw me approach, he almost looked worried. I raised my left hand above me; foam item still grasped tightly in my now clenched fist… and brought the item down hard, directly on top of his head.

William stumbled, surprise evident on his face. I brought my right arm round a moment later, hitting him again. William fell to the floor in front of me as the rage took control. It felt good. I hit him again and again when suddenly I felt my body heat up, my veins began to burn as if I was about to burst into flames. The anger was in charge now, my conscious brain had lost control and I knew deep within my soul that I couldn't stop if I wanted to. I also knew that I didn't want to.

"WHAT IN THE NAME OFF!" Mr Singh had arrived.

My anger stopped, I felt the heat recede within my body. My conscious mind returned and I looked down at William who was now cowering on the floor, his face and arms scratched and bloodied. I looked at what remained of the foam items in my hands and realised in horror that it was Mr Singh's piles cushion. One of those soft donuts that people sit on when they can't sit down properly for reasons I don't want to know about. Or at least it had been; now it was just various pieces of foam ripped into small pieces.

"GET TO THE PRINCIPALS OFFICE NOW!"

I sat outside the principals office with William now sat beside me. I knew I was in trouble, how could I not be? It wouldn't matter who had started it, I had been caught red handed, seen by a teacher leaning over another student repeatedly hitting him with the remnants of that same teacher's personal property. This wasn't good. As I sat in the typically uncomfortable hard chair, standard issue for any sort of waiting room across the country, I couldn't help running through the various scenarios, trying to explain that I had been provoked and that I am in fact the victim here. It wouldn't make any difference; our fate will have been decided well before we enter the principal's office. I could hear Mr Singh's voice through the door, his temper hadn't ebbed in the slightest as he'd frog marched us over here, literally by the scruff of our necks. I let the sound wash over me as I tried to calm myself, my stomach felt sick at the prospect of having to go home and explain this to my parents. By parents' standards mine were alright, my dad seemed to have trouble understanding kids and not just in the 'trying to deal with pubescent teenagers' way that all parents do. No my dad had no idea how to talk to kids at all. He'd improved as I'd gotten older being able to talk more as adults, on a level, but during my younger years my dad had adopted a technique of parenting known among a lot of adult men as 'leave it to mum to deal with'. My mother on the other hand was the polar opposite as if having to do twice the work, which I guess in many ways she did. My mother was the most selfless woman I knew, she would literally do anything for anyone if she thought it would help. She constantly fretted, worrying about us and everyone else, constantly trying to do more. She wouldn't take this news well; she'd probably blame herself as she often did when things went bad. She'd wonder what if she had done something different and then maybe this could have been avoided. It was just the way she was, never able to blame anyone else for their failings in life. It was easy to see where I got my neurosis from; my mother literally carried the world on her shoulders.

The door opened waking me from my reverie.

"I will deal with you two in a minute;" Mrs Brewster said glaring at Will and I. "Mr Smith, Mr Singh here is going to take you to your first class while I deal with this matter."

As she said this last bit she turned again to look at us. I felt her eyes burn into the side of my head but I was momentarily too preoccupied with the discovery of the other person in the waiting room that up until that moment, I hadn't even known was here.

"Who's the weird kid?" I heard Will ask, before Mrs Brewster yelled over him.

"Get in here you two, now."

As I walked into the office I glanced back at Mr Smith. I could see why Will had referred to him as weird; his clothes looked old. I don't mean dirty and worn, I mean they were the sort of clothes I'd expect to see my dad wearing, giving the impression of age whilst his face said otherwise. He looked to be of about my age, short, scruffy haired and un-astonishing in every way. Absolutely nothing stood out from his plain dress sense and demeanour; so much so that it was as if he was trying not to stand out, to blend into the background. Oddly this made him stand out more, now that I had noticed him. He stood, gathered his bag and then as he turned to Mr Singh and I caught a glimpse of his eyes as for one awkward moment he looked directly at me. His eyes looked old, I mean really old, showing an understanding of life that was rarely seen in a kid of his age. There was a sorrow within them that screamed. They were the saddest eyes I'd ever seen. I momentarily wondered what his story was before I was abruptly interrupted.

"Get in here James and shut the door." So I did.

6
2010
Red Report

"Red report?" Steve exclaimed that lunch. "I guess it could have been worse."

"How?" I asked, still a little agitated. "I have to get this signed at every class. It's humiliating! I'm nearly eighteen and I've got to have my behaviour signed off at the beginning and end of every lesson and report to Mrs Brewster at the end of each day!"

"You could have been expelled." Steve stated calmly and I had to concede that he was right, on this point at least, getting expelled would have been very bad. This however offered me little by the way of solace as I pondered the thought of having to tell my parents of my crime. I imagined my mothers panic, worrying how this might affect my future as if I'd been sentenced to death. My dad on the other hand would show his disappointment in the same manner that he showed any emotion, good or bad, by lowering his paper down and glaring at me briefly. I had privately hoped to avoid having to tell them at all, but the teachers had clearly thought about this point and had added a little box to the bottom of each report form that exclaimed 'parent or guardian signature.' I guess in their mind this ensured that my parents at least learnt of my little misdemeanours.

That evening I got in around five having lingered as long as possible on the way home. I went straight to my room, postponing the inevitable conversation for as long as I could. I heard my dad come home from work a moment before my mother called up the stairs to me.

"Dinners ready."

I sighed deeply as I perched on the side of the bed before picking up my report and trudging down the stairs. As I entered the dinning room my dad was already sat at the table, paper in hand as he always did, my mum frantically running around the kitchen. I never understood how she managed to get in such a flap in the kitchen, running around it as if the place was on fire and she was forming a one man bucket chain, completing every link single handed. I looked from the frantic sight of my mother back to the tranquil sight that was my father, a serene look on his face. The house could have been on fire and he'd never have known it.

I sat at the table, placing the report face down to my side. My mother, after a lot of commotion, laid the dinner out on the table and joined us. She questioned my father on his day at work to which he answered with typical, quick, one word answers. To an outsider this may seem rude on my fathers' behalf, but my mother had a tendency not to wait for an answer before firing the next question at you. If you went into an in-depth explanation about the point in question you wouldn't get to the end of the sentence before the questions had begun to pile up behind the conversation. One word answers sufficed, enabling the conversation to flow easily, without my mother having to achieve the impossible and pause during questions. After my mother had extracted my father's day from him in no more than five words, she turned to me and began the same process over again.

"So how was your day James?"

"Bad," I replied.

"You always say that, it can't have been that bad?" As my mother said this I handed her the sheet of paper from the table. She went to ask the next question when a confused look crossed her face. She took the paper from my hand, silently turning it over and beginning to read. The sudden halt in questioning was so unusual that my father actually stopped what he was doing and looked up at my mother across the table, a look of concern creasing his brow as he did so.

"Wha...Who…" My mother began before settling on, "red report?" And so I had to explain the story to them, my mother now on rapid fire, the questions hitting like bullets, the disappointment on her face deepening with every answer. After I had finished my mother sat there, silently. This was worse than any amount of outrage I had seen in the past; it was rare for my mother to be speechless. My mother never really got angry, just disappointed. You knew you were in trouble because her enthusiasm to help you waned, your clothes would still be on the floor where you left them and your dinners would be dull. These were her ways of letting you know that what you did was wrong. I suspect I'd be eating beans on toast for weeks after this. My dad however not only listened and I don't mean through one ear whilst reading the paper as he usually did, I mean he actually listened, but after I had finished he said the strangest thing.

"Good on you son." And he actually smiled. "You stood up for yourself and gave this Will character what it sounds like he deserved." The outrage on my mothers face was clear; she opened her mouth once or twice but nothing came out.

"You're going to have to watch that temper of yours though." My father finished before he simply turned back to his dinner and said nothing more on the matter.

I was stunned, firstly by my father's reaction, but also because this was the most he'd contributed to a conversation about me in as long as I could remember. As he had spoken however I had seen something in his eyes, a glimmer of something as he'd looked at me, concern? Worry? Disappointment? I couldn't be sure. I made a mental note of it and went back to my dinner.

7
2010
Birthday Drinks

The week continued in the same vain as so many that had gone before it, each day a constant struggle against consciousness as I tried desperately not to snore in class. I didn't see a lot of Will or his goons either, which helped the days to pass. The nights however had been rough this week.

The dreams seemed stronger than before, more vivid, almost real. By Thursday morning I was deliriously tired, my sleep deprivation had begun to creep into my daily routine and I was beginning to question what was real and what was not. This is why when Rebecca approached my desk that afternoon it took me a couple of minutes to realize she was talking to me. I blinked a couple of times before noticing that I had been staring blankly and that I should probably say something. She really was beautiful, a shining beacon in my sleep deprived vision.

"…. If your around that's all. Well, what do you think?" My hearing refocused just catching the end of what Rebecca had been saying.

"Sorry, what was that?" I asked dazed, I could actually have just been asleep; damn I couldn't even tell if I was awake any more.

"Oh, um nothing it doesn't matter." And she turned to walk away.

What just happened? Rebecca looks embarrassed. I've embarrassed her. How? Think, what did I just do? I wasn't listening as she was talking to me. Why would that embarrass her? Maybe it was difficult for her to say? What could she possibly want to ask me that might be difficult? What would I want to ask her that could be difficult? Well there's the obvious, but I'd never have the guts to ask her out. Oh God.

"Wait," I called to her as my mind caught up with what might or might not have been happening. She turned to face me, already halfway across the art room. I leapt from my desk to talk to her, although I had no idea of what to say. I stepped forward my eyes meeting hers across the room, my mind raced, had I read the situation wrong? What do I say now? For a moment our eyes had locked, a moment shared and then her eyes vanished above me. In my already dazed state I was momentarily thrown, confused, before the floor hit me in the face.

I turned onto my back, my head spinning. In my haste I must have tripped over my bag. I couldn't believe it; that was about my luck. I felt the now all too familiar feeling as my blood once again began to boil within my veins. I felt my face flush red with anger and embarrassment, my body once again began to feel strange. Fear hit my mind as I wondered what was happening, this felt different, like my dreams; was I still asleep? That would certainly explain things.

"Are you ok?" Rebecca asked. She clearly sounded concerned but there was also a hint of a smile in her voice.

"Uh, I, yeah, I think so. My nose might be broken though." I said with a sigh, then the oddest thing happened, Rebecca began to laugh. At first it was a quiet snigger but after a moment she began to laugh out loud at my mishap. At first I was a little affronted as my pride tried to intervene, but after a moment I too joined in. Her laughter was infectious and after a moment we were both laughing loudly together causing my anger to subside and my blood return to a normal temperature.

"Sorry." I said. "So what was it you were trying to say?" I was a little winded and my nose hurt like hell, had I broken it? It was a good job it was there, it stopped my face from hitting the floor. Damn that hurt, my eyes had now begun to water too, just to help things.

"Should I take you to the nurse?" Rebecca asked.

"No!" I almost screamed, I can't think of anything worse than having to replay this botched moment for anybody else. At least in here it was quiet; here my shame was at least contained. "No thank you, I'll be alright in a moment."

"Ok, so it's your birthday at the weekend isn't it?" Rebecca asked hesitantly.

"Yeah, the big eighteen." I said sarcastically.

"What you doing? Are you going out somewhere?" She asked nonchalantly.

"Well Steve thinks we should get drunk as it's my eighteenth, but I can't say that appeals much so I'll probably just stay in." As I said this I realized how sad it sounded, I was going to stay in on my birthday. I should have lied, made something up. It didn't have to be a big lie, just tell her I'm out with friends, nothing much, just drinks. But it was too late; the floor to the face had already ruined any chance of Rebecca actually taking me seriously, so there didn't seem any point in making things worse with a series of obviously transparent lies. "Sad isn't it?" I finished lamely.

"Yeah, a little. Look, I was thinking of going for a drink on Saturday myself, I wondered if you'd like to come, you know, as it's your birthday and all." She asked quietly. It took a moment for this to register with my brain as I lay on my back looking up at her. I had to still be asleep; this was just too much to be true. I considered my reply, multiple things came to mind before it dawned on me; was this a date? Me and her? Or was this a group of friend's thing? Both options scared me to my core.

"Me and you?" I said before I could stop myself, the look on her face changed instantly and I realized suddenly how it had sounded.

"No!" I said, almost yelling. "No I mean Yes! Yes I'd love to go for a drink with you."

"Only if you want to…" Rebecca said quietly, clearly feeling a little awkward at my clumsy reply.

"I want to, definitely. Sorry. I just wondered if you meant me, you and friends, or just me and you." I tried to explain weakly.

"Well if you want to bring friends?" She said confused.

"No. I don't. I just thought you might." This was going badly, the first and now thanks to my addled brain, probably the last opportunity of actually getting a date with Rebecca and I couldn't string a coherent sentence together. Sleep would really help.

"Ok, so pick me up around eight?" She asked.

"Yes, eight, ok."

"I hope your nose is ok." Rebecca said smiling at me as she turned and left.

Her smile stayed with me for the rest of the day. And that night I slept better than I had done in weeks.

The next day I felt better than I had in a long time. I don't know if it was because I'd finally slept, or because I'd somehow got a date with Rebecca. I thought about the potential that Saturday night held, trying to recall the details of how it had happened; only I now couldn't remember, the details seemed to blur leaving me unsure of how it had come about. As I pondered this my mind began to snowball. It did this a lot, facts seemed to merge with fiction and I became flustered as my mind ran away with scenarios that may or may not have happened. As the lines blurred between fact and fiction I would become agitated, hot, angry, scared. This time it was about yesterday. I tried to recall the conversation, that I knew had happened, but the more I thought about it the more it blurred within my mind, It seemed so unreal that I began to question the details. It started simply with whether I was supposed to pick her up at eight or nine? Then did she say the two of us? Or will other people be there? I was pretty tired yesterday, what if I had dreamt it? What if I get the wrong house? What if I turn up at her house and she looks at me blankly, asks why I'm there? Oh God. My mind tumbled on, each scenario getting more and more ludicrous but as my mind got more confused, they seemed more and more plausible. I began to sweat again. These attacks used to only happen while I was asleep but it was getting more and more frequent during the waking hours. I began to take deep breaths trying to get my mind back under control. I'd just ask her if she was still on for tomorrow, simple. Although I knew it wouldn't be, I'd end up stammering or tripping over something again and probably end up accidentally giving her a black eye in the process and she'd never speak to me again.

As I continued the ongoing argument with myself in the privacy of my crowded head, I turned the corner and could see Steve and Ben

waiting for me outside the form room as they always did. I approached them but as I did a strange feeling washed over me.
"What you doing?" Steve asked as I approached. "You look shifty, like your being followed or something."
"Huh, yeah, that's how I feel. I've had it for days, this feeling like I'm being watched." I replied and I really had, it was strange but for days now I'd felt like I was being stalked, a deer in the headlights of a trucks inescapable course. I turned around, not really sure what I was expecting to see. Maybe I'd hoped to see someone dive for cover, but no such luck. There were a few people from my class loitering around. Some of the younger pupils crossing to their form room on the other side of the courtyard and that new kid, leaning against a wall on the far side. No one suspicious although the weird kid, that name had sort of stuck; was odd, but then that's why we called him the weird kid. I shrugged off the feeling and walked into the form room.

That night the terror was stronger than ever. I dreamt of being torn apart, I felt as if my body was blowing up internally, exploding out, growing, ripping, tearing. The pain was excruciating, or at least I imagined it had to be; the dream seemed so real that I wasn't sure that I wasn't awake. It felt like a beast was trying to tear its way through my body. I awoke at three am, once again lying in a puddle of my own sweat. I tried to sleep again but every time I shut my eyes I saw claws flash across my mind.

8
1010
Cursed

I know not how much time had passed; we could have lay there for days for all any of us had known. When I awoke the Warlock had gone and the men around me were beginning to stir. As I emerged from my own insentient state something stirred within my mind, creeping into the corners. I knew then that I had not done enough, that a curse had been set. I could feel it. As I took in my surroundings I noticed that the Vikings were also beginning to rise. The significances of this didn't occur to me in that moment but in the following years I had given a great deal of thought to the fact that the Vikings were indeed lying amongst us. Was it possible that the circle they had formed around us before I intervened would have been safely out of reach of the Warlocks curse? My intervention however had caused them to run into the centre to stop me, so it stands to reason that they too may have been affected by this curse that the Warlock had summoned, whatever it may have been. In that moment however the urgency of the situation was paramount and my main concern was getting my fellow men clear of the area before the Vikings regained enough composure to realize what was going on.

The sun had risen and it was around mid morning, it had been hard to tell more precisely as the sun was not visible through the dense foliage of the trees that surrounded the little clearing but the shadows that were visible were elongated enough to suggest that it was still early. I had worked quickly releasing my fellow men from their binds including among them the King that had led this disastrous plight. We left the Vikings where they lay and moved swiftly from their location, from the clearing, from London and from our failed attempt to stop our enemy.

I returned home later that same month, our group now disbanded. Although we were at this point unaware of the exact details of this curse that had been placed upon us, we were beginning to get a good idea.

It had been a strange and difficult journey as we'd travelled back together, hoping to finally return to our families and homes whilst praying they would still be awaiting our arrival. It was not long after we set off however that the curse had begun to reveal itself and it became clear that all was not well. At first we had not known the extent of what the Warlock had done many of the men had seemed to be afflicted by something but showed nothing more than subtle signs that things were not well within them. Some had hoped that as we were able to walk away that the curse may not have been set however it was soon clear that my intervention had only prevented the curse from taking full and immediate affect. The burden did not appear to influence two men the same, some apparently more inflicted than others that did not appear any different. As we had trudged the long days and nights covering the distance back from London we talked only of this curse, each man could think of nothing else. We speculated as to its purpose, its affects, its duration and often we would ponder over the original intention of the Warlock. It was the general consensus at the time that his purpose had been to turn us into forest creatures, a common theme among the stories of Danes that were told to children in order to scare them, in turn keeping them inline. When I look back now this seems unlikely, it is far more probable that whatever the intention it would have resulted in a slow and painful death, but whatever the original objective what happened was definitely unexpected.

From what we could piece together on the long journey the curse appeared to cause some sort of a transformation in its host and was seemingly influenced by something specific to the individual. Many seemed to simply change in mood or temperament, uncontrollable outburst of anger or fear were common place and several of the men's personalities appeared to flip without warning, becoming savage, beastly. Occasionally, although rarely, a member of our group had even, triggered by God only knew what, run for the cover of the trees only seemingly to be replaced with some sort of goat.

Their outward form had appeared to morph, changing before our very eyes, a terrifying sight to behold. Fear and mistrust had quickly spread through the group and people had quickly begun to distance themselves from others. Brom, Rowan and I began to wonder if the beast inside each one of us was no longer just a metaphor but a real life danger to every man among us. Most of us did not change outwardly, not on that journey anyway. Many showed no immediate effects of the curse, but as we knew not what triggered it or if indeed we were all affected similarly, none of us felt safe and we never dropped our guard.

The knowledge of this curse, combined with the fear we now all felt of our brutal enemy, no doubt now searching for us, meant the journey home was long and tiresome. We barely stopped for food or sleep, always fearing the next assault and unsure of where it would come from. Our number grew smaller by the day as we each went our separate ways and as our numbers diminished we had to keep an ever more vigilant eye on our surroundings. The Vikings moved continually onwards advancing from two sides. The Norsemen from the north and the Danes from the east causing an increasing threat to us, particularly as our throng dwindled. Not that we would have stood a chance even together; the thought chilled me to the core.

It seemed as the days passed that a pattern emerged. The men that had transformed did so again but only into a single beast, although the beast varied for each person. Some of the transformations appeared random, others in accordance to some sort of emotional trigger of some type. We began to speculate that if a man was nocturnal at heart he might transform only at night or an angry man when angered, whilst the whole time we were all on edge, each waiting, wondering what might trigger their own sudden attack. I had yet to set off any trigger of my own but whilst I had not discovered where my curse lay, I knew, despite the murmuring among some of the men, that I had not been fortunate enough to evade the curse. I could feel it at the back of my mind, a small part of me that was different now, a shadow of something else now sharing the same space within my head.

After twelve days and nights we had made it home, Rowan, Brom and I each returning to our families a mere shadow of the men we had been when we'd first set out. I found my wife and son stood in the very same spot that they had when I'd left, beaming at me and for the first time since the day the army had trudged through our burh I felt joy, my heart lifting instantly at the sight of my family. That night I held my son in my arms; unable to put him down for fear that if I did I might wake up from this dream.

9
2010
Date Night

Saturday came and I was terrified. I'd spent most of the day fretting and after searching the wardrobe for an outfit I decided to pop into town to find something that didn't make me look like I'd gotten dressed in the dark. My wallet had been looking pretty tight lately but never the less I'd managed to get a casual collared t-shirt that I hoped said smart casual without saying, trying too hard. I also managed to get a fresh new pair of jeans that were baggy enough to allow me to be comfortable without being so baggy that I looked untidy. The current fashion is tight 'figure fitting' jeans but I'd tried a pair on in Topman and to me jeans should hide what's underneath, not highlight it. I'd caught up with Steve and Ben for a quick burger but was too anxious to eat so I quickly made my excuses and left.

Seven o'clock arrived. I was beyond nervous, my mind scrambled with panic. I was half cut from the lack of any real sleep as last night the nightmares had been stronger than ever. They'd been building in intensity all week with the exception of that one peaceful Thursday night. I looked up at the clock. I knew Rebecca lived just around the corner; she'd lived there for as long as I could remember. My family had known hers for years as we'd gone to the same schools our whole lives, I think we even went to the same nursery. It was a five minute drive but as I considered what time I should leave I managed to over think it again. I didn't want to be early and look to eager or weird if hanging around outside, but being late looks like I don't care. So I've got to time it right, maybe I should do a practice run now, but then someone might see me turn up early and then leave again only to return later like I'm casing the joint. Damn, if I couldn't get my head around arriving I had no chance of going a whole evening without screwing this up.

I arrived dead on eight. Rebecca thankfully stepped out through the door and hopped into the car before I had even had time to get out which saved me from the potentially awkward scenario of running into her parents at the door, a moment I had also been dreading. I took her down to a pub in Tinley, the Queens Head or something like that, it was a bit of a posh pub which of course looked good on my behalf but also meant that the chances of me running into someone from school were slim. It wasn't that I was embarrassed to be seen with her, quite the opposite in fact. It was more concern that I might be made a spectacle of in front of Rebecca.

We took a table and I went to the bar to get drinks. I ordered a Fosters for myself and a Bacardi and coke for Rebecca feeling seriously young compared to the other people around me, a thought also shared by the barmaid who proceeded to ask for my identification prior to pouring my order. Great I thought, trying to find my ID whilst also trying to keep the fact hidden from Rebecca, sat across the other side of the bar. As I returned with the drinks Rebecca smiled that familiar warm smile of hers before asking.

"ID'd?"

"Yeah." I replied feeling my face flush. It turned out that Rebecca was easy to talk to and conversation flowed readily. I was surprised how natural it all felt, as the topics arose I found myself being able to talk willingly and openly with her, something I struggled to do with most other people. We even laughed from time to time either at a joke or two or a shared story from our past. It was interesting sharing stories of our childhood; we had grown up in the same area and gone to the same schools. Although we were never friends growing up our paths had crossed regularly, whether at school events or out of school activities. It was funny for me to see the occasions through someone else eyes, their memories. It intrigued me to see how time had distorted her opinion of the events, some details differing or lost, while other remembered fondly, vividly. I had to admit that our childhood had seemed happier through her eyes; she recalled past events with a rose tint that made me wish I was there with her. Only I had been, but my own recollection tended to seem bland by comparison. My confused memories seemed to cast a dull grey fog over the events and precious details that she'd held dear had long been forgotten from my own account.

The evening went so well that neither one of us had noticed the time, at a quarter past eleven the bell behind the bar was rung causing us both to look up at the clock on the far wall.

"Wow, that time already." I said, genuinely shocked. "I should get you back."

"There's no rush. My parents are all right, they won't have called the police yet." Rebecca replied with a smile. I returned the smile as we both stood and collected our coats from the stand by the door. I held the door open feeling the blast of cold October air hit as we left the pub. We walked to the car and I put the heaters on full; my old car had very little by the way of insulation and the heaters were crap. Rebecca pulled her coat up around her neck, fighting back the cold as I started the engine and reversed out of the car park pulling away from the pub. I decided to drive up around the pond as it was a cold but clear evening. The village was deserted as it always was at this time of night; once the few local pubs had closed there were little other incentives for people to be out and the village quickly grew quiet. As we passed around the pond the heater kicked in and the windows began to steam up, quickly obscuring my view. "Damn," I muttered pulling over to the side of the road whilst digging around for the window rag, every old cars best friend.

"Here." Rebecca said handing me the dirty old rag from her side door pocket, which I took from her, thanking her in the process. As I wiped the window she wound down her own, staring out across the less than impressive pond before her.

"It's beautiful." She said. "At night I mean, the moon light reflecting off the water is the most gorgeous sight."

I stopped mid wipe. I was no expert on romance but there was an alarm bell going off in the back of my head that was telling me to drop the dirty rag and stop with the window, which I did. I shuffled slightly across my seat towards her, attempting to subtly close the distance between us, under the pretence that I was trying to see what she was referring to.

She turned in her seat to look at me. Had I read this wrong or was this about to happen? She leaned closer still.

I leaned in. Oh God it really was. My head was spinning wildly, my blood pumping, I wondered if she could hear my heart thumping in my chest.

Our lips touched, gently at first, testing, searching, awaiting a response and then there it was, we were kissing. I was kissing this wonderful, beautiful girl. I had thought about this so many times but I had never dared to dream it might actually happen.

The pounding of my heart continued, rapidly increasing with every beat. My mind span on, elated and scared at the same time, nervous but thrilled. A cacophony of emotions swirling around my brain, my blood began to boil, but not in the same manner as before, this feeling was no half hearted anger, it was ten times stronger, causing my veins to rage with emotion.

My head span on, out of control, but it was changing, no longer the enjoyable sensation it had just been. Dizzy. Sick.

I felt Rebecca pull back from me, confused. But my brain could no longer process this. My heart pounded now unbearably, it felt like it was swelling out of my chest, growing, tearing.

I heard the sound of twisting metal and a distant scream registered at the back of my mind, but the fire inside burned on regardless engulfing my senses.

And then it all went black.

10
1010
Brom

Brom didn't fare well over the weeks that followed. The year had turned and the freezing weather had truly set in. Brom, Rowan, I and the other men of the village had turned our hand to ploughing the land ready to be sown in the spring. Brom had suffered greatly trying to control his anger, his moods turned swiftly and as his mood grew darker his strength had seemed to increase. Brom ploughed the fields with more and more vigour as the days passed, channelling his anger into his work, pushing the horses beyond their capabilities. The other men watched this strange behaviour from afar unwilling to become the focus of Broms' wrath, but the horses were too important to the livelihood of the land to allow Brom to continue pushing them the way that he was. If one horse was to be out of commission, the cost to our little community would be devastating. It was for this reason that on one cold morning the men, oblivious to the curse that ailed him, all gathered to talk to Brom and try to curb his frustration from the fields.

The men had approached Brom as he finished the furrow on which he was working and they confronted him. They had only asked him to go easy on the horses, nothing more, but it had proved to be one step too far as Broms anger broke through its boundaries. The curse took hold of Brom. It was as if it had been lurking, waiting for its moment. It seemed to grasp Brom like a fever as his body began to boil, his face grew red and he appeared to swell. The men had seen this reaction begin and through fear of the unknown had turned to run from the scene. Broms body seemed to grow and grow, increasing in mass to an unthinkable size. I had watched this from the edge of the field having chosen not to be a part of the intervention. I knew all to well the feeling in Broms head as I felt it too, tearing at the back of my mind, wanting to be free. Brom had held out all he could, he had fought the transformation but on this fateful day he had lost control just long enough and a moment was all it took.

Broms body suddenly exploded outward in what I now know was fur, each hair shooting from his skin in a fraction of a second, his face distorting in shape and growing, elongating. As the men ran from the field Brom roared, a huge bellowing growl that rang out across the village and there, where Brom had stood only moments ago, now stood a huge black bear rearing up onto its hind legs.

The bear turned, faced suddenly by the two terrified horses harnessed to the plough. The bear lunged at the first horse slashing a huge gash into its side, ripping open the horses flank. The horse reared up but the gaping wound in its side was too much and it quickly fell to the ground, defeated. The bear's claws ripped through the horse's constraints, the thick white rope of the plough line split in two, before a second swipe smashed through the swingle tree allowing the chains to fall free and in turn releasing the other horse.

I had watched as the horse ran free, the men of the village were now returning, their hands containing whatever weapons they could grab at short notice. These were my friends, my family; I couldn't stand by and watch them fight Brom in this manner and so I had signalled to them to wait, an order that they obeyed gratefully. I alone approached Brom, slowly, holding my hands in a manner that I hoped suggested that I meant no harm. I was anticipating that inside the bear a part of Brom still understood; if I was wrong, I was dead. As I approached, the giant bear watched me suspiciously and I thought for a moment that I had seen a glint of recognition in its eyes. The bear settled gradually, recognising that I held no threat and before I knew it Brom lay on the ground in front of me, his old self again. I helped Brom back to the village but the people of the burh were not welcoming. Terror had gripped them and they had wanted to kill him or at the very least banish him from the village. I argued his case for he was not himself in those days and eventually, reluctantly the men had agreed he could stay in the burh but on one condition. And so Brom had spent the next few months in chains, even his own family were now too scared to go near him.

Brom was a good man and had been a close friend to me through the toughest of times; which is why it pained me to see him feared and in chains. I took him food daily and sat with him as often as I could for nobody else would go near him, not even his wife. Brom had a lot of time to think during those long days and he tried to master his curse, but he seemed unable to control the transformation and after the first time the curse had activated it seemed that it had set in. Many times I had taken out food to see a giant bear curled up on the floor and at times, if I didn't know better, I could have sworn I had seen it crying.

11
1011
Burh Burns

The sun rose daily and life in the burh carried on in much the same way as it always had. Things had begun to settle back into the normal routine that I had known before; before we were damned. Brom still remained chained in place with little improvement in his control. I was beginning to wonder if control was possible at all but Brom continued to try regardless, knowing it was the only way his wife and children could ever begin to trust him again. I spoke often with Rowan about the issue of control for Rowan had discovered his beast fairly quickly. It had been during the long, arduous return home that Rowan had first changed, but unlike Brom, it wasn't anger that had first set his curse off.

For Rowan it was despair.

We had encountered a small scouting party of Danes on the second day of the journey whilst passing through dense woodland. They had been tracking us for a short time and had tried to take out the back few from our pack, planning to diminish our number before taking the main group. Rowan had been the unfortunate man bringing up the rear of the group. The Danes had snuck silently through the trees whilst we'd trudged on, utterly unaware of their presence. They had jumped Rowan, silently grabbing him from the track on which we'd traipsed. In his terror Rowan had panicked, unaware of whom had grabbed him, his mind span and the curse took over. His body gave a violent jolt and a yell filled the air, the noise causing our rabble to turn in time to see his body vanish. His yell had turned into a screech, rising in pitch as his body disappeared in a burst of feathers and suddenly a hawk flew free from the Danes grasp.

Our group reacted instantly. Unaware of their numbers and caught off guard we ran clear of the woodland before turning to fight on a more even keel. The Danes however, clearly shook up by what had just happened, did not pursue us from the woodland. With no sign of

Rowan, we had continued onwards, occasionally we would see what we thought was a hawk following from a distance and later that evening Rowan reappeared as if he hadn't left. We didn't ask anymore about it, we were living in strange times.

Rowan had however faired better with his own curse, although he was unable to change at will he didn't suffer spontaneous outburst and for his part he was able to keep his curse secret from the community in which we lived. I had also told no man of the curse that I knew lived within me; for I knew not what my curse was and even less of what triggered it at this time. It was later that same year that I discovered the truth of my curse and my life changed in that moment forever.

Six months had passed and the evenings had drawn out, the people of the town were enjoying what they could of the lighter evenings whilst preparing for the hardest time of the year. Since the mid summer harvest produced only food for the cattle it was at this point, before the harvest of the spring crop, that food was scarcest and times were hard. People had to find food anywhere they could and it was not an uncommon sight to see them scouring the woodlands for much needed sustenance.

Whilst Rowan had not learnt how to control his curse, he had found that he could activate it now at will, although how he discovered this fact he never told. Rowan had taken to scouting duties twice daily, where he would walk to a nearby precipice that over looked the river below and activate his curse by leaping from the great height. Once in hawk form Rowan would circle the burh and surrounding areas, unbeknownst to the other villagers. We were aware that it was only a matter of time before the Vikings reached our home; news had spread down from London from time to time, updates on the situation there. London had been burnt while we were there, but now people were trying to rebuild, despite having to live with the daily threat of Vikings. The North had been lost to the Norsemen by this time and all that was left was for them to work their way down through Wessex, taking our village with them. I know now that our fate had been sealed already and that by the year 1013 Sweyn the Formidable, the King of Denmark would take our country as his own. But even if we had known this then, we would have fought just the same.

Rowan kept a vigilant watch over the village daily, until that fateful day came that he had returned at a run. He told Brom and me of the approaching Danes, two days out by foot and that night we told the villagers to leave. In the face of the impending war the villagers gathered but the consensus was that there was nowhere to run to. By leaving the village they faced a fate worse than the Vikings for they would surely starve wondering the land. It was decided that the women and children would hide deep in the woods, taking with them what supplies were available while the rest of us set about defending our burh.

Two days later around mid morning the first wave of Vikings could be seen crossing the land before us. Brom, now freed from his chains, Rowan and I had seen these men fighting before and had tried to prepare the others for what they were about to face, but in truth I had wanted to tell them that it was futile. The best we could hope was to divert the hordes attention from our families hiding in the woods and maybe buy them some time in the future, but to crush the men's spirit like that would be cruel. At least by fighting they would retain their pride, even if they would lose their lives.

The battle was swift and brutal, the Vikings ploughed through the town with little regard for man or beast, the live stock were slaughtered and the fields burnt. There would be no harvest that autumn. The men fought bravely and held themselves with pride but regardless one by one they fell, viciously cut down by axe or bludgeoned by hammer. Rowan fought well, taking two Vikings down single handed before narrowly escaping a fatal blow as his curse kicked in and his hawk flew free. Brom, with the heart of a warrior and enough rage to compare to the fires of hell fought like a demon. He cut down three men as he turned, ducked and spun through the warriors, the fire in his veins burned brightly in his eyes. I don't think he even knew where he was, these men were to blame for his fate and so with eight months of being chained up, eight months of looking at the fear in his wife's eyes all fresh in his mind, he exacted his own painful vengeance. At one point whilst fighting my own enemy I had turned in battle and seen Brom finish off his fifth victim when suddenly a huge, muscled arm grabbed at his throat choking the life from his body… and then it happened. Brom exploded, violently, his body growing vastly, instantly; his face elongating and his hands turning to clawed paws. I heard the Vikings fingers snap as the beast within Brom broke free of the grasp then watched as the huge bear savagely slashed the Viking that had held him. The bear roared forcefully, terrifyingly and then attacked, Broms death count increased tenfold. The huge black beast tore through the horde as if they were no more significant than a field of corn.

For my own part I fought two men, slaying them both where they stood, before taking a painful blow to my arm from a third. The Viking struck a second blow, shattering my rib cage with a huge mallet before leaving me incapacitated on the floor, gasping for breath. As our numbers dwindled under the ferocious onslaught the Viking horde burned the village to the ground as I lay beaten on the ground and unable to do anything but watch. Eventually their appetite for destruction subsided and they took what silver there was and left. One man stayed however, a sadistic man, not content to leave anybody breathing. He systematically walked to every body sticking his sword deep into the heart of each man, making sure they would never again breathe the air upon this Earth.

He approached me where I had slumped, grasping at my wounded arm. He was a great brute of a man, his face clearly battle worn and his left eye gouged clean from its socket. The man raised his sword, levelled it with my heart and then spoke the words I will never forget.

"My name is Tilsted, take that name to your grave and spread it through Helheimr, the realm of the dead; for when my time comes they should fear of my arrival."

The words have stayed with me ever since. Tilsted then pushed the point of the blade, slowly but certainly, into my heart. I felt the cold of the steel as it penetrated my skin, broke the muscles in my chest and pushed its way between my ribs and into my heart. My heart jolted as pain shot from it, spreading across my body, my lungs took a desperate last gasp but they no longer functioned, crushed and now also punctured by the blade. I heard the blood gurgle up into my throat, felt its warmth and knew my heart had stopped beating. An eerie stillness gripped my body before finally my brain wound down, my thoughts slowed, my vision faded and my mind went blank.

The last thing I saw was Tilsted grin widely.

12
2010
The End

I don't recall what happened that first night. When I came around the sky above me appeared darker than it had done before as if the light of each star that had previously shone so vividly had been snuffed out in an instant, gone. A sinister chill tore through the air unusual for the season and an unnatural silence hung like fog, a dense, suffocating lack of sound that caused my mind to scream to fill the void it created. The world had changed. It had been torn and twisted, shattered beyond repair. I knew it without question for I could feel it within every inch of my being although at the time I knew not what the change had been.

She lay on the ground some distance away. As my mind registered my surroundings I became aware of her presence and I knew at once, even from this distance, that she was dead. The wound in her chest made me gag, choking back on the sick sensation as bile rose from the pit of my stomach. I had never seen so much blood; it flowed out around her body, running out as if searching of a new host having abandoned its previous occupant. My eyes flicked from one part of her body to another and I was dimly aware that a small part of my brain was cataloguing every detail; the mud matted into her long blonde hair, the position of her body, twisted and torn, the broken rib visible through the wound and the blood stained trainer no longer attached to her foot. As the images overloaded my senses I felt my knees hit the hard ground below me although I did not register any pain. My mind spun trying to piece together the events leading up to this, trying in vain to make sense of the scene but it just came up blank, no answer was forthcoming as to what had happened here.

The sound of sirens wailed out in the distance, drawing closer with every moment. The remains of my car were visible to my right but it was going nowhere, torn apart as if it had been made of paper. Panic gripped me; a primal desire to flee rose inside. I looked once again to the body of the girl I had known and cared for, my body convulsed violently in response, repulsed by the scene. The horror of it all crashed in waves against my consciousness, each wave bringing a new bout of nausea to the pit of my stomach. What had I done?

I ran to her but as I knelt down at her head I knew there was nothing I could do. I lifted her lifeless head in my hands and the tears welled in my eyes.

Oh God, what have I done?

Panic gripped me inside, stronger than anything I had ever felt before, my fear for Rebecca hurt unlike anything I had felt before, a deep pain burning inside my chest. My head grew dizzy as my brain tried to process the scene. I had no recollection of what had happened, pain; pain was all that I remembered. I knew that this time was no nightmare, none of the terrors had been this real, they'd felt it at the time but now that they had been realised; now I knew how far from the truth they really were. I let a scream erupt from my chest, a scream that changed, deepened, I began to roar. I felt the horrid feeling grip me once again as the terror inside me rose to an uncontrollable level. My body once again began to shake and it took every ounce of strength left within me to prevent another outburst of whatever had happened before.

I picked up Rebecca's lifeless body and with tears rolling desperately down my face I crossed to the side of the road and placed her body in a clearing under a tree. I don't know exactly why I did this but I just couldn't leave her sprawled unceremoniously in the road. I shut her eyes, placed her hands together over her midriff and said a prayer. The sirens that had before seemed distant now appeared to be bearing down upon me. I didn't know what had happened but I knew it was me that did it; I was dangerous, out of control. I couldn't risk hurting anyone else, so I ran. I ran from the scene, from the police, from Rebecca's lifeless body and from myself.

I dashed into the woods the dark branches grabbing at my clothes and skin as I ran, tripped and stumbled my way blindly down the track. My mind had gone blank by this time, shutting down, unable to process the events of this harrowing evening. My parents lived in the village the other side of these woods but in my terror I got turned around a couple of times and eventually broke cover, scratched and bruised, a few streets away from my intended destination. Having ran the entire distance home I arrived exhausted, gasping for breath as I leaned back against the outer wall of the garage. Thankfully my mother was out still, I don't know what I'd have said to her, if anything. I was running on instinct now and my instincts told me to keep going and not look back. I ran in to grab my car keys but as I opened the larder door my memory threw up a vivid image of my car, sat where I'd stopped with the roof ripped clean off. My mind spun and I stumbled for a second before grasping the larder door for support, what was I going to do now? I couldn't actually *run* away.
"Take mine." The answer came suddenly. I span where I stood to see my father standing in the doorway behind me. Startled, as a deer caught in the headlights, I panicked, about to run, but then I saw the look in his eyes.

My Father stood in the door way holding his keys out to me. He didn't question what I was doing, where I was going, when or if I would return. The look on his face told me that he didn't need to, as if he knew this day might come. I had so many questions but was in no mind to ask them and wondered if he would even answer them if I was. But I had committed a crime; however unclear I may be on how. I knew that it was only a matter of time before the knock at the door would come, blue lights flashing outside, the flashes of navy light illuminating the front room ceiling in short, systematic bursts. My father must have seen the desperation in my eyes as at that moment he pushed the keys into my hand before saying simply, "Get dressed then go."
I looked down at my naked form, confused for a moment before looking back up, staring into my father's eyes. There was so much I

wanted to say but my mind was incapable of stringing a coherent sentence together and my eyes were once again beginning to fill. I know that if I don't leave now I would not have the strength to prevent myself from curling into a ball on the floor and crying until the police arrived. I looked down at the keys in my hand; they weren't to his car.

I dressed quickly, throwing on whatever was first to hand, then ran out through the front and lifted the door to the garage. I leapt over the bike in front of me and fired up the engine, I pulled the helmet from the wing mirror on which it hung and pushed it over my head. I kicked the gear shift down into first and let the clutch fall from my fingers. The bike shot from the garage; I wrestled it out onto the main road before gunning it up through the gears. Gone.

Ten minutes later I dropped onto the M40 opening the throttle up as I went, I had no idea how fast I was going for I didn't care enough to look down at the gauge. I continued to accelerate, pushing the bike faster than it had ever been, just trying to put as many miles as possible between myself and the horror of the evening now past. As I rode I felt the cold biting at every part of my body, the numbing pain of the bitter air however was quickly pushed aside, nothing when compared to the pain that crushed my bleeding heart. As I rode my mind flashed, my memory taunting me; throwing images of Rebecca at me as we sat in the pub drinking, her rubbing her hands together for warmth in the car, the beautiful smile that lit up her face… then the sight of her dead, lying unceremoniously on the floor. The images cut deeper and deeper into my heart, each one hitting with the force of a train against my soul.

I rode on, the sound of the engine drowning out my cries of pain.

13
1011
First Flight

I can’t tell you what came next, not first hand as my body lay crumpled on the floor now bleeding from the hole in my heart. From what Brom had told me later the village had been devastated, burned to the ground. He had searched the dead looking for any survivors although Tilsted had been thorough and none remained, myself included. Brom had found me dead on the floor and despair had hit him, not just for me but for all of the friends he had known now strewn on the ground around him. He tells me that he sat by my side for some time unsure of what he should do next. For his part Brom had rampaged through the Vikings, running many from the village; but there had just been too many of them. Brom had eventually calmed back into human form and returned to the village and what he found there had brought him to tears. He’d considered finding the women and children in the woods, but he knew they feared him already and to be the bearer of this news would see that they never looked at him again.

What I had been told happened next took some explaining. Brom had slumped to the side of my corpse. Despair had gripped him and as he sat there among the fallen bodies of his family and friends he’d prayed for the fallen men around him. As he sat, lost in prayer, the impossible happened. Brom swore after that he spoke only the truth, the truth that as he sat by my side praying for my soul, my body had combusted into flame, the fire rapidly engulfing my entire being. The flames I am told burned with an intense heat, unnatural for a fire of its size, a severe bright white, unlike any normal fire. Brom had scrambled back away from the flames and watched on as my body had been shrouded in the intense inferno before turning completely to ash. I am told that as the final flame died away it gave a last, sudden burst of life from which a huge flaming bird had risen, soaring into the sky, that final flame trailing behind it. It was as if a shooting star had emerged from the cinders, leaving nothing but a pile of ash, all that remained of my body.

From this point onwards I now return to my own memories for my mind suddenly blinked into being. For a moment I thought I was ascending to heaven as my mind took in the approaching sky above. I felt light as a feather as if no longer hampered by my human body or by gravity itself. A serine peace washed over me and I found myself ready to embrace the heaven now rushing forward to welcome me. After a moment however the world levelled out and confused I found myself looking down to the fields below. My memories were my own and my thoughts clear as day. I could remember everything from my life before but now I was soaring through the heavens. I dipped and drifted on the wind for a moment revelling in how natural it was to me. I flew around and around blissfully unaware of anything other than the wind that whistled around me when suddenly I saw from a distance a settlement on fire. My memory threw up the war that had waged and suddenly Tilsteds face filled my mind. I turned in the air and darted down to the village, returning to the ground at its centre. I landed in the burh that I had known all my life but oddly I was seeing it for the first time, from a completely different perspective and through very different eyes. As I stood at the centre of the burh, my body jerked painfully, distorting uncontrollably and a moment later I stood looking down at my old body again, only now I was naked.

As I lingered a moment trying to file what had just happened into a corner of my mind for future analysis, Brom approached holding a pile of clothes out to me.

'So you didn't escape the curse after all.' He said to me while I stared at him, speechless. 'It seems that it just took a dose of death to trigger it.'

'What am I?' I asked.

'I don't know,' Brom replied honestly. 'Some sort of large bird of prey, but on fire.'

After I had dressed I talked with Brom and he filled me in on the rest of what had happened.

After that we had gathered up the bodies of our fallen family and friends pilling them respectfully in the centre of the burh. We would eventually burn them but it would be disrespectful not to inform their families first and allow them the opportunity to say good bye.

14
2010
Alone

I had ridden through the night, I'd had no real direction in mind I just followed the road, followed my instincts. Generally my intuition told me to avoid busy roads so I pushed the bike on through gradually less congested motorways, crossing the heart of the country as I went. I had a lot of time to think whilst riding, which in my book was never a good thing. It was why I had always kept busy in my life before, keeping my body busy kept my mind preoccupied. My mind had always had a second side to it. Side one, my normal side, my human side, ran day to day life; happily going through life in an orderly, responsible manner. The second side however had always felt like something else. I had heard many stories as a kid, tales with a religious undertone that talked of people's conscience sat on their shoulders, the devil on one and an angel on the other. These apparitions would always be depicted making the daily decisions whilst battling for control but always maintaining an equilibrium that allowed people to go about their daily lives. Well my balance was broken. My mind tended to fall from one to the other, crashing down on either side for varying lengths of time. Side one, normal me, the angel. Side two, well, he was certainly no angel.

At first I didn't recognise the difference between the two, the balance would tip and sway, here and there and life would have its ups and downs. But as I grew older, hit my teens, I knew that things were different. My mind didn't seem to balance as well anymore, conflicted. I would be fine one moment and out of control the next and it took only the smallest catalyst to over throw the balance. My temper had always flared as a kid, small things would trigger it off, a disagreement with my parents or an argument with a friend would cause my temper to turn and rage would fill my head. But it wasn't just my anger that I struggled to manage; every emotion I felt seemed capable of spiralling out of control as if a switch had been hit, causing my mind to flip. The second side of my mind felt raw emotion, seemingly lacking the intelligence to control these feelings in the way my human mind did. The raw, overpowering sensation would hit quickly and suddenly, terrifying me, overwhelming me. This was when the second side took control. The beast within didn't like me. He was my devil, the voice in my head that pushes me to do the bad things that I know I shouldn't do, acting on impulse to fulfil its desire. Only my mind doesn't stop there, its continual conflict rages, the beast inside taunts me, while my human side envisions the potential futures that await me as a result of my wrong doing, never letting it drop. Many days I have spent in class, a shadow of the man I normally am, due to the war that rages within my mind. This may sound ridiculous; I know it always does to me when my human mind is in charge. My normal mind, sensible, rational, this side of me simply shrugs this off as ludicrous; when able to suppress the beast I see clearly how ridiculous I'm being about the whole thing. My problem is that my human mind used to be around a lot more than he seems to be nowadays; he seems to have better things to do than to pick up the pieces of my own personal breakdown because in the last few years I've seen all too much of the beast within my mind.

The beast pushed the bike on further now winding down some nondescript, dark country lanes. As I rode the morning begun to break and my surroundings were beginning to become more apparent. Stark looking, baron fields spread away in every direction; craggy rocks jutted out from the ground sporadically, larger than anything I would have ever seen in Tinley but it was the huge mountain range on the horizon however that caught my attention. A sign post flew by and one word caught my eye, Snowdon. I really hadn't consciously selected a destination, I'd just rode, but as the word jumped from the sign I knew that this was where I had intended, something about it felt right and at the moment anything that felt right was good by me.

I eventually stopped the bike down a typically generic back road at the base of a mountain track. The track wound up though the Welsh mountains ultimately ending at the peak of Snowdon, but I had no intention of going up that high, it would be flooded with tourists, even at this time of year. I rode the bike on further, following the dirt track as far as the bike would allow before abandoning it and continuing on foot. I don't know how but I knew that my father would not tell that I had taken it, so no one would be looking for it. I continued by foot for an hour or so, winding my way up through the Welsh hills heading further and further from the beaten track. I crossed rugged terrain, as I went, clambering over the large rocks that were strewn across the landscape. Eventually I found what I was searching for, a small cave in an outcrop of rock. I'd had no idea that it was here, but I knew as soon as I saw it that it was what I had sought. Set within the shear rock face that reached up to the sky above and far enough off the beaten track to avoid any unexpected passing hikers, perfect. At first I was unsure why I had rode out here but as I had climbed the winding track I had felt as if I was returning home. I couldn't say why as I had never been here before but something inside me was drawn to the wild terrain of this mountain. I'm not entirely sure if I liked the idea of being led by what might reside inside me, but right now I just needed a purpose, a destination.

I sat in the corner of the small cave just out of view of the mouth for what felt like an incredibly long time, constantly replaying last night in my mind. I ran over every detail, the drink in the bar, the drive home, the kiss… the death. I questioned what had happened, how I had killed her, Rebecca. My mind kept throwing up the same images over and over again, my car; how had it gotten so badly damaged? The roof torn from the body, the metal frame ripped like paper, the glass shattered into a million pieces. What could do that? How much strength would be required? The worst image that my mind continually offered up were the claws, quick flashes of razor sharp claws raked at my mind, my gut flinching sickeningly with each image. I looked at my hands, it couldn't have been me? And for a brief moment I almost believed it; but the image was too vivid, seen through the eyes of the monster, not from the view of a bystander.

I hadn't witnessed the attack, I had caused it.

15
2010
Despair

The day turned into night and I sat still in the same spot that I had been all day. The war was well under way, my mind now in full swing, taunting me with images of the inside of a prison cell, the court case that would lead to my incarceration, my parents in the gallery watching on, disgust and disappointment clear on their faces; their son, a murderer. Normally when my mind ran through such scenarios I knew that they were nonsense, but this time was different. I knew this time that I had no escape, that I had killed Rebecca, that I was guilty and that I would pay for my crime. This knowledge spurred my mind on, punishing myself for what had happened. And there was no respite, I couldn't make any sense of that evening, my thoughts hit me like a fever. I knew that Rebecca had been killed by a monster whilst simultaneously knowing that that monster was me, but I still failed to see the connection. I began to tire as the mental onslaught continued. As the evening drew on I dozed for what felt like only a minute, but in that minute my mind whirled, only now, without the input from my eyes the images in my head seemed to take over, engulfing me. Images of great beasts filled my reverie, wolves, bears and crocodiles flooded my subconscious, teeth and claws slashed at me from within.

I awoke suddenly, vowing in that moment to never again shut my eyes. It had to be around midnight now. I figured that no one would be around and walked from the cave, heading further up the mountain. Again I had no particular direction but had to clear those images from my head, get some air. I walked on clambering up the rocks, before eventually reaching the peak, Snowdon. There was an old train track that I assumed brought tourist up that weren't able to walk it and a café now long closed for the day. The moon was out, not full, I tried to remember my science classes, waning? Waxing? Something like that; either way it gave enough light to see by, not that I would care if I fell off the edge. I stood for a moment at the small monument that crested this mountain, something for the tourist to touch and say that they had made it. I could picture them all standing here celebrating their achievement. I'm sure there would have been a time when I too would have celebrated such an accomplishment, but as I stood here now, in the shadow of what I had done, it just seemed trivial. No great feat of charity work would rectify this transgression.

As I stood looking out across the moon lit landscape that stretched away below me I considered my situation; it looked grim. I could see no way out, no repenting for what I had done, nothing would bring back Rebecca. I could barely bring myself to think her name now, the shame and fear hitting me in the gut every time, causing me to double over where I stood. I threw up all over the floor, hands pressed against the cold stone. The wind was blowing across the peak and my body was shaking with cold, warmth seemed a million miles away now, I didn't deserve it. I would take the cold as it ravaged my skin, I couldn't justify the comfort of warmth ever again.

She would never feel warmth again; because of me.

I knew in this moment that there was nothing for it, that as I knelt over my own vomit, looking out to the lights of the village below, miles away in the distance, that I only had one choice. I stood, wobbling at first, before I walked to the edge. The wind blew at my jumper, catching the hood, dragging at my neck as I walked. I stepped to the edge, despair had gripped my soul. I was no stranger to depression, it had accompanied me through many of the last few years, taunting my daily routine; but this was different. Depression was often unfounded; it grew in the mind of the victim like cancer, often from something small. This however, this desolation was born from the worst imaginable scenario, the truth and it was unfixable, inescapable, life shattering for both of us.

I stepped forward.

"I wouldn't do that if I was you."

16
1011
Family

Later that evening Rowan too had returned to the burh. He had fought bravely against the Viking foe but after narrowly missing death he had taken to the air and not a moment too soon. He had seen the burh burn but had been unable to prevent its fate single handed, a fact that I knew weighed heavily on his conscience. Rowan had followed the horde for some time as they moved on from our village, eventually however he had turned back to help the women and children here. Rowan caught up to us as Brom and I prepared to return to our families hidden within the woods. We would stay with them this evening in the safety of the forest, before deciding on our next move. The three of us walked quickly to the edge of the woods as the day had begun to elude us and night would soon be here. As we entered the tree line we knew something was amiss, the woods were quiet, quieter than normal. The sounds of the forest usually filled our hearing, the variety of small, subtle noises normally all combined to make a cacophony of natural back ground noise that echoed through the woods. Today however was silent, it was the kind of silence that screamed, setting off alarm bells within my head. Brom and Rowan felt it also; we shared a questioning glance before setting of at a run directly for the point where our families had said they'd set up camp.

What we found when we entered the camp I wouldn't wish on my worst enemy. I have lived with the pain of this memory ever since and the thought still brings a tear to my eye. The memory of that moment had been seared onto my mind for ever more, as poignant now as the day it had been formed. We had run blindly into the camp all caution thrown to the wind, shouting the names of our loved ones as we entered. I remember the feeling of despair as at first we found no one there, the makeshift huts were abandoned, the fire burnt out, what little belongings they had taken left untouched. My mind raced frantically through the possibilities, but before I could conclude the thought the worst sound I'd ever heard filled the air. A guttural cry of despair echoed around me, engulfing my mind. Two things were abundantly clear to me at that point. One was that Brom had found them and the other was that my worst fears had been realised.

I stopped for a fraction of a second that felt at the time like an eternity. A voice at the back of my head, the part of my brain that I know was trying to protect me from the truth, was telling me not to go, not to answer the cry. I knew that to go would be to confirm my worst fear, that if I didn't see it for myself it may still not be so. A second later I knew beyond any shadow of a doubt that I had to go. I had to see for myself, to confirm what I already knew in my heart and find what had caused Brom to cry out with such intensity. I could tell from the howl itself that Brom had felt in that moment more pain than I had ever thought it possible for one man to bear. I ran to where Brom now knelt, looking only at him; Rowan arriving at the same time. I looked to Brom, his head in his hands, openly crying into his palms, before I looked up at Rowan, hoping to find answers within his face and I did. His expression said it all, he'd seen it instantly and his face now stared blankly, his mind still processing the scene in front of him.

I turned where I stood, my gaze taking in the surroundings. We were at the edge of the camp now, some distance away from the main fire pit at its centre. The shadows here were darker. I assume now looking back, that the night had been rapidly drawing in, but at the time it felt as though the darkness had been flooding into my mind as I had turned to take in the scene directly in front of Brom and Rowan. I turned to face the gloom and for the first time my eyes took in the view. There must have been thirty of them, women and children, each one hung by their necks swinging from the trees surrounding the camp. The sight was horrific. In that moment it burned onto my brain where it has resided ever since. Then my world fell apart completely and I thought that I would never be able to breathe again, for there amongst the dead, now hanging lifeless from a large oak tree, were the bodies of my wife and child. My heart died; the epitome of my world, the sole purpose to my otherwise meaningless existence, now gone. I felt the world fall away and in that instance I fully understood Brom's cry of pain. I must have hit the ground at some point, but I wasn't aware of it.

I laid there for what felt like a lifetime, certain that I would never be able to move again.

17
2010
Visitor

"I wouldn't do that if I was you."

The voice sounded from behind me, startling me. I turned, instantly losing my balance and scrabbling for a footing on the edge of the precipice on which I stood. As I wavered precariously, my mind reeled, screaming at me, you were about to jump! Why fight it now? But now someone else was here, involved; their very presence integrating them into my fate. I wouldn't ruin someone else's life, one life was enough.

I threw myself forward, landing face down on the rocky turf in front of me, anger flooding through me. How dare this person interrupt this moment!? How dare they take this from me!? The pain returned to my mind instantly. The images hammering against my brain so hard that I could barely concentrate long enough to look up at the dark figure silhouetted against the moon. The rage flared within my body as I tried to focus my eyes on the stranger before me; since my birthday my temper had become impossible to control. It used to be just my mind that would swing in temperament, but now it seemed that my body followed. I began sweating heavily, my blood boiling, my muscles tensing to the point of snapping, my heart pumping faster and faster, my arms felt as if they were being stretched on and on and my back contorted, tearing as if something was breaking from it.

"I'd watch that temper of yours if I was you." The stranger said unfazed by my anger, his voice barely audible over the din in my head.

"Leave now!" I yelled, my anger now consuming my body, the excruciating pain filling my mind… Before suddenly, everything went black.

18
1011
Travelling

After what had felt like a lifetime in agony, a dead, iciness seeped into my veins. My mind felt removed from my body as if I was watching from afar. Emotionally overloaded I was unable to comprehend what had happened but somehow, with strength that to this day I do not know how I summoned, we'd carried our family and friends back to the Burh. Rowan, Brom and I united in our grief, had one by one placed the bodies of our friends and family with the other dead, before burning the remains of the village to the ground, our loved ones along with it.

Nothing would ever amend the wrong that was done to us in those early days. Our families were gone, we had no home to return to and our curse insured that we would never again settle into society. So we'd wondered the land with little purpose. For Brom and Rowan it was about survival, but not for me; for me it was about answers. I am not proud of the way I acted in those days. I had suffered more than I could bear and at times, when I was at my lowest, I took actions that I regret to this day.

I had died nineteen times by this point, each one different and each as painful as the last. This was the only way I knew to activate the curse and although I tell myself now that this was why I took my own life, it doesn't detract from the fact that every time I wished that that time, would be the one from which I didn't return. The one in which I would be reunited with my wife and child.

In those early days I had travelled with Brom and Rowan. We wondered the land passing from village to village without any real direction, spending little time in any one place. We'd stayed just long enough to hear the stories of the time and tales of the Vikings latest movements whilst also keeping an ear open for anything strange, signs of our kind. Broms temper never ebbed and he showed little by way of restraint. The loss of his family weighed heavy on his mind and occasionally he would lose control. During these episodes Rowan would take flight and I would stand clear. Sometimes I had managed to avoid any repercussions, other times I was not so lucky. Brom would slash out in anger, his beast knowing no self-control as its temper raged and occasionally he would tear open my side or rip off a limb and then I would die, once again.

Broms temper would eventually recede and he would always return to sit by my side, sorrow clear on his face, as he waited patiently by my body until it burst into flames and I once again would return from the ashes.

“It’s lucky that I like you,” I'd joke with him half heartedly. “For whom else would you play with?” And he would apologise to me once again, before we continued onward towards the next destination.

This was how our days continued as we tried to come to terms with the loss of our families, our friends, our homes and the curse that forced us into the shadows of the world we once knew.

After a long time that felt like forever I awoke from the despair that riddled me. We approached a town on the edge of the Danelaw, if I recall correctly now it was Chester, the town in which I found a new purpose. Brom, Rowan and I had been so caught up within our own grief that it had not occurred to us that the other men that had been with us that fateful day were undoubtedly also struggling with the curse. As we entered Chester the place was alive with concern, a buzz was spreading through the town, leaving fear in its wake. A giant wolf had terrorised the place, killing people in the dead of the night. Savage and out of control the beast tore through the town, killing everyone in its path. I knew by the description that it was one of us, the ferocity of the attack, the randomness of its victims and the monstrous size of the beast being described all pointed to the curse. The locals were terrified, locked in their houses through fear of leaving after dark. I didn’t know why this wolf was only seen at night but I suspected that his trigger must be related to the evenings, a fear of the dark or some lunar cycle perhaps.

That night we lay in wait and we weren't disappointed. First we heard the howl, a blood curdling cry that echoed the anguish within the beasts mind. I felt his pain in my soul, brothers in the fate we shared; I would not harm him unless I had to. Just as the locals had described a huge wolf had ran through the town destroying everything in its path as it lashed out uncontrollably. We had set a trap in the town and now I stood in the centre of the square, bait being my most useful commodity at this time. Brom and Rowan were ready to act and so as the beast charged me they waited close by, holding a large fishing net ready to trap the wolf.

Looking back it wasn't the best plan we'd ever had, but it was where it all began.

The wolf charged and as it closed in on me, stood out in the open, Brom and Rowan had leapt. The wolf was huge; they'd had no chance of holding him and were dragged from their feet, trailing behind the wolf whilst becoming more and more tangled up within the net as they went. The wolf bore down on me, growing immensely with every leap. I can't deny that I was scared. Its razor sharp claws had slashed through the net that had utterly failed to contain the wolf. Its first slash had cut the net; the second had cut my throat.

Twenty. I had died so many times that the speed of the process had greatly increased. Only moments later I had burst into being once again, both physically and mentally. As I soared skywards I looked down to see a colossal black bear wrestling the biggest wolf I had ever seen. A hawk that I knew to be Rowan shot out before me as I flew, soaring on the cool night air. I knew he was staying clear, Brom was stronger than anything I had ever seen and Rowan did not regenerate as I did, he only got one chance. I signalled to Rowan and he nodded his understanding before I turned back to where the fight was in full flow. As I sped down to the spot I took in the scene below me seeing the huge bear lash out, throwing the wolf through a nearby house, its inhabitants scrabbling from the wreckage. The wolf was quickly back up and into the fray and the beasts clawed at each other, a vicious assault between two colossal monsters, teeth and claws were everywhere I looked. The speed of the two took me by surprise and although the wolf was huge, Brom was bigger still; he seemed to grow with every transformation. I shot down towards them, the wolf in my sights, I slowed to ensure that I timed it just right; Brom saw my approach and I thought for a moment that a flash of understanding crossed between us. Whether through understanding or just through fear of the flaming bird that was bearing down upon him I was not sure, but either way at just the right moment the bear rolled, throwing the wolf clear from him. I watched the wolf land, sprawled on the floor and knew that this was my chance. I hit the massive wolf clean in the side, driving my flaming bird into his chest, the fire engulfing him in the process. As my feet touched the ground my body returned to its human form and a moment later the wolf followed suit; on the ground before me now lay a man about twenty five in age and of medium build. I recognised him from the day we were cursed but I knew not his name, he had been just a face in the crowd to me that day. As he lay there on the ground I took in his form and saw that he had slashes across most of his body from the fight, but they paled into insignificance when compared to the huge wound in his side. His skin had burned clean off, the flesh blackened around the edges, burnt away and his bottom few ribs clearly visible through it all. I was no man of medicine but I knew instantly that he had no hope. I knelt by his head and looked into his face.

"Kill me." He pleaded, his voice a whisper, the gurgle to his tone suggesting his lungs were punctured. I knew then that it was not his wound that caused him to beg for death. The pleading tone of his voice told me that he had wished it for some time now. He would die soon enough on his own, but I could not leave him here to die a slow and painful death. Rowan stepped up behind me, handing me a knife, a tear in his eyes as he looked to his fallen brother. I took the knife from him and quickly ran the blade across his throat, silencing his pleading whispers, permanently.

I knew not what the future held for me from now on, but while I waited for God to see clear to let me join my family once again, I would help those that I could. I would either help them to control their burden, in the manner that Rowan seemed close to achieving, or I would offer them the escape that is not available to me. I knew then that this was my duty, that I would continue the work we had done here tonight. The suffering had to end, the curse had to be broken and I would ensure that no more of my brothers would suffer as he had, as I had and as Brom and Rowan had also.

19
2010
Truth

I awoke some time later, I wasn't sure how long I had been out but the sun had not risen and so I reasoned that it could not have been any more than an hour or so. My head was groggy as if awaking with a hangover and I could feel a lump on the back of my head beginning to throb. I looked up, confused at first, before realising where I was. I looked around the cave that I had spent all day in, wondering how I had gotten back here. Nobody had known I was here, had they? As my eyes readjusted to the light my mind suddenly caught up to my eyes and it dawned on me that there was light, not daylight, it was more like firelight. I looked around the small cave, searching for its source and sure enough, in the middle of the little cave was a fire and a man sat beside it. Now that my body had caught up with my brain I could feel the warmth against the skin of my hands and I could feel the cold air of the night outside as it fought against the heat of the fire within the cave.

"Join me." The man by the fire said, presumably to me as I saw no one else in here with us. His voice was young, it didn't sound deep, as a middle aged mans would be and it wasn't so young as to be a boys voice, twenty odd I would guess. As I looked at the man with his back to me, I wondered if I should be afraid. I knew I should be; he had after all already knocked me out once. But I had little room in my heart for fear. It was full with anguish and I no longer held enough regard for my own life to care if this man took it from me. I worked a kink out of my neck and walked around the fire taking a seat opposite him, as I sat I looked up and saw, for the first time, the face of the man before me and I nearly choked.

"Weird kid?" I asked, genuinely surprised. "But… How…" I stammered on before falling silent, my mind filling with questions all bursting to get out at once.

"Smith, if you don't mind, I'm not keen on 'weird kid.'"

"Um…Ok." I truly didn't know what to say next, what was he doing here? He must know something. But how did he know where to find me? He couldn't have followed me. Nobody would have kept up with me through that traffic, not the speed I was going. Why would he track me down? Was there a reward on my head? How would he have found me this quickly? "Why are you here weird… Smith?"

"I'm here to help you." He replied as if it was obvious before leaning over to poke the fire as if we were on some sort of camping trip.

"Help me how?"

"Help you to understand."

"Understand?" I replied questioningly, whilst being careful not to say anything that might insinuate me in anything he didn't know already. What did he know?

"Understand what's happening to you. Understand why your, changing. Understand why, how Rebecca died."

I froze; the cave fell silent, the only sound coming from the crackling of the fire. After a minute I remembered to breathe.

"Don't worry." He continued. "I'm not here to hand you in to the authorities." I took a moment to recompose myself, breathed deeply, then replied.

"How did you find me?"

"I followed you." He replied quickly.

"Impossible, no car could have followed me through that traffic and if a bike had kept up with me I'd have noticed."

"I have… Certain talents." I wondered briefly what he meant by this but decided not to push the point further, his intentions were what currently interested me.

"How exactly do you intend to help me?"

"I will start by telling you the truth."

Smith sat in front of me and began to talk. My head still span at this boy before me, he was my age, he had just started at my school, what could he know about what I was going through? I'm beyond sceptical as he started talking, this kid couldn't help me, but I had nowhere else to go. I knew that his proximity put him at risk and that the longer he spent in this cave, with me, the more likely that he would fall victim to me, to whatever was happening to me. But he had claimed to know of it? He certainly knew of Rebecca. I decided it was his risk to take, besides, I knew that if I told him to leave he wouldn't, there was a steely determination in his eyes that showed strength far beyond his years, a certain terror that screamed from inside, tormented. This is why the kids at school were nervous of him, in this stark cave, away from the trivialities of school I could see this clear as day, I wondered how I had possibly have missed it before. So I settled in to listen to what he had to say before deciding a further course of action.

"I have been watching you for a while now." He began, instantly making me feel uneasy; I had felt it over the last couple of weeks, an anxious feeling of being watched. "I was waiting to see if you would turn." He said as if in response to the unspoken question in my mind.
"Turn?" I asked simply, the word seemed odd, what was this? Star Wars? Was I expected to turn to the dark side?
"Yes, turn. But to understand what this means you need hear the tale from the beginning. It was a thousand years ago when the curse began, England was at war from all sides, the Norsemen captured Scotland and Ireland while the Danes swept through the centre of England, controlling the north and East, known as the Danelaw. The Normans were also soon to invade from the south and battles for territory were common place, each mob fighting for control of their part of England. The English people were far and few between, simple folk forced into the southern most tip of the country. The massive forces from overseas made short work of the English, rapidly taking over the country and by 1013 England was under the

control of the King of Denmark, who had invaded with a huge horde of Viking warriors.

The King of England in the year 1010 had tried to fight back, to regain some control, but it was too little too late. A group of men were assembled from across what was then Wessex; the men were farmers mostly, not fighters. They had marched on London to face the Viking foe, but fear ran through the ranks as an armada larger than anything these simple folk had ever seen, breached the Thames. The Danes were colossal Vikings, men built for war and they quickly drove the English from London, slaughtering hundreds."

I had no idea how this story had anything to do with my current situation, but the tale was quite something, intriguing me. I found myself wanting to know what came next, imagining the scene. It must have been terrifying, for the English anyway.

"So what happened next?" I asked curiously.

"Those English still standing fled, only to be captured later." Smith continued. "The Danes in those days knew of monsters, fairies, Gods and demons, magic wasn't the stuff of fairy tales as it is perceived today, magic existed, people now have just forgotten how to harness it. The Danes watched the English turn tail and run before later deciding to punish the English that they'd caught for their cowardice. They believed that death was a release and that people moved onto one of seven varying levels of after life, determined by their actions during their life on Earth. As a result death held no fear for them as it does for thc English with their Christian beliefs of Heaven and Hell. No, they had ways of punishing people that went beyond mere death and so their sorcerer cursed the English that had opposed them, a curse that would see them unable to live a normal life, unable to return to their families, their homes."

"Cursed?" I asked, mockingly. "A bit of voodoo and off they walked? They got off lightly!" As I joked of this scenario I realised that for the first time in a while my head didn't hurt.

"So you would think, especially in today's world of sceptics. But back then people believed it with all their hearts; and with good reason."

"What? You're saying that they were actually cursed?"

"Yes, they… And you." I didn't say anything to this at first as it sounded ridiculous, curses, magic; nonsense. But something in what he said settled into the back of my mind, an idea, taking route and beginning to grow. It would explain a lot?

"So what was this curse that these Danes inflicted upon these men?"

"That's where it gets complicated, after much deliberating on that very point I have concluded that the original intention was to turn the English into forest creatures. Many Viking legends tell of their enemy being turned into creatures, but the Warlock was interrupted and the curse never finished. The English fled in the ensuing mayhem but they later discovered that the men that had walked away that day were not the same men that they had been when they'd first set out. Something within their very nature had changed."

I sat listening intensely, it sounded like a tale from a kids book, but I could here the truth in this mans words as he spoke. He believed it and he believed with conviction, with his entire soul. This wasn't a fairy tale to him.

"Each man that had been in that clearing that day was inflicted by this curse, a curse that would turn each man into the very beast that resided within his soul. The affliction appeared at first to take the form of the worst part of its inhabitant, the part of each man that he keeps buried inside, the part he most fears. The curse activates by a trigger of some kind, usually an emotional response to a situation will trigger it and the beast within will break loose, causing mayhem until the trigger subsides." Smith's voice trailed off with this last sentence. The anguish on his face took me by surprise, the firelight casting a shadow across his cheeks and the remorse in his eyes said more than I could bear. His eyes looked to me how I know mine have looked ever since that fateful night with Rebecca. In that moment I knew that Smith too had suffered a great loss.

"So where does this fit in with me?" I asked after a moment.

"You James are a descendent of the cursed men." Smith said this with a heavy heart, as if delivering news of the death of a loved one. "And you too carry the curse James."

20
2010
Test

"Me! Cursed!" I was getting angry, confused. It was preposterous, cursed by some ancient Viking Warlock! What was this 'Smiths' game? What did he want from me? "Why are you here?" I demanded of him. He calmly sat, prodding the fire as if he had seen this a hundred times before. Some how his calm attitude angered me more, his smug manner as if he knew better and was waiting for my tantrum to end, fuelled my temper. I once again felt the horrific sensation of my blood boiling. I fell to my hands and knees, my body trembling with fever as something gripped my body…

This time I was only out for half an hour or so, another lump forming on the back of my head.

"You have to stop doing that!" I said to the world in general.

"If you won't try to control yourself, then I will do it for you." Smith replied casually.

"What do you want from me?" I asked "Leave me; let me do what I had planned on last night!"

"It's an interesting concept, I wonder if it would work?"

"What? My intention is death and that fall would certainly deliver the required effect."

"Yes, if you were just human, but you are not and the usual rules may not necessarily apply."

"And we're back to this again, the curse, so what am I if I am not entirely human?" I asked testily.

"That is for you to find out; we have a lot of work to do, if you are to learn."

"Learn what?"

"Control."

"Ha! Control. Is this a joke?"

"Look James, it's this simple. You are cursed. When triggered your body alters, turning into that of a beasts, an uncontrollable monster that will destroy everything in your path. My job is to ensure that you don't and I can do this one of two ways; you can learn to control it, or I can kill you. Either way is good with me, but let me make one thing clear, your previous life is over. Your friends, family, loved ones, they are no longer a part of your life, you may never see them again. This life is too dangerous for the world to know about, we live in the shadows, staying out of sight."

I knew the truth in everything he said now, I had known that night that I would never see my family again; I had known I was leaving for the last time. The thought saddened me and I sat once again by the fire, considering my options. They weren't good; it appears my only choice stood before me now.

"So where do we begin?" I asked dejectedly.

"By discovering your trigger, although I think in your case it's fairly clear."

Later that morning as the sun began to peak over the horizon, I stood with Smith outside the entrance to the cave. He was in front of me looking directly at me, his face told me that he was contemplating something, but I didn't know what. I stood there for a minute feeling particularly silly. Hours had passed since we last talked and as my brain processed what he had told me it began to seem less and less realistic. Cursed? What next? We're going to test it? Trigger the curse? Intentionally? This seemed crazy to me. If I was indeed a monster then the last thing I needed was to be let loose. Initially I just felt stupid, standing in a field trying to release my inner beast with my self help guru in front of me. The whole thing just seemed ridiculous in the cold light of day, even if the evidence was being thrown against the forefront of my mind by way of painful images of Rebecca's body lying dead or of my car torn to pieces.

"Ow!" I yelled as Smith punched me in the face, causing me to double over. I looked up just in time to see his boot follow, hitting me once again in the face, breaking my nose and knocking me to the ground. What the Hell was he doing! Was he trying to get himself killed? I felt the anger swell inside me, I knew that anger was a part of this trigger, the thing that set me off, but it wasn't the whole of it. My mind was confused, spinning, images of Rebecca drifted across my vision, intertwined with the sight of Smiths boot as it came in for another shot. What was he playing at? He wasn't a big man although he was stronger than he looked. He shoved me back to the ground as I tried to stand, my mind reeled, the pain of the last few days resurfaced in my mind and the anger flared again, stronger this time. The beast reared again, my minds balance had realigned over the last few hours, I hadn't noticed at first, but it was now, as the beast returned, that I first realised that he had left; fleetingly but none the less I had been myself for a little while. Now he returned with full force and despair gripped me once again. Rebecca. Fear hit my mind and anger fuelled it, my vision blurred as the boot hit again, my blood raged as the fever hit my skin, both freezing cold and burning in the same instant. I felt my arms jerk from my side as I hunched over, falling to the floor. A guttural cry left my lungs, fear of the unknown, panic and pain filled into a roar as it erupted from my chest, echoing around the mountain. I felt my skin crawl down my spine, my fingers seeming to break, distorting horribly as my eyes caught glimpses of them in between the visual onslaught of my worst moments. I could have sworn in that moment that my back broke, I felt something tear from it, it had to be my spine, what else could it be?

I waited for death to take me. No one could survive this, the pain was unbearable.

That part of my brain that held onto the human bits, the bits that in my mind made me sane, gave in, shutting down.

I dreamt of claws, of huge wings beating the ground, of teeth, large, razor sharp teeth.

21
2010
Results

My mind returned some time later, slinking back into the corner as if waiting to be excused, waiting for the beasts rage to subside. I lay on my back, once again staring up at the ceiling within the cave. Smith didn't say anything but I knew he was here, the fire still crackled on and I could hear him preparing something over it. I stood carefully and returned to the fire, sitting gingerly to the side whilst letting the flames warm my body as my mind regained composure.
I was naked, again. The realisation hit me suddenly and my head darted around looking for anything I could use to cover myself.

"Try these." Smith said pulling some clothes from his bag and throwing them at me. "They'll be useful, until you gain some control. If you gain some control."
I looked at the clothes in my hands, it wasn't the best looking stuff I'd ever seen and it smelled like hand me downs but right now I was naked, so I put them on anyway. As I pulled the trousers on, beige, bland, generally non-descript, I noticed that they had poppers up both legs.
"What are the poppers about?" I asked automatically.
"They should mean you don't need a new outfit every time your temper flares." Smith replied.
"My temper?" I asked curiously. "So that is the trigger then?"
"Yes and no, anger is very often the trigger in transformations as it is one of the strongest emotions that people feel, but in your case it is not the only factor. Anger certainly initiates the transformation, but it seems that confusion is also a trigger. When angry or confused you turn, this could be a good thing, I would say that your trigger is in fact not anger or confusion exclusively but more pride. It seems that your pride is what controls you."
"Pride?" I said doubtfully.

"Yes it appears that if your pride swells or is knocked then you transform, many things could contribute to this, anger, confusion, betrayal, but it seems to works the other way too, exultant joy seems to work just as well, although this is harder to test. I knew that your trigger was related to you being upset or angry but anger alone didn't appear to be enough. What ran through your mind when you changed?"

I paused for a moment, although the answer had come to me instantly I found it difficult to say aloud. "Rebecca." I finally whispered.

"Yes that would do it. Your lowest moment, the farthest from proud that you have ever been. Anger, resentment, shame, as your human minds pride diminishes the beasts strength grows." Smith turned the rabbit that he was cooking over the fire. I hadn't even noticed it before now but as it caught my attention I wondered how I had missed it. The smell of it filled the cave. I should be starving by now but food was the farthest thing from my mind.

"So what am I? I don't seem to remember anything, I remember the rage, but then my mind goes blank."

"Yes, that will happen at first, your human mind is overrun by the beast, but with time and practice you will learn to focus the human side, to stand your ground and possibly even to work with the beast."

"Really? Right now that seems like an impossible task, it's too much to control."

"Yes, for many it is too much, control is a pipe dream and impossible to master, the beast is too strong, or they are too weak. But many have managed it."

"What's your story Smith? Why are you helping me?" I asked him directly.

"I'm helping you because I too am like you. It seems that you are a rare beast indeed James, a beast that was thought to have been extinct hundreds of years ago, your bloodline I thought had expired. In my time I have seen a few like you, but not for many years. You James are a majestic beast; the pride that triggers your transformation is a very well known attribute of your animal. For you James, are a dragon."

I considered this, I went to speak but nothing came out, stunned into silence.

"A dragon?" I eventually managed to say. "Are you sure?" I then asked rather stupidly. It was a ridiculous question of course he was sure, it would be hard to mistake such a thing. "But they don't exist." I said; the stupid, unconsidered comments continuing in an uncontrollable stream from my mouth, of course they exist or else I couldn't be one. Suddenly, as my mind processed this, I realised that not only was Smith right, but that I had known it all along. I had dreamt of dragons my whole life but I'd just put it down to having an overactive imagination.

"You said you were like me?" I managed to ask when I could organise my thoughts into a coherent sentence again. "Are you a dragon too?"

Smith laughed at this, although I failed to see the funny side.

"No James, I am not a dragon. I am in fact rarer still for there is only one of me." He paused as if deciding the best course of action. After what felt like an age he seemed to reach a decision.

"You should know the truth James. My name is not Smith. I am a hunter; I hunt our kind, following the bloodlines from the men originally cursed. Watching, waiting for the change to occur and when it does I train those that can be trained and I kill those that cannot. My real name is Eadric."

—

22
1012
Trojan

For a year I travelled with my two companions, both proving to be good friends in what was the worst year of my existence. A shared past and shared grief bonded us closer than almost any bond I had known before, second only to the bond between a man, his wife and his child. I knew without a doubt in my mind that I would lay down my life for these men, if it were at all possible and that they too would do the same for me; if of course it were necessary. We knew each other well, knowing each mans own strengths and weaknesses in hunting, tracking and fighting. Brom proved a formidable adversary to any foe we fought but his ability to hunt left a little to be desired. Whilst Brom could hunt huge prey in his bear form, his uncontrollable rage in this form meant that little survived of the intended meal and we often ended up with nothing left to cook. Rowan however would take flight and return four or five times in an hour with multiple rabbits; we knew when Rowan hunted that we would eat well. I myself, unable to easily activate my own beast tended to stay close to camp, setting the fire and such things. In truth I often wondered where my beasts use would lay if I were able to change at will. In hunting the meat would return burnt beyond any edible standard; useful in a fight maybe but it meant that I had to die mid fight which in turn tended to end the tussle abruptly, at least for my foe who would suddenly find himself without an opponent and believing that he'd won. So I reasoned that my gift in this was the same as my curse, it lay with my inability to die.

That year we'd fought many a foe, none a match for Rowans speed or Broms immense strength. Mostly it was Danes or Norsemen that tended to cross our path as we travelled from town to town, listening to the gossip as we passed and searching for signs that would lead us to our next calling. Mostly the talk turned out to be just that, stories of beasts were all too common in a time when every aspect of life was thought to be the work of some devil of deity. So we listened to the stories and followed up on trails, Rowan proved to be an excellent tracker, his knowledge of the land and his ability to fly above helped him immensely. We occasionally found signs that a brother of the curse may have been around, but they proved difficult to track down. It was a time when word of mouth was the only tool at our disposal and people only had first names and there wasn't a lot of variation in those. So we checked every trail for the truth in its midst and occasionally we would believe we were close, only to be disappointed once again.

The first that I believed we had found had not turned out well. He had been turned on by his own town folk, witchcraft had been blamed and he had suffered the awful fate deemed appropriate for a witch; burnt at the stake in the town. The scorch mark was still visible in the square, a reminder to all that witchcraft was not tolerated. It was an awful fate for any man to befall and my minds eye could almost see him burning and hear his screams as I looked upon the scorched earth. The town folk talked of a large cat that had slunk through the town from time to time, hunting and of how the burnt man would later be found laying naked on the moor with no recollection of how he got there. I do not know if he was indeed a cursed man or simply in the wrong place at the wrong time, but it didn't matter in those days, it was deemed that his behaviour was definitely bewitching and to the superstitious town folk of the day that was all the proof they had needed. I never committed his name to memory; I thought of those that we hunted as brothers, but to know their names would make it too personal and if I then had to intervene and take their life from them it would be that much harder.

Eventually we found ourselves travelling down the Danelaw heading to the southern coast, back past London where we had stopped for supplies. After the fire had engulfed the city those two years past, the town had flourished in the way that only London seemed able. The town had rebuilt itself quickly; the trade opportunities that London provided proved a worthwhile and profitable business, so London saw people returning promptly and it had grown vastly as a result.

We travelled quickly through London, picking up the news as we went. Mostly it was the usual talk of the invading Vikings, pillaging another town here or there, but two points had stood out, two tales that caught my attention. The first was that a rumour had spread that the Danes where preparing a vast army for a last push at securing England for themselves and the second was a tale of a magnificent war horse that had been seen running wild in the forests south of London. At first there seemed little strange about this horse, but the tale talked of it being vastly bigger than any horse seen before, some thirty hands one man claimed. The folk talked of the horse leaving flaming hooves as it galloped, that it had the strength of ten horses and that it would take no rider. I knew that these tall tales might have led us nowhere but we agreed to check the area regardless. Rowan had heard talk of some barbaric men planning to capture the beast and keep it in chains and the thought of one of our brothers in chains was one we could not bear. Brom had known this fate himself and did not wish it upon another.

So we travelled south, leaving the sprawling town of London behind and moving back into the country. We all felt more at home in the country. Whether this was due to the painful memories from our last visit to London, an animal instinct to avoid built up areas or just that we were simple village folk at heart I did not know, but my mind rested easier when London was well behind us. We travelled two days and nights, when a passing tradesman on his way to do business in London told us that he had heard claim of this horse in the woodland to our east and so we headed onwards following the trader's advice.

We came to the land that the traveller had spoken of and it did not take Rowan long to find tracks that supported the tales. Huge hoof prints scattered the land, it seemed that this horse cared nothing for subtlety, which, as Brom suggested may indeed point to the fact that it was just a horse after all. None the less we followed the most recent tracks and some hours later, Rowan, in hawk form, spotted something entering the woodland across the field from our very position. Brom and I hurried across the meadow and as we approached the edge of the woodland our search was abruptly over, for there, just visible beyond the tree line, was the biggest horse I'd ever seen.

The horse watched as we approached, I didn't know what to expect so I advanced with my hands held open and no weapon drawn, hoping that he would know we meant no harm. Brom and I stopped twenty feet from the tree line, not wanting to spook the beast. We'd suspected we were not far ahead of the men that wanted to imprison this magnificent creature and such might not have gotten a second chance. The beast watched us warily and then after a moment he took a couple of steps forward, stepping clear of the tree line and for the first time we could see his huge form. I realised in this moment that the tales were true, thirty hands may not even be sufficient. This horse was beyond large and it was clear then that this was no ordinary horse. I observed its massive form, the huge muscled neck that held the war horse's giant Roman head, its powerfully muscled legs that looked capable of running forever, its great mane and tail giving it a magnificent, majestic appearance. It clearly wore no halter, no saddle, for this horse would not be broken, we could see that instantly, no man deserved a beast this fine. In this moment as we both judged each other where we stood, Rowan flew down to my side transforming in front of us. This wasn't something Rowan would ordinarily do, he felt his transformation to be a private matter, particularly as it left the person naked and vulnerable; but this was his way of showing this majestic beast what we were, that we too were like him. I handed Rowan his clothes as he stood at my side and he accepted them gratefully. The horse stared at us; I could see him reading the situation, the intelligence clear in his eyes.

"We mean you no harm friend, brother. But we come with word from the town. There are people in London that are conspiring against you. They do not know what you are but they intend to capture you, to chain you up and keep you a slave to work their fields. They seek you as if a prize, it is discussed with much vigour and we fear that you will be outnumbered greatly."

Brom took a step forward at this point and uncharacteristically he spoke to the great horse. “I know what it is to be chained and I wish it on no man or beast. I ask you to travel with us, to leave this place where they will most certainly hunt you.” Brom bowed his head respectfully before he continued. “If you choose not to leave, I will stay with you and fight off your foe, for no beast deserves chains.” And with this Brom did something I had never seen him do before. He stood perfectly calm and changed smoothly into the giant black bear that we now knew so well. The colossal bear then roared an almighty roar that shook the ground on which I stood before his form receded and Brom once again stood at my side. “Brom of the bears, at your service.” He said bowing once again to the horse.

The horse held his ground through all this before his head tipped back and his huge body raised its massive form onto its hind legs. As he had reared up in front of us his form had begun to shrink and a man stood where the horse had been only moments before.

“My name is Trojan and I am grateful for your warning. I wish not to spend my days in chains and I commend your bravery Brom of the bears, I see you three are men of honour. I feel sure that the two of us Brom would see no trouble in fending these hunters off.” Trojan said with a grin on his face. “But I fear they would return with more men and we would eventually be overrun. So I accept your offer to travel with you, but I warn you that I am more comfortable in my animal form and as such will not make for good conversation whilst travelling.” And so with that Trojan had joined our band of brothers as we travelled down to the south coast to continue our search.

23
2010
A Fellow Beast

"A hunter?" I asked him incredulously. "Like a monster hunter? Or dragon slayer? But this is the modern world. People no longer believe in monsters or people that change into beasts, I mean are we talking werewolves?" I still didn't get this; it was too far out there, too much for me to believe. I'm a dragon?

"Yes, sort of, but not just wolves, everybody's different. I did meet a werewolf once many years ago. It didn't end well for him."

"So monsters exist and I'm a dragon, fact."

"Yes. I must say that most people have grasped the basic concept by now." Eadric said mockingly.

"It's a lot to take in." I replied sullenly. "And you say that I will be able to remember being a dragon when my mind stops cowering away from the beast?"

"Basically, yes."

"How long did that take you?" I questioned.

"My beast was different, not so aggressive, I remember the first time it happened, but I was prepared, I had seen my friends go through it already. It took about two years to learn to transform at will however." Eadric replied calmly.

"Two years!" I exclaimed a little louder than was intended.

"Yes but we didn't have anyone to teach us." I considered this before another thought crept into the back of my mind.

"You have never told me what your beast is? And you said you were one of the original fighters? You said this curse was set a thousand years ago but you are what, twenty?"

"I am eighteen, but I have been eighteen for a thousand years." I sat and looked at him as he said this, scepticism once again clear on my face, how was I supposed to believe this. When I didn't reply he continued. "And as for your other question, I am a phoenix."

I didn't say anything to this either, I'd seen Harry Potter and knew that a phoenix was a mythical bird that burst into flames when it died or something like that. They no more existed than dragons did. I went to speak but Eadric had stood and walked over to the fire in the centre of the cave. I leapt to my feet but before I could stop him he'd stuck his hand into the fire, his hand beginning to burn. I could see the skin blacken, it was grim. What was he doing? He was clearly nuts.

"Stop it!" I yelled, stepping forward to pull him from the flames.

"After a while pain becomes mute." As he said this he shut his eyes and his body, without warning, burst into flames, white hot, the fire burned with an intensity I had never seen. The suddenness of the fire sent me stumbling backwards, tripping over my own feet in the process and landing in a heap on the floor. I looked up to see the outline of a huge flaming bird as it filled the entrance to the cave, before flying clear from it.

"Wow!" I said whilst taking in the scene. I leapt up as fast as I could and ran to the entrance of the cave to see the phoenix ducking and diving playfully in the sky above the entrance before it turned back down towards me. I leapt clear, landing face first in the mud outside as it shot back into the cave. I stood and cautiously entered the cave to see Eadric standing in front of the fire once again, his body returned as he pulled some new clothes from his bag.

"You must go through a lot of clothes?" I asked because it was all I could think to say. In that moment I believed. It would be impossible not to in the face of the evidence. "Does that hurt?" I asked curious.

"At first it did, my beast rises from the flames of my dead body. I die every time I change and I am reborn, I have control now and the death is very quick, so the pain is minimal."

"You die every time?" That sucked. But yet he was an immortal, as the thought crossed my mind the words followed from my mouth.

"Immortal? No. I can die the same as you, but I am then reborn. My body however is frozen in time it seems and I return to this form every time I regenerate."

"Now that is cool. You can't die! Well not for long anyway." I said carelessly, the wonder of his talent filled my mind, it was incredible. He didn't need to fear a thing.

"Yes, very cool if you *want* to live forever." Eadric said in reply, his tone catching my attention. He clearly wasn't as chuffed with this talent as I thought I would be. "My curse does not lie within my beasts form as yours does. I have watched my family die and seen my friends die over and over again. Unlike yours, my curse lies within my very beasts nature, my curse is eternal life."

I considered this as he spoke and saw the pain that he must have suffered, I thought again of Rebecca, of the pain that her death caused me and wondered if I could watch others die, over and over again. The beast inside returned and despair once again sunk into my bones as my mind clouded over with darkness. I wish I could never again think of Rebecca, but I knew that to lose this part of me would be to give up my soul. I know that this is what Eadric felt, I could tell by his tone when he spoke of his family. He knew what I felt.

"I'm sorry Eadric, I didn't think." I said to him as he stood watching the flames of the fire flicker.

"I have come to terms with my past. Now it is time for you to come to terms with your future. We must leave now James, for the police will be looking for you by now and it won't take them long to find you here."

"Where will I go?"

"I know a place."

24
1012
Trouble Ahead

We travelled south in the weeks that followed our encounter with Trojan. He rarely changed to human form over the duration, always favouring the safety of his animal. Trojan showed a great understanding of his curse, he seemed at ease with the beast within and he accepted it as part of him, as if it was simply an extension of his body no different to an arm or a leg. It seemed this acceptance was the key to his control. His trigger it appeared was linked to his instinct for self preservation, a desire for flight and on occasion, in those rare times that he would change back to share a conversation with us, we would witness his returning transformation and it was quite something. Trojan would stand in human form talking one moment and then he would turn and run as fast as his human legs would enable, once at full run his body would blur and suddenly four hooves would hit the ground and his speed would increase ten fold. Trojan was a magnificent, proud beast; it was easy to see why he preferred this form. Brom, Rowan and I had often talked as we walked on along the coast of this transformation and the ease with which Trojan managed it and it was during one of these talks that I'd asked Brom of his control on that day that we'd meet Trojan. I remember the conversation well as Brom's advice has stuck with me ever since.

"You never did say how you changed so effortlessly the day we found Trojan, Brom." I began, wondering if he would be willing to discuss the matter. To my surprise he answered willingly.

"The moment I saw Trojan a thought hit me, I realised that we had been looking at this all wrong. As I looked into Trojans eyes I saw no internal war raging as I have always seen in the eyes of each one of us."

"Yes I too spotted this, but what conclusion did you draw from it?" I asked curious.

"I reasoned that his beast did not run at our approach, it did not act on instinct and unlike normal horses it appeared to be a solitary figure. Horses are naturally flighty, herd animals that choose to run in great numbers, this beast stood alone and showed no fear as we approached, so I reasoned that the mind was not that of the animal." Brom spoke with admiration in his tone and as he talked I realised how right he was, a part of me scolded myself for not also making this connection; our animals had always acted true to their animalistic nature.

"I wondered to myself if his human mind had managed to control the beast, as we have often pondered the possibilities ourselves, although with little success. When in bear form my human mind is lost and the beast takes control, until I saw Trojan I had assumed that this was the way of the curse and that the best I could hope for was to contain the beast within. I know that you and Rowan have always had more control than I from the start and my assumption had been that this was due to your beast being of a less dominant nature; that your human mind was able to restrain your beasts easier. But when I saw Trojans control of a beast of his size, I knew that this was not the case. Initially my mind was ashamed of my lack of control, but as I pondered it in that moment I suddenly knew the truth."

"Which was?" I prompted intrigued to hear more.

"That the beast inside is not a monster at all, just an animal. I have spent every moment since the day the curse was set hating the beast inside, hating it for what it made me, I waged war against it internally, detesting myself for what I had become. But the anger only fed the beasts rage and he broke out, filled with the hate and savage as a result. Trojan showed me another way, acceptance. I saw all this the instant I looked into his eye and in that moment I knew that the beast was me and I he. And so was born Brom of the bears. Our human mind is not meant to fight the mind of the beast, join him and share control, I have learnt a lot from him and he from I and now we have reached an understanding."

I was impressed and deeply pleased for Brom, he had found what we had searched so long for, the answer was not to fight, but to let the beast in. Rowan listened to Broms every word as did Trojan. Neither said anything but I know that both pondered the information, understanding now dawning in all our minds.

Later that same day we had an opportunity to test this new found knowledge as we crossed a band of Danes heading back towards London, having plundered the southern villages. We saw their horde approach in the distance, their large number giving them away from afar. They moved swiftly towards us, following the track that led along the coastal cliff on which we travelled. Rowan removed his clothing in an instant and leapt from the cliff, free falling at first before soaring upwards a hawk once again. He flew above the band as they moved ever closer, before returning to us and taking human form once again.

"There are maybe thirty of them and they have with them a great number of carts full of silver and such, they must be returning it to London, but for what I do not know." Rowan reported. It was strange behaviour, for whilst the Danes where renowned for their plundering, they rarely transported such vast quantities, preferring instead to disperse their treasures, burying them in various banks around the land for collection later when required.

"There must be something going on in London soon, a treasure of that size must be a gift to an important man, a feared man; a King perhaps." I pondered aloud.

"Perhaps it is this vast invasion we heard talk of in London, it must be sooner than they believed." Rowan added.

"Possibly, we should not let them pass regardless; we must stop them from joining the mass assembly in London. Leave one alive though; we must know that our suspicions are correct before we decide upon a course of action."

And so we sat in wait of the band as it worked its way to our location. Trojan, in a rare instant turned to human form and asked that we leave the horses alive, if at all possible; his beast demanded it of him and he thought that they would hasten our travel in any case. We agreed to save what we could but that he had to understand that our own control was not equal to his, He'd nodded his understanding and returned to his animals form once again, awaiting the ensuing fight that would be upon us shortly.

The band turned a bend in the track; they were only moments away from where we lay in wait on the edge of a gathering of trees, just out of sight of the track. Brom crouched beside me ready to run, Rowan had gathered a vast pile of rocks, each easily big enough to bludgeon a man to death and he now perched at top of them ready to take flight. Trojan just stood by in horse form, serene, as if this was just another day for him.

They edged ever nearer and suddenly without any signal from us Trojan trotted clear out into the open and onto the track in front of the Danes.

The Vikings halted at the sight of this magnificent beast before them, each man staring, dumbstruck by the great beast. Many of their men looked on with greed in their eyes; this beast would make a magnificent gift to a King. Others were more wary, they had been brought up on stories of magical creatures and monsters and they knew that no normal horse would stand so tall. Brom didn't give them the chance to think anymore on the matter for his human form tore from the tree line, the muscles in his legs pumping as he ran, pushing himself onwards faster and faster, he looked like a mighty warrior raining down upon the men. But they were not small men themselves, great Vikings, instinct hit them and they turned to fight Brom in combat. I saw instantly his plan for them; they would see one man running from the tree line assuming that the horse was his and thinking it an easy fight. He saved the bear for when it was too late, if they had seen the bear running from the tree line they may have turned and fled; but a mere man they could handle. The instant they turned on him he too had turned, letting the beast loose upon them. The colossal beast ripped from his body mid stride, his fist had pulled back to hit the first Viking but it was a claw that connected with the mans face, tearing the flesh from his skull. Chaos erupted.

Trojan had charged directly at the pack splitting them through the middle, the horses reared in fear at first but Trojan turned at the back of the pack and ran once again through them, knocking Vikings to ground as he passed. This time the horses followed; herd animals, instinct kicked in and they followed Trojans path, running to keep up with this great beast. The Vikings had no chance, they were stampeded by there own horses, trampled to death under hoof. The great bear of Brom however got his fair share and Rowan too picked out the odd stragglers as they attempted to break clear from the carnage. One Viking ran for it only to find himself inexplicably dead, bludgeoned, a huge rock now embedded within his skull. I walked clear of the tree line, my intention had been to fight believing we would be evenly matched with their number, but I could see now that I was not required, Brom and Trojan could defeat an army if required. Trojan circled around bringing the carts and horses with him and Brom returned to his human form, still dripping with the blood of his enemy.

"Well we have enough money now to buy a Castle if required," Brom jested as he approached the carts. In that moment a man dropped from the sky, landing on his face in the mud at my feet. I had asked for one man alive and Rowan had delivered. The great hawk took a perch on one of the carts, choosing not to return to human form whilst an enemy still remained.

"What is your name?" I asked of the Dane now lying at my feet.

"My name not matter. Me loyal to Sweyn." The man exclaimed slowly in broken English.

"Then where are you carting these spoils and why?" I asked patiently, but the man said nothing more. I looked to Brom who understood and walked forward, clenching his massive fist. I do not take pride in the beating of a man that was already defeated, but information was what we needed and this man was a hardened warrior. There was only one language that he understood. Brom slammed his massive fist into the Vikings face once before bringing his fist around for a second time. This time I heard the crack of his nose, but the man still did not talk. Brom tried a variety of other ways of inflicting pain but the man seemed impervious and after a while I asked Brom to stop. As we stood there a thought occurred to me and I wondered if this man was as strong mentally as he was physically. I stepped in front of where he now knelt, bloodied and beaten.

"Are you a family man?" I had asked of him. Looking back now I regret what I did to this man, I played on the worst fear possible, a pain that I had known myself all to well. He didn't reply but a new glint of fear appeared in his eyes and I knew that he was.

"Did you not see what happened to your men?" I asked him. "What we are capable of?" I saw the fear build as I spoke; I knew he thought us monsters, now I would confirm that belief, I would make him believe I was the devil. "My fate will be that of yours and your family if I do not get the answers I desire." And as I said this I brought forth every image of death I had seen over the last two years to the fore front of my mind. Thoughts that I had worked hard to suppress flooded in, images of my towns folk burning, my friends dead on the ground around me and my family hanging in the woodland all flashed before my eyes. I had considered what Brom had told me and reasoned that if I let the transformation happen it would trigger far easier; I had always fought death before but not this time. The thought of death was all I needed now, surrendering my body and mind to it, grieving my loved ones and giving up on life itself was enough to trigger the beast within. My body burst into flames in front of the Viking, his eyes opening wide as he watched my body burn intensely and turn to dust. A moment passed before a huge winged beast rose up into the air, burning white with heat and scorching the ground below me. I didn't fly clear as I would normally do, my mind now balanced with that of the birds, we agreed to stay put and as our tail feathers grazed the ground, my body returned and I stared once again into the eyes of the warrior.

"Now tell me what I want to know." I knew he thought me the devil. Only stories of the most hell bound creature's depicted men bursting into flames.

"We ride to London, deliver our bounty for Kings arrival." The man exclaimed, terror now evident in his eyes, not for his own safety though but for that of his family. I knew that he held his own life in little regard, to die in your duty was an honourable death, but his family was a different matter and that is why I knew that I had to threaten more than just his own life.

"When do you expect him here?" I asked.

"Six full moons from now." The man said, defeated.

After this I let him go, he had suffered enough and I felt disgusted by my threat on his family and with my little trick. His death I knew would not appease this guilt. He would tell all he met of this encounter, some may believe him, others will not but I had suspected at the time that it may do some good to spread a little fear through their ranks.

We set up camp after that, a little way off the beaten track, to take stock of where we were at.

"I say we meet the King face on and kill him as he steps onto our land!" Brom said enthusiastically. "We may not get another chance at the King himself, their hordes will be lost, disbanded; cut off the head and you will kill the beast."

"I agree with Brom," Trojan added, taking human form for this exchange only. "But we will need more than just us to fight this foe. His numbers will be vast and we will fall quickly."

As Trojan spoke I knew the truth in his words for we had seen such an enemy before.

"We have six full moons to gather an army capable of defeating this Sweyn. Can it be done?" I asked.

Rowan looked to me at this point and provided an answer. "We may not need an army of men if we could band together those that fought beside us before; we could perhaps regain the dignity we lost last time. We may be greatly outnumbered, but we now have something extra. They turned the curse upon us to begin with; can we turn it back against them now?"

"We would need almost all of them, we know two at least are no more for this world, what if others shared a similar fate?" I asked.

"And we would not have enough time to hunt them all." Brom added. "We have searched for a year long and we found only two!"

We considered this for some time before Trojan spoke up once again.

"I may be able to offer some assistance there." he said with a knowing smile.

25
2010
St Michaels

We left the cave that had played home to me for the past two nights and worked our way back down the mountain. As we headed back to the tracks leading down, we began to see people trekking up, taking the main track that led to the peak. Each group that passed by were dressed in hiking boots and full walking gear, prepared for the late October weather. We definitely weren't dressed appropriately and occasionally I got an odd glance as a passer by in full waterproof gear would notice my light linen trousers with quick release poppers.

"Why did you choose to come here?" Eadric asked me after a while of walking in silence.

"I'm not sure." I answered honestly. "I just found myself here."

"Interesting." He said and did not elaborate any further.

"Why is it interesting?" I asked him, curious to know what he was thinking.

"It's just that the Welsh mountains were once renowned to be the home of the dragons. I wondered if you had known this?" I hadn't. It could just have been coincidence but somehow I doubted it, lately I've felt that I'd had little control over anything in my own life, why should this be any different.

"So where are we heading?" I asked ten minutes later.

"To see some friends of mine, they should be able to help you. We cannot train here, if you were seen, it would mean trouble for us all." He replied and then said no more.

We eventually returned to the dirt track where I had left the bike and I pulled it up, getting on and placing the helmet over my head.

"Uh, I've only got one helmet. We won't get a mile riding without a helmet; the police'll pull us for sure. You got a car?"

"No, Head south to the tip of Cornwall. There is an Abbey on the hill, St Michaels, I shall meet you there." Eadric said confidently as he turned to leave.

"What if I decide not to go?" I asked, merely to see his reaction, where else could I go? If these people could help me then I had no choice, I needed all the help I could get.

"Then we won't be able to help you. I'm sure the police will be very helpful though." Eadric answered with a smile. We both knew the police would be useless and I would rot in jail for a murder that… well, that I did in fact commit. When you think about it that's exactly what I deserved. For a moment I considered handing myself in anyway, perhaps paying for my sin by rotting in jail would ease my conscience but I suspected not.

I started the engine and gunned the bike down the track. I glimpsed in the wing mirror just in time to see a flash of light and a burning flame rise into the air. I found myself wondering how he carried his luggage as I pulled of the dirt track onto the side roads leading from the welsh mountains.

An hour later I dropped onto the M54 pushing the bike far faster than I should, I tried to keep it under a hundred, trying not to draw attention to myself, but my patience was wearing thin and I knew I had a long way to go. I pulled into the services on the M54 the tank was running low and I had a good few hundred miles to go. I decided to avoid the main services and head straight to the petrol pumps to prevent any unnecessary contact; I was feeling pretty anxious amongst all these people. I filled the tank and headed into the pay station, the whole while looking nervously around at the other people filling up, watching their faces. I don't know what I was expecting, someone to shout, 'there he is!' and sirens to swiftly move in? I pictured myself being surrounded by police, made to lie face down on the floor of the forecourt, before being carted off in a police van.

"What pump?" uh? I looked up. The station attendant was looking at me in a very bored manner, waiting for me to say something. "What pump sir?" he repeated.

"Oh, four, Sorry." I said, handing over some cash and walking swiftly from the station. As I walked out I caught the headlines on the papers by the door.

'Boy still missing in savage attack.'

I read the first few lines of the article, boy still missing… girl found dead… animal attack… police following up leads. It chilled me to the core, there it was, a stark reminder of my crime. I think I had begun to tell myself that it wasn't real, that it couldn't have happened, but there it was; in ink. My head began to spin, I couldn't think, I couldn't breath. I ran to my bike, fired it into life and gunned it from the petrol station. The beast filled my mind. I hit the motorway at a hundred, pushing the bike on faster still. I tried to push the beast back, to keep my human mind in charge, to keep control; but the fog began to drift over my mind and I could feel the shame in my head as it began to throb. I felt my skin begin to burn as the beast inside pushed at my human side, trying to force me from my own mind as he attempted to take control of my body. My human consciousness tried to fight back but the animal was too strong and control was hopeless. I pushed the bike on and suddenly I saw blue lights flash as sirens began to ring out behind me.

"Damn!" I yelled as loud as my lungs would allow. My mind panicking as I thought of the cops. I would be pulled for speeding initially but they'd soon know who I was, I knew I couldn't pull over but this was getting out of hand. I pushed on faster still, hitting the M6, the motorway was crowded now and I wondered if I could lose them in the traffic but then I remembered that cops show from the television and I knew that this was one of those moments. Soon there'd be a chopper over top and a tailback of cop cars behind and trouble would be unavoidable. I had to do something and soon.

I shot through the traffic the speedometer blurring somewhere around a hundred and ten, I held the bike to the right of the centre lane, allowing myself to drift from the central to the outside lane as required, enabling me to glide through the traffic; the occasional horn dying away in the distance as I caught a driver off guard. The cop car kept up with me well considering, but the traffic was getting denser and I knew I would lose him shortly.

I leaned left, then right, guiding the bike swiftly through the traffic, which had begun to back up as I neared the M5 junction, it was always hellishly busy here and I wondered if I could get through it quick enough. The traffic now filled all three lanes and I pulled my arms in for fear of catching a wing mirror as I passed. The sound of the engine roared as I entered the now stationary traffic, bouncing back at me in the confines of the queued cars. I dropped my speed to a still breathtaking ninety miles an hour, my heart pumped to the point of bursting; I was terrified, but despite that fear I couldn't help grinning from ear to ear, the first time I had smiled since Rebecca. Rebecca, the memory caught me off guard and I narrowly missed a large mirror protruding from a truck. Rebecca… the police… the paper… my head swam and I lost concentration for just a moment. It was all it took.

I didn't see the car as it pulled out from the central lane and in that split second the world slowed, I saw the car pull across at the same time that I felt the fear flood my body. I went cold despite the burning flames that then crawled through my skin. I felt my mind change gear fully as the beast won, taking the controls as my conscious, human mind flinched away. I saw a terrified face in the reflection of the rear view mirror as the driver saw me all too late.

I felt the impact like a train as it pounded into the bike, the front wheel and forks vanishing instantly.

I saw every shard from the front fairing, the lights, the dials, the wind shield and every other generic plastic component as they flew with me, over the top of the car. My body turned in the air, my feet going over my head. My eyes were dimly aware of the roof of the car before they were all too aware of the remains of my bike, the fuel tank, seat, frame, engine, swing arm, sockets, rear wheel… all following my slow motion ark over the roof of the car that I had surely just written off.

The beast acted impulsively but my human mind, for fear of my life, stood firm. My back tore open, my arms snapped back and my figure grew, crawling, burning, a fever worse than anything I had felt in my human form. But my mind took it all in. Suddenly I knew what was happening, understanding dawned as a sharp awareness hit my brain. I felt the tips of huge wings stretching out from me, effortlessly pushing aside a truck on the inside lane. I could feel the boundaries of my human form stretch beyond anything they had known before, my feet grew, changing, tearing at the car below me as I righted myself in midair. Suddenly the beast took off, soaring up and away from the scene of the crash.

As I shot up into the air my head dropped just enough for me to see the remains of my bike bury themselves into the side of a coach in the outside lane. My human mind was in shock from the crash and also because it had never seen any of this before; I was flying. I don't know how, the details were being taken care of by the beast, but flying none the less. I felt like a passenger in my own body, not in control, but no longer suppressed either. I could feel the two minds barely tolerating each other like two dogs squaring up for dominance, but I knew now that an understanding had been reached, I was here now. I watched through the windows that were my own eyes as suddenly a huge flaming bird rose up elegantly in front of me, its head turning to me just long enough for me to see its expression. Oops.

As I flew I tried to remember what he had said about keeping a low profile; he was not going to be happy with me when we landed.

26
1012
The Monk

We continued south, but we no longer stopped at the settlements we passed, we no longer had time on our hands, the deadline had been set and we had a lot to do in the little time we had.

We gained speed by the way of the horses, we had taken one each to hasten our journey and the others were hitched up to the carts to bring with us the pay load that we had gained from the Vikings. Trojan rode with us for a while, selecting himself the largest of horses and settling in for the journey. I felt that he was beginning to trust us a little more as he began to spend more time in his human form, even seemingly enjoying our trivial conversations and occasionally chiming in with a story of his own.

After a while I'd turned from the back of my small grey cob to face Trojan who'd appeared at ease a stride the large horse as it trudged on. I could see Brom to the back of our pack following behind the carts of silver, looking uncomfortable as he rode another horse. Rowans steed I believe was an Ardenne, rare for that time as it would have been an import from Belgium; but it often walked alone, Rowan preferring to fly above watching the road ahead for any unexpected guests.

"So where is it we are heading?" I asked Trojan conversationally. We had set off straight away and he had as of yet to explain our purpose.

"We are heading to an old friend of mine. Do not worry, he should prove to be very useful." Trojan said jovially.

"And what is it that makes him useful to us in this situation?" I asked warily.

"He is one of us for a start my new friend, but I must warn you that he is quite strange, but none the less an honourable man."

"Which one of our fighters was he Trojan, I remember their faces well." I had enquired.

"Oh he is no fighter; no he is a learned man, a teacher, a man of the cloth. I knew him simply as Monk, he is able to read and write and as such he was asked to record the names and details of each soldier as they joined, he also maintained a record off those that died. I believe this enabled them to send a messenger to the village and inform the families of the deceased, he should have information that could help us locate our cursed friends."

"Well that certainly is going to be useful. Where will we find him?" I enquired.

"I travelled back with him after the curse was set and he talked non stop, the whole way back, of his Abbey on the bottom most peek of the country. So there I am heading. I warn you though that he's a talkative soul." Trojan laughed as he said this last bit.

"You said he was one of us." Brom interceded. "What is his beast and can he control it?"

"Well he is no fighter, so unlike us the instinct to fight the beast inside never occurred to him, he simple looks upon it as something else to learn about. I have not seen him since we parted ways that day but I should think he has a good grasp on things by now. As for his beast, well I'll let you see that for yourself."

"Will he be safe in his Abbey?" I had asked the concern clear on my face. A lot rested on us finding this man and a lot of time had passed since he was last seen.

"They are men of the cloth; they will not harm a person if at all possible. He's as safe there as anywhere." Trojan answered casually his relaxed manner when human was quite refreshing from the intensity of Rowan and Brom, not that I blame them, the last few years would have destroyed lesser men.

We had travelled by horse moving as fast as the track had allowed, winding our way down the country following the coast all the way to the very lowest point. The weather turned for the worst slowing our progress but after three days and nights travelling, with very little sleep, we'd arrived. We stood at the edge of a sandy shore that overlooked an island in the mist, detached from the mainland with no access but by boat.

"So where now?" I asked Trojan, raising my voice over the rain that had poured heavily, soaking us to the bone.

"There." He replied, pointing over to the dense foliage at the centre of the island, I looked closer toward the island and began to see shapes in the mist. As I watched the wind shifted, momentarily clearing the fog and revealing a huge Abbey at the centre of the island, visible even at this distance. We stood in stunned silence, staring at the vast building before us, we had seen very few buildings of this size, churches mainly and only ever in London. But this Abbey rose into the skies, perched upon a vast hill and stranded alone out in the ocean, impassable by any that would try. The wind shifted and the rain poured down, once again obscuring the abbey in a huge veil of mist that had risen up from the sea. It was truly menacing. The island itself was also vastly populated more complex than any village I had seen outside of London and it was fortified on all sides by a huge stone wall that circled the island. I had never seen anything so daunting in my life, it looked impenetrable.

"How do we cross?" Brom asked all confidence in his voice gone.

"We wait." Trojan replied, not elaborating any further. So we did, we set up camp, Rowan hunted and a few hours later as the day began to draw to a close the strangest thing happened.

We'd stood and watched for some time as slowly the land began to rise from the sea. I know now that this is natural, that twice a day the tides come in and go out, but at the time it'd appeared to be magic to us simple folk. What else could explain it? We knew nothing of the ocean having never seen it before this past month and as such it held wonder and mysticism within its vast expanse and threatening nature and then to see this stretch of land rise from its depths was quite a sight to behold. We stood and watched as the path wound across the sea in front of us leading directly to the huge walled island, running right up to its gates.

As the path rose from the sea Trojan set off across the track, a moment later the rest of us followed trailing the carts as we went and eventually we approached the huge doors that barred the only entrance onto the island.

"Do you know his name?" I asked Trojan as we approached the doors.

"No." He replied simply, "I just always called him Monk."

"There must be hundreds of monks in there! How will we know which one to ask for?" Rowan asked, astounded at this over site.

"Easy." Trojan said as he banged on the huge doors. Rowan huffed a little but let Trojan go ahead, keen to watch him flounder in the face of his oversight.

"Can I help you?" A voice called through a little hatch in the door.

"Yes." Trojan replied. "A monk once travelled with me and said if I ever needed him again to come here and he will be here. So I'm here and I need his help."

"What name would this monk go by?" The voice replied.

"His name I do not recall, but he talked non stop the whole way back, I have never met a man that could talk like him."

"Ah," The voice said. "That will be Thomas." He continued mumbling to himself as he walked away, then as the voice faded into the distance I faintly heard the man saying something like. "He never shuts up that Thomas."

"They could have let us wait out of the rain." Brom mumbled huddling into the wall for shelter. Ten minutes or so passed, I'm not sure exactly how long but I remember being soaked by the time another voice spoke through the hole in the door.

"Hello, Hello, any one there?" it called cheerfully through the gap.

"Monk my old friend." Trojan called jovially, "It is good to hear your voice again!"

"Ah, Leofrick, old friend!" The monk called back cheerfully. "I trust you are well?"

"Leofrick?" Brom sniggered before being silenced by a glare from Trojan.

"Its like I said, he talks too much." Trojan said, grumbling now. "May we enter my old friend, these people travel with me and we require shelter for a night."

"You may by all means enter friend." As the monk said this he must have signalled someone because as soon as he'd spoken the huge gates began to open. We entered through the large arched doors into a courtyard with a maze of passages leading off between a network of huts and buildings all intertwined together. I turned to watch as the huge door shut behind us, closing with an ominous thud that resounded through the courtyard in which we stood. I knew by the shift in Broms stance that he too felt the confines of this muddled town to be claustrophobic, after a life time spent in the country this walled compound felt as if it was closing in around us. Rowan went to take flight but I put a reassuring hand on his shoulder to calm him.

"Patience my friend" I said quietly to him. "We are here for their help."

Rowan said nothing but nodded enough that I knew he'd heard me. Thomas led us through the maze of huts that surrounded the lower half of the island, talking of something to Trojan but I could not hear what they spoke of. After a minute he led us into a large clearing and I felt the tension around me ease as the sky came back into view again.

"I see you have huts on top of huts?" I heard Brom say to Thomas confused. In modern times this is standard, two floors, three floors, fifty floors, but in those days we rarely saw anything above ground level and the height from the second floor would have made Broms head spin.

"Yes, we are quite apt at it now, although it was not without its troubles, people fell through the floors regularly at first. You should see the Abbey itself, it is quite something!" The monk laughed at the thought. I remember thinking at the time that this man must never be sad, for to see his cheerful nature removed would be a crime against humanity. Thomas had a way about him that made people around him cheerful; I could see why Trojan liked him, even if he didn't say so himself.

“Welcome to my humble abode.” He called as he led us over to a large three sided shelter on one side of the large open space. “I did live up in the abbey with my fellow men of the cloth, but with my new talents I found this to be more fitting a home for me.” As I took my surroundings it occurred to me that this was no accidental clearing within this village.

“Is this a training ground?” I asked Thomas as he entered his shelter.

“Ah ho! It was, until I returned. They still try to use it occasionally but mostly its mine. If they want to train I make them fight me! After a while they stopped challenging! Ha ha!” He finished. I looked at the small frail frame of Thomas in front of me. He surely posed no challenge to anyone? I pondered this a moment before conceding, at least not in this form. He walked to a small desk in the back corner of the shelter, rummaging for something upon it before giving up and pulling up a couple of stools for us all to sit on.

“So come now Leofrick old friend, you and your companions will stay as my guests for as long as you require and when the sun does rise tomorrow I shall show you around our great village, but for now please curb my curiosity and tell me how it is I can help you.”

“It is Trojan now dear friend if you don’t mind, Leofricks days are behind me now.”

“So be it.” Thomas replied without giving the matter a second thought. “So my help is required I gather.”

“We have travelled long and far to see you Monk. We have heard news of an impending attack on our country; the King of Denmark is planning to take our country by storm.”

“I see, the monk replied. “And I can help you how?”

“We are all survivors of the wave of Vikings that came up the Thames two years previous.” I interceded. “We all have… talents. As I hear you have also.”

“Ahem, I see, that is why I now reside out here.” Thomas said smiling and signalling the area around him.

“We plan to fight the Vikings head on but we need fighters to help. We are trying to reform the original men that were cursed that day to persuade them to fight by our side, to turn back the Vikings at our shores." I finished.

"We had a few hundred men the first time round and it was not enough. Not even close. Only twenty odd were cursed, what makes you say that we have any chance?"

"I have never seen anyone fight like these three do now." I said, signalling the three around me.

"But that is only three men, three men against an army."

"Three beasts against mere men." I replied.

"And you have all mastered control?"

"It took time, but yes." I said earnestly.

"Then tomorrow you shall show me, but for now eat and sleep, I can get you whatever you require in the morning."

27
2010
Hunting

The dragon followed the phoenix onwards, staying above the cloud cover to avoid detection. Every now and then Eadric would drop into the clouds and I would follow to let a plane go by unaware of our presence. My head was a mess as I flew and after a while I began to wonder who was really in charge within my head. I was indeed willing the direction but I don't know if the dragon was listening or simply hunting, the phoenix looked appetizing and the beast was hungry. As I considered this I began to notice details within the way he moved, it certainly had a distinctive stalking quality to the action and I could here his hunger calling him. It was a good job Eadric was fast, it would take some explaining to turn up at St Michaels without him.

As we soared onwards I could feel my mind settling in, gradually feeling more comfortable around the beast; the beast too seemed to accept my presence, no longer trying to tear at me subconsciously. I probed around this strange mind as I flew, trying to sense this new form by pushing my thoughts into every corner and feeling the power that the beast held within its bones. I had never felt so strong, so powerful, this beast seemed capable of anything and I could feel my pride swell as I took in its majestic form. Its wingspan must have been thirty feet at least and as I felt the bulk of its body I could feel him using the vast tail that trailed behind us. The tail acted as a sort of rudder catching the air as we flew. I could feel him making subtle alterations in the angle of his wings to gain or lose height, his tail swaying left and right to counterbalance his bodies' movement as he shifted our mass in the air whilst collecting heat from passing thermals. Occasionally he would beat his wings and I would feel the sensation of lift as this new body would soar upwards. It was out of this world, I knew in this moment that I would never travel any other way again. I occasionally caught glimpses of the landscape below and I could see the coast now, off in the distance. This high up we covered the land quickly, flying as the crow flies, or the dragon of course. Eadric indicated a small island off in the distance but didn't approach it directly, so I continued to follow him as we flew past and out across the ocean. I wondered at first where we were going, when my heart leapt with a sudden jolt of joy as I realised I would never need my passport again. I could already see France off in the distance and knew I could make it there easily. Eadric suddenly dropped from the sky, down through the cloud line in front of me and I quickly reined my thoughts back in as the dragon turned to follow him. We skimmed low over the water and after a moment I realised what he was doing, avoiding being seen as we flew back to the island out of sight of the mainland.

We soon hit the beach of the mainland and Eadric flew clear over the wall to land on the ground just inside of the vast boundary that surrounded the complex. He dropped from the sky onto a large patch of dirt that had been roughly marked out as a sort of helipad, delicately transforming from beast to man before landing lightly on his feet and walking to a large shelter that stood off to one side. I watched as he took what looked like a robe from the shelter and wrapped it around his now naked form whilst still holding his back pack.

I followed his lead and the dragon led us into the landing patch. I was nowhere near as graceful as I landed but was pleased with myself for landing at all and I felt the beast ebb as my body began to return.

Suddenly a huge roar filled the air and I felt my mind tear to the left as my body abruptly jolted to the right. I felt my wings beat heavily as the dragon returned unexpectedly, the beast now in full flow. I got my mind together just in time to see a herd of cattle off to the side of the landing area and I felt the beasts mind roar as he saw his lunch. I felt the hunger fill his mind and for a moment the desire felt so strong that my human mind also felt the temptation to eat.

No! My mind yelled as the dragon continued on his course, nothing else mattered to him in that moment except lunch. I hit his mind as hard as I could, pushing him from control as I fought to prevent what was about to happen, but I was too weak. I felt our claws open, felt my huge jaw gape widely and felt my teeth sink heavily into the hide of the nearest cow. It didn't stand a chance, I was a hunting machine. I wondered in that instant how I had not caught Eadric earlier before realising that it had simply been a game, the dragon enjoying the chase. If he had wanted to he would have caught him. I was not strong enough to hold back the beast as it feasted heartily on the now limp cow in its jaws.

Only after his hunger was sated and he grew tired was I able to push him far enough from my mind to regain my human form, my shape changing back before my naked body hit the ground. Eadric stood over me looking down at my blood stained body. I could hear others now entering the clearing around me and I felt shame fill me deeply, I knew again the sensation of wanting the ground to swallow me whole, to never have to face the world again.

28
1012
Base Camp

The next morning we awoke well rested. Monk had been true to his word and we had been well fed and for the first time in weeks we had washed thoroughly. Monk had offered to find us all a warm bed for the night but each one of us refused, simply lying under the shelter with a bed of straw such as he himself did. We all, I was sure, felt safer for not having four walls hemming us in and slept better as a result. As we awoke Monk was already busily working at his little desk, his job to document detailed accounts of various aspects of the daily lives within the city walls. People would come to him with requests for land usage or something similar and he would document it all and take each request to the senior monks up in the Abbey above.

He had shown us around the island later that day, a sprawling metropolis compared to the burh from which we had come. The main town surrounded the base of the island where town folk went about daily life, working, trading and whatever else was required. They did a little farming on the island and kept livestock, to minimise trade requirements and negate the need to travel to the mainland or trade with the nearby town, although occasionally they did still have need to. After we had completed a brief tour of the village Monk led us up to the Abbey that dominated the town, visible from anywhere within it. We walked up a long, sprawling, beautifully kept path, the only track that led up through the sprawling woodland that surrounded the Abbey on all sides. I remember how Trojan had sighed deeply as we entered the woods, reminiscent of the woods he'd once roamed and all of us felt better still as we climbed the track out of the town, leading up to the Abbey.

The Abbey above was incredible, a huge building, easily the size of a Castle with turrets and chimney stacks reaching for the heavens from every wing and tower that rose from the mighty, multi story bulk, of the building that was literally built into the rock of the island itself. Monk led us through the vast gothic entrance to the Abbey and past an assortment of smaller passageways that I assumed led off to the various wings of this place. We followed through the main vaulted passage and after a few minutes we stepped out into a vast hall, so big that at first I thought it was a courtyard.

"Wait here a moment and I will get my acquaintances, if your need our help it would be wise to get them on side." The Monk said smiling widely and walking off, leaving us stood in the centre of the vast hall, alone.

Monk returned some half an hour later. We had gotten comfortable sat off to one side enjoying the rare morning sun as it shone through the large gothic window. Trojan had stood out on the grass to the front entrance, longingly watching the woodland below, he had been human now longer than he had been in years and wasn't happy about it. Monk walked over to where we sat, with two other monks at his side.

"May I introduce to you Abbot John the third." Monk said holding a hand up to the monk on his left. "He is the Abbot of the Abbey. And this is the Claustral Prior." Monk said conversationally. Rowan, Brom and I leapt to our feet, although unaware of the exact protocol here, we knew that bowing at least was required to show the appropriate respect for a man in his position.

"Please, that is not necessary." The Abbot said as we raised ourselves back up into a standing position. "I do not care for formalities." The Abbot turned then and began to walk before continuing. "Welcome to St Michaels, please, let me show you around."

We all followed behind the three of them, Trojan joining us as we left the main hall. The Abbot proceeded to lead us around the vast facility. We'd passed through the main courtyard and through the various working rooms to the Abbey, the refectory, the dining room, the kitchens and so on. Eventually he'd led us into a vast library, walls lined with books like nothing we had ever seen before.

"Now gentlemen, we should be able to talk in private here." He said taking a seat at a large desk at the centre of the huge library.

"So Thomas here tells me that we are facing a war, that Sweyn himself is heading up this charge and that England will be lost."

"Yes I believe this to be the case." I answered gravely.

"And you require our help?" The Abbot asked rhetorically.

"Yes although we do not ask a lot, we hope to ascertain from Thomas a list of the men that like us were cursed. We have been led to believe that he possesses such a list."

"Ah yes, Thomas tells me that you are all men of the curse like he."

"Yes."

"He tells me that you have learnt control. That is very difficult and takes great strength. I saw first hand as Thomas learnt to live with his beast; I have seen the torment it can cause."

"That is very true and it has taken a lot to overcome, but we have managed it."

"Show me this control that you talk of and the beast that reside within you. After I shall tell you if we may help."

One by one each of us stepped to the centre of the vast space in front of the Abbot's desk. Rowan stepped up first, took flight and soared around the ceiling of the vast library before landing back at the desk. Brom followed next, the Abbot grinned widely at the size of the bear before Brom too returned to his human form. Next Trojan changed into his giant horse, but chose to remain that way, trotting to the side to allow me to walk toward the centre. I had transformed then, bursting into flame, raising only a few feet off the floor in flight before returning to the ground again. The Abbot, unable to hide his surprise, stood up quickly knocking his chair to the floor. As I returned to human form I looked down to see an expensive looking rug smouldering below me.

"Sorry about the rug." I said before stepping aside.

"Well that was a surprise." The Abbot exclaimed joyfully. "The gift of flight is a useful one." The Abbot said looking toward Rowan. "The speed of the horse and strength of the bear, great assets you will be to our side." The Abbot continued. I noted his use of the word 'our.'

"And you." The Abbot said turning his head towards me. "A phoenix; my God. You are the stuff of legends a phoenix has not been seen for hundreds of years. Some believe they died out long ago; others wonder if they ever existed at all. According to legend they are said to live forever, did you know that?"

"Forever?" I said half to myself. I knew before this that I couldn't die, at least not for long, but to live forever? That hadn't occurred to me before that point. "I knew not what I was, a Phoenix you say? It is good to put a name to my beast. I do however know that death appears to elude me."

"A useful talent to say the least but it's not without its own price." The Abbot said before sitting back down on the chair that had since been picked up by a servant that had been loitering in the back ground. "You know that they will not be easy to find, even with the list and that's assuming that they have not already been discovered and killed?"

"Yes."

"You understand that six months is not long enough to learn complete control?"

"Yes."

"That you will need a place to train them… Somewhere safe from harm… Safe from the brutality of the Vikings that roam the mainland if you are to stand any chance…"

"Yes."

"And you understand that if you manage all of this, you still have a battle that you cannot win ahead of you?"

"Yes."

"But yet you are still willing to try?"

"Yes. What option is there but to try?"

"So be it, this is what I can do for you. You will need a base, somewhere to train the men; you will not be able to do this effectively whilst travelling. You will take a small band of men and hunt each man on the list that Thomas will supply. You will send each that will come back here, where Thomas will begin training, I will also prepare a small band of our best fighters to assist you where they can. We will prepare to help your cause in any way possible, it's like you said what choice do we have?"

"Thank you Abbot." I said before we turned to walk from the library. As we reached the door the Abbot called to us.

"May God be with you." He said and with that we left. Thomas had guided us back through the maze of corridors that led to the main entrance of the Abbey, talking incessantly the whole way. I heard little of what he said but I did hear Trojan ask him why the Abbot was so willing to help us, why he assisted monsters and the simple reply spoke volumes to me.

Monk simply asked in return, "Are we not all Gods creatures?"

29
2010
Training Begins

Eadric led me through the main buildings that congregated around the lower quarter of the island. There were maybe twenty mid sized buildings made of old stone that formed a small fishing village sat just inside the large boundary that surrounded the island. I guessed the buildings had to be maybe two hundred years old but I couldn't say for sure, the main wall however looked a lot older. The village was friendly looking but the evident fortification made sure that people knew it wasn't, nothing said stay out like a fifteen foot wall surrounding the island. As we walked through the main town I gawped up at the huge Castle? Monastery? Abbey? Whatever it was it was impressive, a huge vast building that dominated the landscape around it, clearly whatever this island was, it was all about that building.

"What's that?" I asked Eadric as we entered the main village.

"It is the Abbey." Eadric answered. "The island belongs to the church and the church, support our cause." He continued.

"What? They know about us?" I asked curious.

"Yes. They understand the threat that we pose and are keen to help us to control it; they have been with us since the beginning, a great resource to our cause."

I didn't ask any more on the matter, I'm sure I'd get my head around it all in time. As I looked up again to the building I wondered how old it was, it was clearly a lot older than the village below, eight hundred years I guessed, but I couldn't tell; parts of the main Abbey were crumbling away, reminiscent of an old Castle from the days of knights and dragons. I laughed to myself as I thought of the tale of St George and wondered what he'd make of me.

"It's dinner time." Eadric said to me, as he entered into a large building that over looked the bay. "Although I see that you've already eaten." He then added, laughing to himself.

I had apologised to him about the cow but he had just shrugged it off saying, “That’s why you’re here, better a cow than a person,” and said nothing more of it. After that incident I had cleaned and put on one of the robes from the shelter before following him through the streets to here.

“I will introduce you to some friends of mine.” He said as he walked through the door and into a large mess hall. We walked into a canteen of some sort, there must have been forty people sat on a large, central table, all eating together. Each one of them looked up at Eadric and I as we entered but no one said anything as we sat down on a couple of spare seats at the end of the table. No sooner had we sat down when two plates of food appeared in front of us, I looked up to see a man dressed in chef whites who spoke to Eadric as he placed the plates before us.

“Eadric my *old* friend!” He clearly emphasised the word old as he said this, enjoying his little joke. “How are you today? We haven’t seen you around here in a while.” He finished.

“I have been out on business Paul, thank you for lunch; I have missed your cooking whilst away.” Eadric said in reply before tucking in.

“Anytime.” He called as he walked back to the kitchen.

“Is this the new guy?” a big man asked in a gruff voice, leaning over from further down the bench to talk to Eadric as if I wasn’t here.

“Yes. Ben, this is James.” Eadric said jabbing his fork in my direction. “James, Ben here will be training you.” He said to me before turning to this Ben guy and saying “I think we should begin right away.”

“No problem.” Ben said, gulping down a mouthful of what looked like beer.

“So is everyone here like us?” I asked Eadric as I took in the surrounding table. It was the strangest assortment of people I had ever seen, fat, thin, tall short, some looking angry, twitching, I guessed they were newer to this life, others looking casual as if this was all perfectly normal to them.

"Yes most." Eadric replied. "But not all, some are friends or loved ones that know of their fate, that said, most of us are loners. We are a small community here and we rely on each other to help run this place, whilst here you will work with them during the day and train in the evenings until you master control. Once fully in control you may make the choice to leave if you wish, but not before.

After they had eaten they all began to stand, one at a time and gradually left, leaving me alone with only Eadric and three others.
"We will begin training right away." Eadric said to me after we'd finished eating. "After dinner the beast is at its calmest, this should help you with your control."
"This should be good," Ben said grinning. "What is your beast?" He asked me, but I chose not to answer.
"You will see Ben, be patient." Eadric answered jesting with him.
"Hi, I'm Tabatha." One of the others called across the table at me. I looked up to see who had said this and I saw a woman on the other side of the table, two seats up. She was probably late twenties in age, pretty and I assume outgoing based on the very forward way in which she'd introduced herself.
"Hi." I replied smiling nervously.
"This is Aaron." She said pointing to the other man at the table. He raised a hand at me but did not say anything, still finishing off his meal.
"We are going to the fire pit." Eadric said. "I'll warn you now; we don't get new people here that often and the unveiling of a new beast is quite exciting to them.
"Them?" I asked my concern clear.
"Them. Everyone." He said.

We got up together and the five of us walked out past the dock and out through the small town. I looked up at the night sky above me, surprised that it was dark already whilst marvelling at how clear the sky was now. We entered the woodland at the bottom of the hill walking for only a few minutes before we came to a clearing in the trees. I figured we had to be around the back of the island now, out of sight of the mainland. I could hear the voices before I saw the people, it sounded as if a party was kicking off. As we entered the clearing the sound stopped abruptly and an eerie silence fell over the place. I could feel every eye upon me as I followed Eadric to the centre of the clearing. It was a strange place, I assumed man made as the trees lined three sides in a perfect square at least a hundred feet in length and the fourth side was created by the huge outer wall. Eadric and I stood in the centre, the others had stayed at the perimeter and there had to be a further fifty people surrounding the outer edge of the clearing.

"This is James." Eadric spoke clearly to the assembled crowd, I felt like I was in a playground and a fight had broken out. "He is new here and is here to learn, as you all once were, please show him the appropriate respect." After he had spoken he turned to me. "This is a bit of a ritual here now; we have had trouble here in the past with not knowing who people were when in their animal form, so any newcomer now has a sort of unveiling ceremony if you like."

"Ok. So what do I do? I can't change at will."

"Well that's lesson one." He said and then three people stepped out of the crowd. "They will see that no harm comes to you or anyone else."

The first man to step forward was Ben who stood to the east, another man, the one called Aaron to the west and another lady that I didn't recognise stood to the north of my position.

"But I could hurt someone, you saw the cow earlier." I was getting panicky; did they really want a large dragon to be let loose here?

"Trust us; you are not the first or the biggest beast that we've had to train." As he spoke I heard a noise rise up around me as the crowd cheered abruptly. I turned around the circle to see Ben's body suddenly grow, morphing into a huge grizzly bear, the transformation only took the briefest of moments and I could tell with the swiftness that he had done that many times before. Aaron followed suit, but his body grew out slower taking the form of an enormous Rhinoceros, it was a terrifying looking thing with its giant horn protruding into the clearing. Next it was the woman I didn't know. She looked so slight in frame that I couldn't tell what she would become, but as I watched and with lightning speed she turned into a glorious golden eagle. The light of the moon above seemed to glint off her feathers; she was truly a glorious beast to behold. The three stood around me ready for whatever I became, only Eadric and I knew of my beast and I got the impression that Eadric wanted to hold the suspense. I wondered if they'd ever seen a dragon before, but as I processed the thought I realised how ridiculous it was, dragons didn't exist.

"Triggering the curse is usually pretty simple." Eadric said turning to me. "We know what your trigger is so you just need to think of whatever it was that set you off the last few times. Let the thoughts fill your mind but don't try to fight it, let the beast in and remember you're among friends here."

"Ok." I said uncertainly. "Right now?" I asked and he nodded. I thought of Rebecca and the guilt flooded in, I felt the dragon rear his huge head, but this time I didn't fight him. He slunk warily into my mind, not happy that my human mind stayed but not trying to fight it off either. And then, as easily as that, I began to change. I heard a whisper rising up from the crowd as my body began to convulse, the fever gripped me, my body grew larger as I spread my wings out and began to take form and before I knew it my transformation was complete. I heard gasps and cries ring out around me.

"Is that…"

"What…"

"Good God!"

"It's… a dragon!"

I stretched my body out from where I stood. I could feel the beast eyeing up the crowd but we had eaten, twice and wanted no more. I stretched my wings out to their full thirty feet, only I felt bigger now, was that possible? I saw the eagle in front of me twitch nervously at my size, she was big, but I was considerably bigger. The crowd, having thoroughly confirmed that I was a dragon now cheered an almighty cheer. I felt the chorus go right through my body, swelling my heart with pride and with that I beat my massive wings and took to the skies in one huge leap. I flew up into the air rolling on the cool wind, ducking and diving over the island far below. As I flew back and forth I saw Eadric join me, the huge flaming phoenix unmistakable and then the eagle too flew up to join. Gradually, one by one, at least four other huge birds of prey joined in ducking and diving around me.

Five minutes later I landed back in the clearing to yet another almighty roar. The beast sedate from lunch I was able to easily change back into my human form, pleased with the progress I had made. I would think of this moment again, try to replace the thought of Rebecca with this brief moment of pride.

30
1012
The List

We had returned to the monk's quarters around midday, the sun was shining clearly in the sky above and the day had looked more promising than the previous rain soaked days had done. The Abbot had agreed to help us, which was more than I could have hoped for. Monk hustled around us talking to himself, constantly mumbling of one thing or another. Trojan, Brom and Rowan had begun to gather what little they required for the journey ahead of us and after a while Monk took us to eat with the other residents down by the dock. The other residents were all men of the cloth and had vowed to a life of dedication to God and silent prayer and as such they said very little while we ate. Monk however seemed ill at ease with silence and felt unabashed at filling the otherwise quiet room with his continually jolly queries of one thing or another.

My mind however had been on the task ahead, I see now looking back that I thought of nothing else in those early days, but if I had allowed myself time to stop and think I would surely never have found the strength to continue. I wanted revenge on these savages for all that they had done and I wouldn't rest until I had got it, even this lunch felt like a waste of time, a betrayal to my families memory. As we finished eating we stood and returned to the training ground that played host to us this past night where we prepped the horses to leave.

"We will ride out this afternoon." I said to the others whilst loading a small amount of the gold from the horde into a pack on the horse. "We must make up every moment we can to stand a chance in the battle ahead." The others nodded in agreement before shifting the carts into the corner of Monks training ground for safe keeping.

"Monk, is the list available?" I called to Monk who was shuffling through the parchments on his desk.

"Ah ha." He'd called pulling a large roll out from under a pile of similar parchments all stacked randomly in the corner. I looked curiously towards the pile as I walked to the desk, he must have noted my expression as he answered my unspoken question.
"It is only temporary, I was staying here whilst I trained my own beast, I knocked down too many walls when inside." Monk said, laughing at the thought. "I keep my main work in my original home, but since the curse I tend to prefer to work out here."
"I understand." I said by reply and I truly did. I believe we all felt better outside after the curse, our animal instinct was to resist the confines of walls or cages.
"Is that the list?" I asked, prompting him to return to the task at hand.
"It is, or at least this is the full list of men, I documented each man as we marched through each burh. It will not take me long to write out the list of men that were in the clearing that day." He unravelled the list as he said this and began to work down it.
"How do you know those there from those that were not?" I'd asked, curious once again.
"I have always had an impeccable memory." Monk said tapping his quill to his head. I knew most of the names and there weren't many of us left that day. I have already marked off most of the departed, see, there is your group. I was unsure of your fate until now… oh and you say that you know of more dead since I last updated the list?" As he spoke he pointed to the list, at this time I was unable to read and could not understand the markings, but I committed the strange scrawl to memory none the less.

Robin – Wareham – Deceased

Eadric – Shaftesbury – Fate Unknown

Brom – Shaftesbury – Fate Unknown

Rowan – Shaftesbury – Fate Unknown

William – Shaftesbury – Deceased

Nicholas – Shaftesbury – Deceased

John – Shaftesbury – Deceased

Walter – Shaftesbury – Deceased

Benedict – Shaftesbury – Deceased

Gregory – Winchester – Deceased

Peter – Winchester – Deceased

As my eye wondered over the page the Monk pulled out a fresh piece of parchment and began to write a new list of names, this one considerably shorter. As I watched Monk write Trojan had approached the little table.

"We are ready to depart Eadric. Your horse is waiting when you require it. Damn! I do wish you'd stop using that name Monk." Trojan said as Monk added Leofrick to the list.
"You can read?" I'd asked Trojan surprised, only the monks learnt to read and write in those days. Words held power and it was generally thought that only men of God should hold such power.

"I have learnt a little in my time, certainly enough to read that list." Trojan replied.
"Then you will prove yourself useful once again, for this list means little to me." I'd then told him. The monk handed me the list a moment later.
"There is the list of those that were in the clearing that day, the cursed men."
"Thank you; this will help our quest greatly." I said opening the list to look down it, despite it meaning little I felt better knowing I had committed it to mind.

"Do you know of these places?" I asked Trojan as he too took in the list.

1. Alric the afraid – Corfe Castle
2. Ulric – The Burh of Wareham
3. Tybalt – The Burh of Wareham
4. Forthwind – The Burh of Wareham
5. Sadon – Swanage
6. Terrowin – Portland
7. Eadric – The Burh of Shaftesbury
8. Brom – The Burh of Shaftesbury
9. Rowan – The Burh of Shaftesbury
10. Borin – Exeter
11. Fendrel – Exeter
12. Althalos – Carhampton
13. Hadrian – Gloucester
14. John – Worcester
15. Henry – Chester
16. Frederick – Canterbury
17. Walter – Canterbury
18. Leofrick – Chertsey
19. Lief – Selsey
20. Barda – Selsey
21. Thomas – St Michaels

"Yes." Trojan answered simply.

"Then we will work through them in order of distance, Monk said that thc first is four days away by horse, we must set off for time is against us now." And with that we finalised preparations to leave.

"One more thing Monk?" I asked as a thought hit me. "Before we leave, I am curious to see the beast that resides within you, if you would not mind." We had heard of this beast on a couple of occasions but still knew nothing of it.

"Certainly." He replied and walked to the centre of the training ground.

"Why do you need all this room?" I asked as much to myself as to Monk, but he'd heard it none the less and laughed at a private joke that at the time I did not understand.

"I do not yet know myself of the name of my beast for neither I, nor anyone else here, has ever seen one before. It is certainly a curious beast, much like myself I fear." As he said this he laughed to himself and then his body began to shudder.

His body changed slowly, the transformation was controlled and appeared to be painless, just slow and careful. I watched on as his body began to swell, he fell forward onto his hands, only by the time they'd hit the floor his hands were no longer there. His body and head grew onwards; every time I thought he'd stop, he grew a little more. He was at least the size of Brom or Trojan, only he continued to develop. Suddenly he was twice the size of Brom, dwarfing our human forms. His skin had turned leathery; thick, grey and still his size increased. The huge form of his body caused me to take a cautious step back from him as something began to grow from his face. After what seemed like an age his size halted, his head was big but his ears were bigger, huge things that stuck out proudly from either side of his head. His body was massive filling the training arena that now looked small against his form. An oddly small tail appeared to protrude from his behind while a distinctly larger tail now hung from the centre of his face. We all simply stood and stared at him. At the time he was breath taking, easily six times the size of Brom or Trojan and I knew then why he could not live indoors.

It was Trojan who broke the silence. "I told you he was odd." He said laughing at the expressions on our faces.

We left not long after that, Monk had returned to his usual frail frame and gave us a generous amount of bread for our journey before we were then on our way, leaving before the land once again fell beneath the sea. I thought about Monks form often over the weeks that followed, pondering what the beast was, Monk never found out, it was only many years later that I was able to put a name to his animal, Elephant, he was the first Elephant to ever grace the English shores.

31
1012
Borin and Fendrel

Four days later we'd arrived in Exeter as night fell, the sun just disappearing below the horizon as we stepped into the centre of the Saxon town. The journey had been a long and tiring one, travelling by day and resting by night. The horses had been heavily laden with our men and their supplies and we did not wish to push them faster than was necessary; they'd still had a long journey ahead of them that month.

There were ten of us that had ridden into the town that evening, but as fate would have it we didn't all leave. I realised later the mistake that I'd made by brazenly walking into the town such as we had. It was a mistake I wouldn't make again, a mistake that a solider of the Abbot's paid for with his life.

The thing came from nowhere, a black shape darting from the shadows before a muffled yell was abruptly cut short as the life escaped from the fallen victim. The horses to the back of our troop reared up throwing their riders to the ground in the process.

"Calm! Hold your positions." I heard one of the men shout, trying to retain order among his men. The horses skittered on the spot but their riders were able to hold them now that the initial surprise had passed.

"What was that?" Brom had asked from atop his own horse.

"I do not know, but I'm sure it is what we are here for." I replied as the Abbot's men formed a defensive circle around us. Brom dropped from his horse, tethering it to the side of Rowans steed, before walking out into the open in front of our pack. I too dismounted and stepped out to join him. I saw Trojan in horse form also move to follow, but I signalled him to halt where he was, being in horse form meant that our attacker was as yet unaware of his presence, which we could use to our advantage. Brom and I stepped forward, I could feel the tension in the group as we left the safety of their number but I knew we were in no harm, Brom was stronger than most, man or beast and I had my own defence mechanism built in. We walked up the main street of the town, timber framed houses lined each side of the street and a mid sized church sat at the centre of the town. We approached the church anxiously. Over the years many people have asked if I fear anything, for many believed that the knowledge of eternal life would inevitably lead them to lose all fear of death. I always answered them the same; death may not be permanent but death itself still hurts. I expected something to attack, anticipating a sudden movement from the dark corners of the church or surrounding buildings; I knew we were being watched, I could feel it.

Suddenly movement came from a side passage by the church, I tensed, ready. Brom in an instant burst into the colossal bear, gasps of surprise rang out from our own band, many having not seen the bear before now. To my surprise however, it was not the dark flash that we had seen before that emerged from the alley, instead something small ambled casually out from the mouth of the alley and trotted up to us as if we were no more significant than the trees that were scattered about us. The little thing meandered towards us and after a minute it sat in front of me about ten feet away, it was a mangy little terrier dog. I looked at the thing surprised by its seemingly relaxed manner. As I recollect the same thought occurs to me now as it did then, I thought that the thing looked smelly.

"What business do you have here to bring your men into our town like this?" I looked at the dog; I remember briefly wondering how he had spoken, before quickly realising that he couldn't have. Brom was still on full alert and I realised that this little dog did not fool him for a moment.

"We mean no harm." I called to the surrounding building. "But be warned I will not tolerate another death, come out now so we may talk, if you do not show yourself we will find you." With this Rowan took to the air, the hawk flying straight from the back of the horse that he sat astride a moment before. The large hawk circled the town quickly before swooping down to me, changing in the air and landing on his human feet at my side.

"He is by the building to your right, hiding in that large shadow there." Rowan said pointing to a building to the side of the church.

"Thank you Rowan, your eyes are second to none, especially at night." And with that he took flight again.

"You see that we too can see you and we are well prepared." As I said this I walked over to where this man was apparently hiding, the little terrier watching the whole time. It could have been my imagination but he appeared to grin as I approached the shadow hiding our adversary. I stopped five feet from the dark shadow, I could see very little but it seemed that the centre of the shadow was subtly darker than the rest.

"Show yourself." I demanded and as I said this I too changed form. The white hot flames of my transformation lighting the entire alley instantly where I saw, slinking in the shadows and crouched as if ready to attack and snarling viciously was a large black cat.

The cat, startled by my sudden burst of flame, ducked to its right and fled the alley, running straight past me. He must have been blinded by the light because he ran straight into the clutches of Brom, now in bear form. The huge bear grabbed the black cat in its grasp before falling to the ground, crushing the cat within its inescapable grip. The cat had no chance. It was big for a cat, not your typical house cat; it had a large muscled body clearly built for speed and agility. It was not far off the size of your average pony only longer and sleeker, vast by cat standards but Broms bear was bigger and the cat's vicious teeth and claws lashed out hopelessly as it remained trapped in Broms unbreakable grasp. The cat soon realized it was beaten, the huge arms of the bear retaining their grip until the attacks subsided and as its breath was wrung from its body it slumped into Brom's arms, not dead but unconscious. As the fight left its body it began to change returning to a mid sized human form, now lying naked on the ground as Brom released him. For the first time the dog that had just witnessed all this seemed to express some concern. It ran to the body before standing over it and growling at the giant form of Brom's bear as if to challenge him himself.

Brom did not retaliate.

The cat's human form awoke about an hour later, confused at first but his memory was quick to catch up and he looked around himself suddenly, as if searching for something. His eyes darted left and right before stopping on the terrier that lay at his side, now wagging its tail happy to see its master alive. We had taken his body into the church; the huge vaulted ceiling had loomed ominously above our heads. The dark now truly set in for the night, the town was quiet and the church deserted. Brom had wrapped the man's body in a spare robe and carried him in setting him down on a pew once inside, the little terrier following obediently never letting the man from his sight.

"Are you Borin or Fendrel?" I asked the man as he took in his surroundings including our band of men all now settled down around him. The man did not answer at first, squinting to take in the faces of the men around him, barely visible, lit only by the light of the moon streaming through the large slits in the surrounding walls. His head had turned as he took in each of us, hesitating momentarily on Brom's face before his gaze stopped on me.

"I know some of you; it has been a long time. I see earlier that your destiny was also altered as mine was on that fateful evening." The man said to the group in general.

"Your memory serves you well." I replied.

"And how may I help you now that you have my full attention." He said trying to portray a relaxed tone as if unbothered by the nine of us that surrounded him. The tension in his body however told otherwise.

"We came here searching for you. We have received news of an impending attack. The Danes intend to breach our shores with a huge force and take what remains of our land. They will enslave our men and women; take our homes and our way of life from us. We intend to stand against them six months from now; we are reuniting the men from that day. The curse that was put upon us has given us an edge that they will not be aware of. We lost a great deal that day, but we have also gained a great strength, we owe them for both and we will repay them by turning them back from our shores."

"And you want me to fight with you." He replied. It wasn't a question.

"Yes. With our new talents we may have the edge that we did not last time."

"How many of us are there so far? I see Brom there, I remember his face and that bear is incredibly strong but still I've seen only four of us, that is not much against an army."

"I am Eadric, Brom you know and this is Rowan and Trojan." I said pointing to Trojan now in his human form and standing to my right.

"Ok. So we have five cursed men against an army of savage warriors. And what, a few fool hardy guards?" He replied after looking beyond us to Trojan and the Abbots men.

"So far." I replied. "We have a list of those cursed and hope to number considerably more before the time comes. We also have others training as we speak including amongst them another man of the curse. As we travel others will join for we must defend our home." As I spoke the man sighed deeply clearly considering what I had said.

"The country is lost either way so I will fight with you. I am Borin."

"We have a record of two from this town. Is Fendrel with you?" Trojan asked over my shoulder.

"Yes, Fendrel is here." Borin answered before pointing to the little terrier by his side. I was momentarily surprised unsure why Monk would have included the mutt on the list but pushed it to the back of my mind. I'd ask him when I next saw him.

"Then we must leave soon, you may either travel with us, to gather more men, or join our friends at St Michaels where they will give you shelter and allow you to train if you wish. Do you control your curse or does it control you?" I asked him, whilst the men around me prepared to leave this town.

"No, I must admit to being a slave to my curse, it seems to activate when trouble arrives, it appears to be a defence mechanism. I have used it for the past two years to protect the town. I am safe here with them and they are safe here because of me, but if what you say is true, it will take more than just me to prevent what is coming. I will travel with you. I may be able to help and I do not wish to be cooped up waiting for what is to come."

"As you wish." I replied. We gathered the horses and prepared to leave. Borin fetched a horse from the stables and gathered some things from his residence before he too was ready to leave mounting his horse and following us from the town. As we left the main entrance to the town the little terrier ran behind for a while before Borin threw him up onto the back of his horse where it sat happily as the horse trotted on.

32
2010
Smug

The first week went by quickly; I spent most of the daylight hours working the fields, helping in the kitchens or out fishing on the boats. I got to know a few of the people that populated this place, some working within the Abbey, trusted consorts of the church. Others, like me were here for either their own safety or the safety of others, earning their keep and their protection hidden away from the world. Eadric had told me that it wasn't always this way, that there had been a time when we had run free without fear of persecution, but the human species had grown in number and strength and if we were discovered today we would likely never see daylight again. Apparently people had been caught in the past, never to return. The children told stories of secret government experiments and the like but Eadric had assured me that these were only stories designed to keep the children in check. I worked hard whilst I could here, it served to both take my mind of my troubled past whilst also allowing me to train more efficiently in the evenings. I was tired of course; but so was my beast and so after dinner every evening I would go and work on my control with Ben out by the fire pit. That evening we arrived late from dinner and others had already begun their training. I watched as a kid my age stood by the fire before suddenly exploding into a flurry of fur and suddenly there was a rabid looking dog where he had just stood. The dog turned to me at once smelling my presence, but a look in its eye told me all I had needed to know, he knew who I was, what I was and respect was paid accordingly. Dogs knew when they were outmatched. I had learned a lot in the short time that I had been here. I found now that even in my human form I had developed certain senses, dragon senses. The beast and I shared head room and he sniffed the scents on the air disgruntled by the inefficiency of my human nose but none the less using it to sense our surroundings, watching warily. The dragon inside me never rested, always alert and as I learnt more of him so did he I. I found myself ever alert, reading situations, preparing to react at a moments notice. The dragon inside was smart, which I hadn't expected. He took in situations and considered them, weighing up the options before settling on what he felt was the appropriate course of action before enlightening me. This exchange however seemed to flow. It wasn't as a conversation between two people, more of a shared consciousness we deliberated together and came to joint conclusions, often without even being consciously aware that the exchange was even taking place. I know the others didn't think like this. I had tried to explain it to Eadric, but it seemed to concern him. I had thought this was what they wanted, they kept telling me to work with the beast, but their animals were dumb, just animals, this seemed in my opinion to hold them back.

"Are you ready James?" Ben asked me. Ben had descended from some guy he called Brom. He spoke of him often and seemed to live by some sort of code that Brom had taught to his children and so forth, through the generations, a long ancestry of bears that had always fought beside Eadric. Or something like that anyway. I found it hard to picture Eadric's past; he'd said he was a thousand years old? Now that was a long time, too long to imagine, he'd have seen it all.

On Bens command I changed, growing rapidly into the dragon and I let him spread his wings, stretching out across the training ground. It felt good, I didn't exactly feel cramped when human, but I felt it when shifting. I could suddenly feel the outer extents of my body stretch out from me, a release that made my body and mind feel suddenly free and made me want to take to the air. I felt the dragons' power surge through me. This was something that still took me by surprise, the surge of strength that hit me as my muscled legs grew out and my huge powerful wings expanded. I could now control this process well, no longer fighting the beast. He understood that there was no rush for control now and I could savour the moment.

"Ok, now fight the urge to fly and change back to human form, don't let the beast have his way, show him who's in charge." Ben said. They treated this like training a dog; you told it short sharp commands with an air of authority, show it who the alpha is. This is what leads me to think that their animals are stupid, that their beasts obey their simple commands. Dragons were majestic creatures, every time I changed I could see the history of the beast fill my memory, magnificent, proud creatures, they would not listen to barked commands. Nether the less I changed back to human form.

"Good, now do it again." Ben continued. As he spoke Ellie entered the clearing. Ellie was the golden eagle from that first day, she was about my age and was beautiful, I had seen her once or twice over the week she appeared to have learned control quickly but she still seemed to come out to train here a couple of nights a week. The sight of her boosted my confidence, eager to impress I turned back into my dragon and stretched my wings to full length, filling half the clearing.

"Now back to human." I heard Ben say, but the urge to fly hit me and I didn't see what harm it would do. So with one huge beat of my giant wings I shot up into the air causing a bellowing wind to fill the clearing. I could hear Ben grumbling as I soared into the air. A moment later I saw a golden streak as Ellie shot past me and I turned in the air to follow her, both me and the dragon eager to chase, to play. I shot past her as she slowed and she watched me go. As I flew higher and higher I changed form back into my human form allowing momentum to carry my human body to the pinnacle of the arc before gravity kicked back in. My human body fell from the air, I threw my arms out to my side into an elegant dive position, mimicking an Olympic diver, or at least in my mind this was the case. I fell through the air falling faster and faster, the air rushed at my human face and a small part of my brain yelled at me, knowing this was stupid. But I had control and as I bombed it back past the eagle I smiled a wry smile into her beady eye and when only a couple of hundred feet from the ground the dragon surged forward once again, sweeping terrifyingly close to the people still training below. I heard gasps and screams as I passed and the dragon grinned. I just caught the look on Bens face as I passed that told me that he'd like to rip my cocky head off.

33
1012
Althalos of Carhampton

We travelled north moving swiftly towards the town of Carhampton. I knew nothing of Carhampton but our new companion Borin told us a little about the town as we travelled. He seemed unimpressed with the place in general telling only of is diminutive size and lack of hospitality. He did however talk of this Althalos, the man we sought. It seems that the men had travelled together, for he had returned home those two years previous with him in his company. He said nothing of the mans appearance or mannerisms, speaking only of his ability to ascertain information from people. It appeared that this was what Borin remembered most of this Althalos, his way with people. Described as a charmer that spoke with a silver tongue this man apparently set people at ease, prompting them to talk, leaving them safe in the knowledge that they had nothing to fear from his knowing of their knowledge. He sounded dangerous to me, a man that could make you divulge your inner-most secrets and do so without you realising that you had done so; you couldn't trust a man like that. I asked Borin earlier that afternoon if he knew if the curse had triggered within this Althalos but he could not say for certain, only that he had not seen any evidence of it himself.

As we had closed in on the town of Carhampton we'd discussed how we should approach the town. I had not wanted to make the same mistake that we did with Borin. We had decided that Brom and I would enter the town alone and that the group would stay outside the town's perimeter for the time being, much to Trojans anger. He did not take well to being left out through fear of being hurt and made it quite clear that he was unwilling to miss out on a good fight. Fortunately the point became mute for as we stayed the horses just outside of the town, a man left the main entrance and approached our group casually as if we were no more a threat than the local seamstress.

We stopped and watched as the man approached. He was a relatively small man, but he walked confidently, approaching our group as if we were old friends, a group of ten armed strangers and without a single weapon to hand. Strange behaviour indeed. Borin had changed form, he and his dog had run to the surrounding woods as we approached as they'd planned to hunt and eat whilst Brom, I and possibly Trojan had he had his way, went to search for this Althalos. So we had no way to know, among those of us there, if this man was the man we were searching for.

The man strolled right up to us, brazenly entering our makeshift camp, before declaring, "I hear that you are here to see me." He was small and unthreatening; his slightly stooped posture gave the impression that he was weak. His whole appearance made the Abbots men around me swell with confidence; they knew that he posed no threat, that he would be easily overpowered if he were to try anything and as such their guard relaxed. It was then that I knew that this small, insignificant man was Althalos. He had already unarmed my whole guard without them knowing it; they had already mentally given up the fight, confident that it wasn't necessary. It was quite a ruse; only a well trained eye would notice the sinewy strength within his arms and the vigour that was present in his eyes.

"That we are Althalos, I hope you are well." I replied. I would not give him the satisfaction of showing my surprise although I must admit now that at the time I had had no idea how he had known of us ahead of our arrival or of the task that we had embarked on.

"So when do we set off?" He asked casually, before settling in by the fire that the men were preparing to cook over.

I remember distinctly how odd this mans presence was, it was a sort of magic spell that he cast over people. Within a few short minutes he had strolled into our camp and taken his place among us, the guards seemingly unaware there was anything odd about this at all and by the end of that afternoon he was joking with them all, telling old tales as if they had grown up together. Borin and his dog had returned some time later and they too talked to Althalos as if greeting an old friend, of course they did at least have some history with this man. I must admit that I too, whilst prepared for his ways after hearing what Borin had said earlier, felt strangely compelled to laugh along with his tales and quips. His light hearted manner and quick wit, making him pleasant company and quite the story teller. I tried on many occasions to find out of his beast and its control over him but each time I found myself laughing along to a tale of his childhood, or some joke about our not so glorious King and before I knew it I had forgotten all about my original intentions. He cast a spell over us all and we had soon all but forgotten the haste of our present situation and had settled in for a good nights rest.

34
2010
Complicated

I landed back beside Ben and I'm sure that if I wasn't four times his size he'd have strangled me there and then. Instead he gritted his teeth and simply said.

"You are here to learn, not to show off, or have you forgotten the trouble you have already caused?" I knew he was right, my little motorway incident hadn't gone unnoticed. The papers had thankfully reported that a gas explosion had caused the accident and that the gas leak had in turn also caused hallucinations, apparently that's why everyone saw a great big dragon fly off from a motorbike. This was a ludicrous story in my eyes and I couldn't help but wonder how anyone would believe such a thing, but as always I had overlooked the human ability to believe anything they were told, especially by the papers, without questioning the obviously flawed facts. Anyway, I had not forgotten how lucky I had been and it had been after this incident that Eadric had told me of the hunts that had occurred in the past as the 'normal' humans had searched for our kind and of the reasons why we now remained hidden. Shame hit me again but not like it had before; this was not because time had healed all wounds or because I had forgotten what I had done to Rebecca, but because I now let the dragon into my mind when I felt like this and looked upon the world through his eyes. The dragon didn't feel remorse or guilt and held little regard for human life. He was smart, but he didn't concern himself with worrying about human emotions, they just confused matters, clouded judgement. The dragon had proven a good comfort over the past week, allowing me to look upon my problems with a clear mind, void of conscience, the ultimate aspirin.

Ben was still berating me about honour and control and about the greater good. He was like someone you found in a movie, the fall on your sword type. It was at that moment that Ellie swooped down passing by me into the clearing before the golden eagle then swiftly shot back up into the dark evenings cloud cover and out of sight. The dragon inside me stirred and I agreed, I ran a few feet before leaping into the air, my human body left the floor by about two feet before the dragon took over and with an instantaneous change we were air born, chasing the eagle.

The eagle shot out over the ocean. She was fast, moving through the air with the grace of a true predator, perfect little movements that enabled her to maximise flight time whilst picking thermals as she passed. Ellie glided gracefully onwards, simple beats of her wings caused her to surge forward, minimal effort for maximum results. I on the other hand by stark contrast powered through the thermals with huge beats of my massive wings leaving claps like thunder in my wake. I tore through the air forcefully, it was not elegant but it was effective. We flew on just enjoying the cold evening's breeze, the freedom that came with flying, a freedom not found on the ground. Humans were bound by too many rules, don't do that, do this, stop that, it was a wonder that they got anything done. When flying free up here my troubles washed away and I found my thoughts unimpeded by the mundane rules of the human world and that I looked on from the hypothetical sideline with indifference. All their rules and regulations seemed so trivial and as the thought passed through my mind I felt the dragons mind huff his agreement; he didn't stand for human rules, only his own. So whilst in flight all of these things fell away, there were no rules to govern the sky, or at least none that bothered us. I knew that Ellie agreed, she'd told me before now, it was as if there was a code among those beasts of the sky. Those of us that could take flight shared a bond; a bond that we felt set us above the others and not just in the literal sense. We felt free, the beasts of the plains or the beasts of the forest seemed burdened to us, grounded. We flew on through the clouds for some time before returning to the training ground and changing back to human form. Ben had left now, clearly fed up with me. Ellie landed at the side of the clearing dropping elegantly through the roof of the changing facility and landed inside through a hole that had been cut specifically for this purpose. The men tended not to be shy, the women however were more careful of where they changed and a moment later Ellie exited the changing block in a robe and walked from the clearing. I ran to walk with her but she was gone before I could see which direction she went. That was the thing about flight, it was different up there. Down here things got complicated.

35
1012
The Royal Court

"Someone one day will provide something better to go under our garments," Borin said jovially to the group in general as he returned from the dense woodland, rearranging his tunic. We had travelled for four days and the going had not been good; the end of the year was closing in and the weather had grown bitter with renewed force. Jack Frost had passed by at some point and the ground had glistened with that morning's share. I remember that journey well as the going had been so trying. We had travelled only a day when the first frost appeared and our pace slowed considerably as the ground became treacherous under foot. On our second days travelling, after a painfully cold nights rest, luck abandoned us once again as we encountered another horde of Vikings, sixteen men in total. We had all leapt into gear as both groups spotted each other simultaneously. Brom and Trojan had charged them head on, both changing mid run and bowling straight into the group. They would have been able to take the group single handed, but Borins beast felt the danger and his giant cats instincts took over. Although his transformation was slower and at a standstill, his speed once changed was unparalleled. The cat leapt forward and charged after the other two, quickly passing them and leaving them behind. The giant cat hit the group of Vikings before they had time to register what was happening. They had seen a group of ragtag men on the track in front of them and had thought it an easy fight, they did after all outnumber us, but they would never know just how very wrong they were. The cat took two Vikings out before Brom and Trojan had arrived at the scene, although they still got their fair share. Trojan charged through the centre of the group, scattering the men closely followed by Broms razor sharp claws. Brom hacked and slashed at one Viking, then another opening huge, gaping, wounds upon the Vikings bared chests through which their lives escaped.

The fight was over quickly and we gathered up what they had by way of belongings. Our next visit was to the King and it would not have looked good to turn up empty handed. We took the cart that they had travelled with and piled the reasonable amount of silver we had taken from them into it before lashing their horses to the cart also. The silver would not impress the King but the horses had been in good shape so I had hoped that they would please him instead.

After another two days of hard riding we had eventually arrived at Corfe Castle, sat at the centre of Wareham. In those days the Castle was just a fairly simple fortification, at least by comparison to the impressive Castle built on this sight in later years, but at the time we had seen very little like this structure. Built up on the highest land mass around, it looked truly daunting as it loomed over its surroundings. We rode into the village of Wareham that resided at its base, the people of the town watching as we passed, curious of our business. It was early morning and Wareham was bustling as we entered. I had wondered of the logic of this after what had happened in Exeter, but the streets were crowded and the town was unfortified, unlike the Castle itself, so I had hoped to blend discreetly into the crowds. We had discussed leaving the main group outside of town, but the King would be heavily guarded and we would be weaker split up, a show of strength I had hoped might also help to show the King that we were serious in our plight.

We rode up to the gates of the fortification and requested an audience with the King, but the guards at the gate stood firm, informing us that the King only takes audiences twice a week. I had enquired when he would next be available and we were told that it would be the next day and so we had ridden back out to the village and used a little of the Vikings money to pay for food and lodgings within the towns stables for the night. We took it in turns to stand guard that evening as we knew there were at least four cursed men in this town somewhere, other than ourselves and we knew that trouble was never far from a cursed man. As it turned out the night had passed with no trouble and we were up to see the King at the Castle at the crack of dawn. A queue had already begun to form at the gates as we arrived but before long we were told to leave the Kings gifts and were led through to a well adorned room, at the centre of which the King sat upon an elaborately carved throne, with two guards at either side.

"And how may I assist you today? I do not recognise your band of men, you are not from here?" The King asked shakily, his uncertainty showing a weakness that he tried to cover with an air of authority.

"No we are not sir," I had replied smoothly. "My band of men have travelled a great distance to meet with you sir. We have it on good authority that Sweyn the Formidable and his band of savage Vikings are to breach our shore and storm our country, in five full moons from now. He is the same foe that we met on the shores of the Thames nearly two years previous." As I said this last bit I had looked into the Kings' eyes, watching for a sign of recognition at my reference to 'the last time' and sure enough, his eyes twitched slightly and fear glanced fleetingly across his face, giving himself away instantly. He did not reply for a moment, his eyes scanning across each of our faces and I knew he recognised a few.

"And this news is reliable?" He asked.

"Yes sir." I replied.

"And you propose what exactly?"

"To meet them once again at the shores of the Thames."

"You appear to have forgotten that that did not go so well last time."

"But this time things are different." I replied, wondering how he would react to our beasts. Would he understand? Was he also cursed? Or would he call the guards in and lock us in chains? "We have controlled our curse, we are stronger now and we have great warriors on our side this time." Again his eyes gave him away with the mention of the curse and I knew that he too was afflicted.

"Get out!" He yelled so suddenly I was momentarily taken aback. "Leave this town and do not return." His lip trembled as he cried out, the fear was now clear on his face. I did not know why he had reacted so fearfully at the time, but I knew there and then that he would not help us and that we would have to save our land without his help.

We walked from the Castle grounds and prepared to leave, no good would have come to us from hanging around there, word would have spread and the town folk would turn on us quickly. We had already prepared to leave and after only a few short minutes we'd gathered up our belongings and were trotting from the town before midday.

As we left the main town a horse came galloping out from the village, a messenger sent ahead to stop us as we left. Our group had been deeply suspicious of this and prepared to fight as other horses begun to emerge from the town. I watched as Brom, Borin and Trojan dismounted and stood tensed to fight, while Borins smelly little dog just sat happily on the back of Borins horse, seemingly oblivious to anything out of the ordinary.

The men slowed their pace as they closed down the gap between us, they had no weapons drawn and did not seem to be preparing for trouble and as they halted fifty paces before us, my curiosity got the better of me.

"What is the meaning of this?" I called to the lead man. "We are leaving as requested."

"I hear that you seek the men of the curse?" The first man asked. There were maybe ten of them in total, all members of the King's guard.

"Yes?" I replied questioningly.

"The King may rule this land, but the curse rules me. I am a man of the curse like you and so are Ulric and Forthwind here." The man said, signalling two others on horse back behind him. "We wish to join your quest. We are not free men while we are slaves to our nature, perhaps in facing the foe that inflicted us, we may learn of a cure. We will aid your quest and these other men also wish to fight for the lands that their fathers before them bled for." The man spoke well, an honourable man, he and his men would prove to be a great asset to our cause and as such we welcomed them with open arms. So as the ten members of the King's guard joined our band we left

Corfe Castle now banished from the town. I knew not what the future held for us at this time but I remember feeling my heart lift as our numbers grew and with it our strength increasing.

36
1012
The Tale of Sadon

"We travel south, Swanage is our next port of call; an easy half days ride from here." Trojan had called cheerfully as we trotted away from the town of Wareham and Corfe Castle. Trojan loved to be out in the open air and was visibly happier now than he had been in the Castle or at St Michaels.

"There will be nothing to find in Swanage." Ulric had said. He had not spoken loudly but his words held weight and we had known instantly that he spoke the truth. Ulric had been one of the ten men that joined us from Wareham, he was a big man, as all of them were and as guards of the King they were good fighters, brave and loyal to the King. That was why they'd had to disobey him, they knew that the best way to protect the land was to fight the hordes back and not to stand aside and pretend nothing was amiss, even if the King didn't see it.

"We should pass Swanage and head straight to our next destination." He spoke again. Ulric was one of three cursed men within the Kings guard another was Forthwind and Tybalt was the third, the one who'd spoken for them outside the Castle. Tybalt was the captain of the guard and Ulric, Forthwind and the other guards followed his command without question, although only Tybalt, Ulric and Forthwind had been inflicted by the curse. Forthwind was a quiet man, I don't recall hearing him speak that whole journey, but at the time I knew not why, he simply followed the other two with a determined stare in his eyes. I remember often pondering what his story must have been.

"Why do you say this?" Brom asked Ulric as we trotted on.

"Because the man you seek in Swanage is dead." As he said this I reeled my horse around and drew level with Ulric who rode at the back of our now fairly large pack, twenty one men strong.

"What happened?" I asked as I trotted with Ulric, Tybalt, Forthwind and Brom.

"I visited the town of Swanage a year past," Ulric began. "I had spoken with Sadon whilst travelling back from London that fateful day. We had not known at first of our curse, although others had discovered theirs on that journey we did not learn until after returning home that we too had fallen fowl of this affliction. For the most part we were able to contain our curse, our beasts are placid by nature, herd animals and we learned to live, for the most part, with them. The three of us were able to contain each other when required, chaining the beasts until the transformation ebbed. After a year of trying to live with our curses Tybalt, Forthwind and I had talked of finding Sadon. Knowing him to be only a half days travel from us, Forthwind and I had decided to set out to find him, to see if he too was plagued by this curse.

What we found was worse than we had imagined. Sadon had lost all control, he'd had no one to help him and by the time we had arrived the town folk were terrified. Sadon when human was full of regret but his human mind had been crushed and he no longer knew what was real within this world. His beast was savage, a monster that tore from him with seemingly little or no trigger, we spoke with him ourselves only briefly before the beast ripped from him and we were forced to retreat. Sadons human mind was weak and the beast engulfed him completely, he would wake regularly with no rccollcction of what had happened, hearing stories of a huge vicious creature that tormented the town, killing randomly. He knew that it was him and the knowledge ate at his conscience. The guilt and fear only weakened his human mind further and eventually his beast had control more often than his human form. The town folk had at first known nothing of Sadons true nature but they quickly made the connection and after one particularly savage night, after the beast had run riot through the town, they had followed him and waited for him to change back. Once asleep the town folk had bound him and dragged his body to the town square; he awoke once only to be hit savagely with a rock until unconscious again. Forthwind and I had witnessed their return, we had seen them drag his body into the town where they had set up a large fire and he was burnt as a witch. The screams that filled the town that night will haunt my dreams forever more, a sound I can never forget." Ulric spoke quietly but his words echoed in each of our minds having seen for ourselves such horror. "I regret to this day not interceding that morning, but I had seen the damage Sadon had done and knew that he was a danger that could not be left unresolved. But then the town folk went too far, for unbeknownst to us at the time Sadon had a son, only a year old, born after the curse. The town folk feared that he too would grow to be a monster; they spoke of the child as the son of the devil, shouting of beasts and demons as they carried the child from his home and approached the great fire that still burned the remains of the child's father. I could no longer stand by and watch, my own beast roared at such treachery and I attacked. If it wasn't for Forthwind here I would have died with Sadon that day, the town folk had believed Sadon to be alone so the sight of my beast charging them took them by surprise. I charged directly for them, knocking people to the floor before my beast turned on the man with the child. The other town folk had fled and the man holding the child quickly followed suit, dropping the child and fleeing. I had changed back to my human form and scooped up the child within my arms when two of the braver town folk had crept up on me whilst my attention was turned to the child. Forthwind here disposed of them swiftly, his beast tearing them apart before I had even been aware of their presence and for that I owe him a great debt. We took the child with us as we left and to this day I remain his guardian, I do not know what the future holds for this child, but Sadon was a brother at arms, his fate was tragic and I will not let the same happen to his son." As Ulric said this I noticed for the first time the small bundle that was wrapped up lovingly and cradled upon his back. I had assumed it was his belongings before but as I looked closer I could see that it was a small child.

"Then we will travel directly to Portland." Trojan said after a minute, the story settling on all of us, a heavy weight on our hearts at the knowledge that another of our brothers was gone.

Our band continued onwards, Portland was a day's ride away and we had to push on to reach it before nightfall. The weather stayed at bay for the remainder of the day and it had not been long after the sun had hung directly above us that we had reached the point in the land where our band was to part ways. As we had ridden we had discussed our options, we had gathered quite a band now but many where yet unable to control their beasts and although we had thus far had no outbursts I became concerned that after many days of travelling tempers will begin to fray and a fight, no matter how trivial the reason, could indeed prove fatal. The beasts that lurked within us were incredibly strong and would not be easily tamed if angered, therefore it was generally agreed that those without complete control would travel to St Michaels to learn with Monk under the Abbots care.

Tybalt, Forthwind and Ulric took their leave, taking the seven guards that had travelled with them and Sadon the second, still lying silently in his sling on Ulrics back. I did not know what Ulric intended to do with the child for it would be too dangerous for him to travel with us, but for now I did not mention it, we needed all the fighters we could get and I felt sure that if Ulric left our cause then the other nine would follow. The rest of our band continued onward towards Portland, travelling around the coast, Brom, Rowan and Trojan with me and the Abbots' five remaining guards. Althalos also came with us although we still as of yet had no idea of his beasts nature and Borin insisted on accompanying us too, against my better judgement. He was not as of yet in control of his beast but he was insistent, his little dog following him as always.

37
2010
My True Nature

The next time I saw Ben was at breakfast and he was not happy.

"Cocky… Grr…" He stewed, growling instead of finishing the sentence. "If I am to teach you to control that beast of yours you have to stop giving in to its every whim. You need to come to an understanding, find a balance." He yelled red in the face, his body started to shake and for a moment I wondered how good his own control was. "When your training you do not go chasing birds!" He continued; I saw Ellie at the other end of the table take offence at the term 'bird' but she clearly decided not to get in the middle of this and turned back to her breakfast while I sat quietly waiting for his temper to ebb. I was due to go out fishing with some guy by the name of Brad and with Ben's mood I'd be glad to get away from him today. He needed some time to cool off. I let him finish his rant and when he stopped for breath I grabbed a couple of slices of toast from the table and fled the canteen like a coward. I felt my dragons disgrace at me for this act of cowardice but I shoved it aside, he was too proud for his own good.

As I walked the short trip to the mariner I considered what today would hold. I'd helped out fishing once before, earlier in the week. The fishermen seemed to be of the usual ilk, a couple of old sea dogs from the Abbey that had fished their whole lives. They talked about fishing, compared fishing tales and drank the evenings away whilst contemplating the next days fishing; if this guy was anything like the rest it would be a boring day. That was why I was so surprised when I got into the harbour and saw a slick looking power boat, clean and clearly fast. I knew nothing about boats but this one sure as hell seemed to beat the usual pop eye style boats the other fisherman seemed to prefer.

"You must be James." A man shouted from the deck.

"Yeah."

"Then get aboard. We're leaving shortly." And with that I leapt aboard. The man was young, for a fisherman anyway. He had to be in about his late twenties, he had the look of a man that had spent his life by the ocean he clearly belonged here. Long blond hair waved down to his shoulders, a torn t-shirt depicting some surf brand or other, knee length denim shorts and flip-flops that completed the look. Clearly a surfer he was a man of the sea through and through. The other fishermen hadn't looked like they belonged in the sea, on it maybe, but not part of it; they weren't willing to get wet. This man however looked ready to go, like he was about to jump in and grab the fish himself.

Ten minutes later we were out in the ocean shooting away from St Michaels, the island rapidly vanishing over the horizon.

"So you fished before?" Brad asked whilst pushing the boat on faster, I felt the sea disappear beneath us as the boat crested a wave momentarily before it split the water once again with a gentle swoosh.

"Yes, I went out last week with Pete."

"Ah Pete, yeah he's old school, you should enjoy today then." Brad said chuckling, I wasn't sure what he meant but it sounded like it was going to be fun.

"Pete fished closer to base" I stated without realising at first that I'd said it out loud whilst thinking that we had gone fairly far from the usual fishing lanes.

"Yeah, the fishing lanes are all a bit busy for my style of fishing, I like seclusion."

Another ten minutes and he stopped the boat in the middle of nowhere and dropped the anchor.

"Here looks good," he said as he moved to the back of the boat, beginning to unravel a huge fishing net from the storage box there. "Most people fish by trawling the bottom of the ocean." He said to me conversationally. "It's a messy process that means they catch a lot of what they want and even more of what they don't want. We don't tend to abide too strictly to the fishing laws as we only catch for our own consumption, but I don't like to kill anything that doesn't serve as food. Standard fishing kills a lot of unusable fish." He finished whilst unravelling the net before he turned to me grinning now.

"So what do you do that's different?" I asked genuinely curious.

"I think of it like rounding up sheep. I set my net like so," he said signalling the huge net that now sat in the ocean behind his boat. "And then I find a large shoal of fish and herd them into the net, that way I only catch the intended shoal." He finished, beaming proudly.

I sat there confused for a moment, "How do you herd a shoal of fish? Have you got a trained fish dog?"

"No, that's my job. This switch turns on the motor to reel in the net, hit it on my signal." He said and with that he turned and leapt from the side of the boat. I ran to where he had just jumped off just in time to see, I think, a fin disappear below the ocean.

Fifteen minutes later, just as I had begun to grow bored, a noise floated up from below me, it sounded like a lot of something all moving and fighting to get passed each other before the net suddenly went tight, pulling the back of the boat down to the level of the sea. A second later a huge shark leapt from the water, arcing over the back of the boat before disappearing under the waves once again. I stood stunned for a moment before the dragon in my mind mentally prodded me back into action and I hit the switch for the net. The net instantly began to retract, closing off behind the now trapped shoal of fish. The shark dove from the water once again, flipping forward and changing in mid air, before Brad landed cleanly on the back of the boat, human again.

"Nice work." he said. "That's it for the days fishing we'll pull that lot in, that'll see us through for today." He said smiling. His beast took me by surprise and after a moment I realised that I was still gawping stupidly, I don't know why it struck me as odd? It's just that I hadn't thought that sea creatures were possible; no one had told me they were. They hadn't said that they weren't either, but still, a shark?

"How come you're a shark?" I asked Brad without really thinking it through. For a moment I wondered if my bluntness had offended him but he didn't seem surprised.
"Eadric believes that the curse brings out our true nature, I guess my nature is with the ocean and a shark is the King of the ocean."
"I thought it brought out our worst bits?" I asked weakly, unsure how to phrase the sentence.
"That was commonly believed at first, but we now believe that the beast is directly linked to a person's true nature, like yours for example. Do you think the dragon represents your worst bits?"
"No." I answered instantly, I didn't need to consider that question the dragon was a proud creature, not my shameful dark side. For a moment I wondered how he knew of my beast but I figured he had been there my first day here, everyone was.
"We are out in the middle of nowhere, miles away from any shipping lanes. Take a flight if you want, just stay low and don't go too far." Brad said and I didn't need to be told twice, I ran to the end of the boat and leapt over board in the same way that I had just seen Brad do, only I didn't hit the water, I soared.

38
1013
Portland

We travelled onwards to Portland, our troop had moved quicker now there were less of us and Portland resided at one of the lowest tips of the land so the going had grown easier as the terrain around the coast flattened out.

"Did you hear what Ulric had said of the King?" Brom had asked me conversationally as we travelled.
"No, I did not." I answered curious as to what had been said.
"He was telling tales of the King's transformation, he said that it was spoken about in hushed whispers among the troops and claimed that Forthwind had been with the King when he first changed."
"So the King is also cursed." I said aloud, pondering this new information. If the King was indeed cursed too, then why did he not want to fight? Surely he too felt aggrieved by these people who cursed us.
"Yes and apparently he was so ashamed he had Forthwinds tongue cut out to prevent him from telling anyone of it."
"That will explain why he is so quiet. But why did he stay with the Kings guard after that?" I'd asked, for I knew that I would have left his guard swiftly if the King had done that to me.
"Forthwind is loyal to Tybalt and they are safer together, I think. They had seen what happened to Sadon after all." Brom said.
"So what is this animal that had made the King so ashamed?" I asked.
"No one knows for sure, but the rumour is that he's a chicken."
"I was aware of that before, but what is his beast?"
"That is his beast; the guards believe he is a large chicken!" Brom had said restraining a grin.

"Oh." I replied surprised. That would explain why the King was so against joining our band. A chicken would be little use in a fight, little use at all I thought to myself as we travelled onwards.

We approached the town of Portland just after nightfall, Brom and I'd prepared to enter the town alone while the others set up camp just out of sight of the fortified towns' main entrance. As we were about to set off however Althalos stopped me and insisted that we leave the scouting to him; he did not elaborate but his tone, as always, was difficult to argue with and so Brom and I stood aside as Althalos set off on foot taking nothing with him but the cloth that he wore.
"Are you not even going to take your horse?" Brom had asked as he left and he had replied with a simple no, before continuing onwards. I watched as he walked away and although it was dark I could have sworn that he'd just vanished into thin air. I ran to the spot where I thought he had vanished and just found the cloth that he had worn now abandoned on the ground. He had proved to be an intriguing man.

Only an hour had passed when Althalos returned. We had all sat around the fire eating a great feast of rabbit courtesy of Rowans incredible night vision. We had left two on the fire, awaiting Althalos to return when suddenly he stepped out from behind a tree as if he had been there all along, only now he was naked. The guards leapt to their feet, drawing their swords in the process, Brom's body tore apart as his bear ripped from him. Borins cat also erupted into the opening around the fire and Trojan, already in horse form leapt to his feet, ready to charge. Only I remained seated, death was no longer a threat to me and as such I was not easily startled. The only other of our band that was not startled was Borins odd little dog, simply scratching his ear and taking the opportunity to get a closer spot to the fire. He really was a peculiar little dog.
"You should know better than to startle a group of monsters." I said jovially to Althalos as he stood, arms raised, in front of a terrifying group of men and beasts.

"Too true," He said edging around the still tense group and helping himself to one of the rabbits. "I assume I have you to thank for the food." Althalos said nodding his appreciation to Rowan who had not changed but had leapt up warily none the less.

"You are welcome." Rowan replied gracefully sitting again at the fire. One by one everyone returned to form and sat back down. Brom, still a little wound up, returned to find a small terrier curled up in his place. A loud growl erupted from Brom's human lips as he looked at the little dog but the terrier had simply looked up at him in a simple, but somehow condescending, way and quickly curled back up to dose off again. Brom was fuming but took it no further and I couldn't help but laugh at Brom, the great bear, being outdone by a mangy terrier but he gave me a look that said that he didn't see the funny side.

"So Althalos, what can you tell us of the town?" I enquired when everyone had settled back in for the evening.

"Its lively, they are all celebrating the new year this evening and the town is bustling." As Althalos said this there were a few murmurs around the camp and I assumed that I was not the only one that hadn't realised that the year had come to an end already. "There is no sign of this Terrowin that we seek, but there is also no scorch mark on the ground in the square, which is a good sign. I should think we could mingle among the crowds without causing a scene and ask around to see if anyone knows of his whereabouts."

"Ok, so Brom, Rowan, Trojan and I will leave soon." I said to the assembly in general, Borin went to speak but I answered his complaint before he could say a word. "You cannot guarantee control and we cannot risk exposure." I finished, Borin had looked dejected but he knew I was right.

A little later the four of us rode from the camp and off towards the town. The celebrations were now in full swing and we could hear music and laughter filling the night time air as we approached. As Althalos had said, the town was busy enough that nobody paid us any attention as we tethered the horses and walked among the people of the town. We walked into the main square where the majority of the people had congregated and purchased a couple of tankards of mead. We began to mingle around the towns folk listening into the conversations as we passed. Rowan and I split away from Brom and Trojan both continuing the search for any sign of this Terrowin. I continued on with Rowan sipping at the surprisingly good mead. I could not remember the last time I had drunk mead and it was a welcome distraction, even if only fleetingly so. We searched for some time for any sign of unrest or news of beasts roaming the town. We spoke to various people who answered our questions, some openly, other more warily, considering our questions strange; but none had seen anything untoward. Eventually we ran back into Brom and Trojan who had also seen and heard nothing of any Terrowin. We had sat down a side street away from the main crowds as we discussed our next move when the strangest thing happened. Borins little terrier wondered up to the four of us and began to pull on my tunic. At first I didn't understand, I just looked at the others confused; but after a minute Rowan spoke.

"I think he wants us to follow him?" he'd said, standing to do just that.

"You're going to follow this dog?" Brom asked incredulously.

"Do you have a better idea?" Rowan asked, the terrier simply watched with a bored expression before turning and walking away and after a momentary pause Rowan followed. A few seconds later I got up as did Trojan, laughing to himself at the situation. I assume Brom must have followed for the next time I had looked he was behind us.

We walked after the little terrier through winding alleyways between the timber framed houses, until he eventually stopped in front of a door.

"I think he wants us to enter?" Rowan said to no one in particular. I heard Brom grumble as if he thought this was stupid. But Rowan went to push the door open anyway.

"Let me." I said to him stopping him in his tracks. "If this is a trap, better I die than you." I'd said and he'd nodded in understanding. And so I pushed the door open and stepped into the room before me.

The room was dark, lit only by a small fire at one end, but it was enough light to see by. As I took in the room I could tell it was a home to someone, but there was little by way of home comforts, a single table, a stool on one side and a make shift straw bed by the wall across from the fire. As I turned back to the flames I noticed for the first time, a man sat on a stool to the side of the hearth. I knew not who he was, or what to say, so I decided to keep the conversation light.

"You are not out celebrating the New Year?" I asked the man but he did not reply at first, simply sitting there staring at the fire. At first I wondered if he was all there, but after a moment he spoke.
"I do not have much to celebrate." The man said.
"But surely we all celebrate simply being alive at the end of another year, do we not?" I replied. I awaited a reply but when nothing came I decided to get straight to the point. I was sure that this odd man had to be that who we sought. "I have been searching for you Terrowin." This got the man's attention and he turned on his stool, looking at our group for the first time.
"And why do you seek this, Terrowin?" he asked.
"We have a proposal for him. We fought with him many years back, on the brink of the Thames." I answered and through the light of the fire I could see the terror in his eyes as I reminded him of that time.
"Terrowin is not here." The man said and turned back to the fire.
"I know of your curse." I'd said to him. "Is that why you lock yourself away in here?" He remained silent. "This is no life for a man of the curse; we can help you to control it, to learn to use it to your advantage and help you to fight those that set the curse upon you."
"I just want to be left in peace." The man said eventually. "I heard what the men did to the man in Swanage; I wish not to be burned at the stake." This sad sap of a man, sat cowering in front of the fire, was going to be of no use to us, so I turned to leave.
"At least with us you could live without fear, for we are like you and we protect our own." I said to the man, looking back over my

shoulder before leaving. "But if you wish to cower in your little room then so be it. You fear persecution from your fellow man for what they fear you might be, but from what I can see you are already punishing yourself worse than any fate they may bestow upon you. In my mind imprisonment is worse than death, even if it is by choice." And with that I left.

"Wait!" the man called from the door as we walked up the small alley outside. "I will come with you," he said. "But I must leave right now, for my transformation is uncontrollable."

"Then we will leave right away, we have a camp outside of town."

And with that the man followed behind us as we left. He carried no possessions but the cloak he wore and he did not even trouble himself to shut the door to his sparsely adorned cell as he left.

The little man followed us from the town. We left briskly, stopping only long enough to collect our horses as we went. Terrowin must have been really fighting the beast in his mind for no sooner than we were out of sight of the entrance his body had burst and a large ram had suddenly appeared before charging off into the dark, Terrowin's cloak tied around its neck trailing behind him like a cape. After a few minutes Terrowin returned to us and although I said nothing I couldn't help notice that the robe was tied tightly around his neck even in human form, clever I thought as we continued onto our camp.

Terrowin's form changed regularly, more so than any of the rest of us. Rowan had said later that he believed that his curse was triggered when he became nervous and it seemed that he was always nervous. His beast however caused little concern to us and so we happily let him work it out of his system in the hope that he would eventually tire, or get used to our presence and relax. There had still been some rabbit left when we had arrived and Terrowin devoured it greedily before changing once again and running into the woods that surrounded our camp.

39
2010
Fatal Flight

That night after dinner I had trained with Ben until late, he had retired to bed now leaving me out in the clearing alone. I lay on my back staring up towards the night sky, it was a clear evening and the stars glittered with a wonderful grace that defied their truly colossal, volatile nature. As I lay there I longed to fly, but the Abbeys rules stated that we were not to fly out at night or alone as apparently it wasn't safe, but I knew no harm would come to me. As I took in the wonder above me, a shooting star shot across the heavens, a beautiful golden streak soaring through the sky, flowing across the dark night and… back again? That wasn't right, I was no astrologer but I knew stars didn't turn in mid flight. Suddenly it hit me, what else was golden and flew? And without another moments thought I leapt to my feet, my body twisting and changing as I rose from the clearing, beating my huge wings as I went. I wasn't up here alone anyway, I thought as I rose to where Ellie circled above. No rules were broken, right?

We ducked and dived in the crystal clear air of the night sky, it was beautiful up here and the beast roared with joy, well awake and revelling in the moment. We flew for what felt like minutes but I was sure an hour had passed, time held no concern up here, nothing did, just the air around us. The golden eagle swooped away from me once again and I felt the dragon's joy at the thrill of the chase and left him to follow as we shot down toward the ocean. Ellie pulled up just before hitting the waves but I wasn't quite as quick or agile as her and my tail crashed into the ocean, my wings having to pump hard to keep my large form clear of the water. We flew along level with the ocean for a while swooping left then right. Every now and then Ellie would drop lower spraying water up into my face before surging forwards once again away from me. I hadn't noticed at first but we had closed into the mainland and before I knew it I was shooting over the cliffs. An alarm rang in my head as I tried to catch Ellie to warn her to turn, if she was seen that was one thing, an eagle was strange but not unfathomable, a dragon however tended to lead to questions when seen flying over the cliff tops.

I pushed on but couldn't catch her, she was too nimble and enjoying herself too much to notice my sudden agitation so I decided to turn back myself, I'd explain to her later. I turned to my left tilting my wings to catch the air just right to lead me back out to sea when suddenly movement caught my eye. At first I wondered if it was Ellie having turned back round, but to my horror I realized that this wasn't the case. The dragon reacted instantly, quicker than I could stop him, he shot down to where a couple stood at the edge of the cliff clearly enjoying a romantic stroll; but they now stood dumbstruck, staring at my dragon as it zeroed in on them. He didn't miss a beat. Excited from the chase and hungry from the exertion the dragon was uncontrollable, his mind blocked mine instantly and it was in that moment that I realized who was truly in charge. He humoured me when it didn't matter, let me have my way, but when he was hungry, hunting, I had no chance. He shut me out, his mind a hundred percent focused on the hunt, the kill. I felt his thoughts salivate as we approached the terrified couple. I saw the look of panic in their eyes and felt shame hit me like a tsunami, crashing against my mind as we cleared the edge of the cliff and shot back out over the ocean. From the corner of my eye I saw a golden streak and I knew she had seen me, seen everything.

I could taste the blood in my mouth; feel the flesh between my teeth and the shame that battered my mind. I knew that I was no more in control now than I had ever been, I felt duped, deceived; beaten at my own game by my own *true* nature.

40
1013
Separate Ways

That next morning on the dawn of a new day and a new but bitterly cold year, we rode out from our camp outside of Portland and travelled north for a few hours heading back to the mainland. We rode on swiftly, our newest recruit Terrowin riding upon Trojans additional steed, Trojan preferring to run in his beasts form along side us. Trojan was strong and never tired, easily keeping ahead of the other horses, his huge beast vastly superior to the domesticated animals we rode. They knew it also and seemed to speed up when Trojan's beast was near as if his presence inspired them to be the best they could be. He was quite easily able to outrun each one of our horses without even trying.

After a couple of hours riding we stopped at a juncture in the track, the track splitting into two. One track I knew went north, the other east, along the coast.

"I think it is time we parted ways." I said to the group as a whole. "We are short on time and we now have the furthest distances to cover. Gloucester is four days to the north, whilst Selsey is four days travel to the east. If we split up we will cover the ground in half the time." There was a general feeling of unrest now flowing through the pack, but they knew that I was right; we were all aware of the timescale that we were up against and if the men we sought were as unable to control their beasts as Terrowin was, then training would be essential.

"Brom, you and Rowan head north to Gloucester and then onto Worcester, find any men that you can and return to St Michaels to begin their training. Trojan and I will run for Selsey and then onto Canterbury. We will meet you in approximately one full moon back at the Abbey."

"Consider it done." Brom replied preparing to leave.

"And what would you have of me?" Althalos asked concerned.

"I would like you and Borin to accompany Terrowin back to St Michaels." Borin looked sullen at this but he said nothing. "I need you to guard the others Borin. They have not a fighting beast among them and the land is littered with Vikings." Borin nodded at this and he and the terrier, turned to leave.

"Please take my horse with you too." I said as they turned and looked at me, understanding my intention.

"Will you not need that?" Terrowin asked confused and I recalled that he and Althalos had little or no knowledge of our beasts having not yet seen them all.

"No." I answered him simply. "How fast do you think you can get to Selsey?" I had then asked Trojans massive horse form. He neighed in response and I knew he welcomed the challenge.

"Take care." I said to the group in general and with that I burst into flames and flew into the sky at the same time that Trojan bolted from the clearing heading for Selsey. I looked down from above to see Terrowin fall from his horse in surprise. He hit the floor at the same time that the ram exploded from his body and bolted into the tree line, cape flapping behind him.

I flew above Trojan as he ran across fields and dales, covering the ground with surprising speed. If he could maintain this pace we would be at Selsey in two days, not four. We stopped that night as the dark closed in around us; I lit a fire before hunting for food. By the time I returned the fire wasn't necessary as the rabbits were well roasted from the heat of the flames that engulfed my beast's body. Trojan just laughed, taking the char-grilled rabbit and tucking in, his appetite voracious after a long day. The next day followed in much the same way, a long days travelling along winding cliff top paths that trailed along the coast. Occasionally Trojan would come across a band of Vikings but they were quickly dealt with, I would swoop down into their midst distracting them before Trojan would storm his way through the centre of them, sending them into complete disarray; we would be gone before they had even registered our arrival.

We'd reached Selsey by midday on the third day of travelling. The journey had taken its toll on both Trojan and I, so we'd entered the town wearily by foot hoping to find ourselves a place to drink. We had made good time and had chosen to rest before proceeding to search out the two we sought from this town. We had known from the list that two men of the curse were known to have once resided in this town so later that afternoon we had asked around. We'd checked the names with the locals to see if the cursed men still frequented the area but the names had not been heard of for a while and it appeared that the men had left not long after returning. One man had told us that the two of them were brothers and that they had returned for only a week. They had had no family to return to and they had stayed not long before they'd left and hadn't been seen since. And so we headed out and onward that evening towards Canterbury. We had rested well and so had planned to run through the night. It was a five days ride to Canterbury and we had wasted enough time in Selsey, so that night I flew ahead of Trojan, lighting the path that he trod as we worked our way across the south of the country to reach our final destination.

41
1013
Canterbury

Four long days passed, we had made good time but the weather was against us as we travelled and the effort was taking its toll on the two of us. Trojan pushed on like a warrior sleeping for only an hour or so at a time and stopping only briefly to eat. Unwilling to give into fatigue he plunged on relentlessly, he was strong and fast, but he was not invincible and by the time we got to Canterbury we were both exhausted. I left Trojan in human form to find us a place to rest for the evening whilst I began the search for the cursed men that we had come here to find. Trojan had told me that Monks scroll listed a Frederick and a Walter to this town and I hoped that the arduous journey hadn't all been in vain. Fortunately, although the town was fairly large, the men we sought were well known if not well liked. I had returned to obtain Trojans help prior to confronting the men. One of the town folks had informed me that these men were not friendly and although I did not fear for my own safety, bursting into flames in front of the town's folk would not have gone down well. If we could talk without trouble then we would be in better stead to rest without having to flee the town. Trojan was, as always, eager for another challenge, always looking to prove himself. We eventually found the two men in what I assume had been Walters's quarters. Frederick was also with him and so were a couple of other reprobates. The men had not looked friendly as we entered their quarters, knocking at first, but after no reply I had pushed the door aside and entered regardless.

We had walked into a smoky, unfriendly room where we found four men gambling over something and laughing darkly at each others misfortune. They had clearly been drinking as old mead tankards lay carelessly strewn around them. The room fell silent as we entered; I took in my surroundings watching the four men until my eye caught the man at the centre of this assemblage.

"And who are *you* to walk into my home unannounced?" The man at the centre bellowed, clearly surprised at this apparently unthinkable action.

"My name is Eadric and this is Trojan." I had replied. "We seek both Walter and Frederick of Canterbury. Have I the honour of addressing either man now?"

"That depends on your business and it had better be good or I will take this intrusion personally." The man replied. He was huge, not built like Trojan or Brom, no he was fat. A repulsive man, the weight of four men easily, his bulk spread out around him where he sat and spittle formed at the edge of his mouth as he spoke. His features resembled a collection of small islands, lost in the vast ocean that was his bright red face and as he spoke I saw light glint from the knives that his associates were trying to discreetly un-sheath. I decided to get straight to the point.

"We are here to talk of your curse." This stopped the man short and he must have signalled the others because they momentarily stayed their blades. The huge man spoke under his breath and two of the three men around him left the room. Once they had left and with a great effort the man rose to his feet, his body unfolding as he stood. My first assumption of this man, although correct, was not the entirely accurate. The man extended as he rose and whilst he was fat he was also at least seven foot tall. Sitting he looked no threat as if he would be unable to stand let alone fight but now that he stood his size was terrifying, a giant by human standards. Now that I could see him clearly I could remember his form from the clearing that fateful day, he was not a man you'd easily forget. Another man stood at his side, I had all but forgotten him, insignificant in the presence of the man mountain that had stood with his head in the beams of the room we were in.

"I am Walter," The larger of the two men said. "And this is Frederick." He continued, signalling the man to his side. "Now tell me why you interrupted my game. I was about to win so you cost me tonight's meal."

"Then let me buy your meal this evening, I will tell you our tale whilst we eat." I replied.

We'd had dinner that evening and had all eaten well. Walter was a man that liked his food and the locals around here seemed accustomed to his ferocious appetite. He wasn't as unpleasant man as I had first feared, he was loud and spoke his mind forcefully, but his intentions seemed genuine and it appeared that he was content as long as he knew where his next meal would come from. Frederick on the other hand spoke barely a word; he just sat silently, ate and answered our queries simply and without the embellishment that Walter seemed to favour. We told the two of our plight, of the reason that we had come to find them and they listened with interest. Walter only occasionally interrupting to show his feelings towards our enemy or to order yet another tankard of mead and eventually they had agreed to join our cause. Frederick had seemed reluctant at first, but Walter was eager and I got the distinct impression that Frederick did not argue with Walter. So the next morning, once well rested, Trojan and I were ready to leave once again and awaited the arrival of Walter and Frederick.

It was some time later when they'd actually arrived, much to Trojans annoyance. He had spoken rashly on a couple of occasions of our new brother's tardiness and whilst I did not agree with his general impatience, I did share some of his concern. We were both troubled by the thought of our diminishing timescale. This would be too long a journey with Walter in tow for he would not fit astride any horse I had ever seen. I suspect that even Trojan would struggle to carry such a man, not that Trojan would ever lower himself to carry a man on his back. This concern was why both Trojan and I grinned widely when Walter did finally arrive. He had clearly thought of this issue long before we had and he came down the main track from the town astride what must have once been an old cart that had been strengthened at some point to carry a heavy load. As I looked closer it appeared that he had hitched a set of harness to a central pole replacing the two standard shafts that would normally fit only a single horse. The cart was now pulled by a team of four horses. It was quite something to behold, this mountain of a man being pulled by his four steeds astride his 'chariot,' he would surely terrify anyone who stood in his way. Closely following behind him was Frederick astride a single horse of his own, blending into the world as if he was no more significant than mist. I had forgotten all about him as Walter rode down and could easily have left without him.

I had not known how this friendship had risen between these two for it was an odd pairing. Frederick seemed somehow unfazed by Walter's presence, despite being a sixth of his size and Walter seemed to regard Fredrick as a baby cub that he would fight to the death for without question. I couldn't help but wonder what Frederick brought to the friendship, Walter clearly offered Frederick protection but what Frederick contributed I wasn't sure.

"It is a fifteen day ride across the width of the country. Are you ready to go?" I had asked them as they'd arrived.

"It's been a while since I have seen outside of these walls," Walter answered. "And we may get to enjoy the company of some of our Viking friends while we're at it." Walter boomed, chuckling to himself at the prospect. Frederick simply kicked his horse into a trot and set off ahead of us.

We travelled for five days, resting as the light receded and commencing as it rose again. The going was slower than our trip to Canterbury had been, but this was to be expected. I'd spoken to Walter often over those five days and learnt a lot of him; he was an interesting man with many tales, a warrior at heart. He had known that this day would come and he looked forward to seeing our foe off from our shores. He knew nothing of his beast and was unable to even tell me what it was as neither he nor Frederick had seen one before him. Walter had no control over his beast and it sounded as if he and Monk would have a lot to talk about on our return. Frederick however had taken to his animal well, apparently, although I had not seen it for myself. He also knew of no name for his beast but had learnt control easily and I figure that it was this control that Walter admired in him, what had solidified their friendship. It transpired that Frederick had often hidden Walter in his times of need, helping him to conceal his beast from the other town folk and I could only imagine that this was no easy task given the size of the man.

It was on the sixth day that we first ran into trouble.

42
2010
Lost

The next morning I awoke early with a heavy head, a black fog hung in my mind before sinking into the pit of my stomach. As the haze lifted, the memories flooded back to me. I lay there for a while wondering how I was going to face the others for surely Ellie would have told them by now. I wondered if I would be exiled, if I would find them glaring at me as I entered the mess hall before being escorted from the island, sent on my way. Or would it be worse? Eadric had said he was a hunter, am I to be his next victim? I stepped from my quarters a short time later. The early morning sun seeming brighter than usual and felt like a search light highlighting my shame as I slunk to breakfast. The short trip to the mess hall took an age and my mind throbbed as I walked. People passed by but I moved on swiftly, too ashamed to look them in the eye. I pushed rudely past a lady and I heard her muttering under her breath as I moved quickly on. I found myself waiting for someone to grab me, to shout, for the crowd to suddenly notice me and turn hostile. I had broken the cardinal rule last night; I had taken a human life, again, two in fact.

As I approached the mess hall I felt the weight of my situation loom ominously, so much so that even the beast, sated from the night's activities, stirred briefly detecting my unease. I took a deep breath and entered the hall prepared for the worst.

I paused for a moment in the doorway. Nothing. No yelling, no screaming, no accusations, nothing.

I moved to a spare seat at the nearest table pouring a coffee on route, food was out of the question as I would only bring it up again. I could still feel the flesh from last night in my mouth, the haunting ghosts of my victims playing on my mind as I sat nursing the coffee. It felt like the only real thing in the world to me as I sat there, the glue keeping my breakdown at bay, as long as I concentrated on only the coffee... I wanted to scream, to confess my shame. I had taken human lives and I should pay. I wanted to be punished; to get it over with, the suspense was always worse for no one could punish me more than I punished myself. I felt the dragon rise briefly, mocking my weak, fragile human mind. He felt no shame, no remorse; he cared nothing for the lives that were lost. I felt a set of eyes bore into the back of my head and turned in time to see Ellie walk away as I looked up. I just caught the back of her head as she left. So she clearly didn't want to talk about last night then.

"You look like crap!" Ben exclaimed sitting opposite me. "You hit the beers after I left?" He asked, not waiting for an answer before tucking into his breakfast. I felt bile rise up in my throat at this everyday conversation, how dare he!? Did he care nothing? But of course he must not know. He was my trainer, my mentor; he would not let this pass if he knew. So Ellie hadn't said anything, yet. So what do I do?

I felt the turmoil rage inside my gut, should I tell him? Beg for forgiveness? Would it be worse coming from Ellie? Or should I leave? Run again. The thoughts rushed through my head so fast it span, the bile I had felt before came back with a vengeance and I stood and ran from the canteen, knocking my coffee over the table as I went.

"Kids!" I heard Ben shout after me as I left. "Learn to handle your drink!" I didn't look back, I had to get away, clear my head.

I wondered around the island for a while aimlessly, walking through the small woodland that surrounded the base of St Michaels subconsciously heading towards the peak. I knew this was the dragon wanting to get to higher ground, he always feels more comfortable higher up and I didn't have the strength to fight him so I just let him guide my body upwards and before I knew it I was standing in the entrance to the large Abbey. I sat quietly on a rock to the side of the entrance looking out over the harbour far below. I could just see the shape of Brad's boat in the harbour and I found myself longing for the simplicity of that day fishing once again.

"Do not punish yourself anymore than you already have." I turned at the sudden voice and saw that Eadric had appeared from nowhere, now stood a foot behind me leaning casually against the outer wall of the Abbey. "The fact that you feel remorse for the couple shows that you still hold on to your human side. It is the reason that there is still hope for you."

"How do you know?" I asked rather stupidly for I didn't know what else to say.

"I saw Ellie, you scared her, she cares for you but she fears the dragon that resides within you."

"And so she should." I replied. "So do I."

"Good. You need to harness that fear, it will help you. It is war and with all war there are casualties. Use this, remember the pain you feel now and ensure that the dragon never puts you through it again. It is not a committee, the beast doesn't get a say. Make sure he knows it."

I did not say anything to this, what could I say? I had been weak and I had lost.

"I knew your father." Eadric said suddenly from out of the blue, the shock brought me out of my reverie momentarily as my ears pricked up to hear what he was about to say.

"He didn't change like you, as the years have passed the curse has begun to skip generations, I have wondered if the curse was beginning to wane but often the next generation would then come back stronger than ever. Your father's beast didn't manifest but his temper had an edge to it. He believed this was just his nature that he just had a bad temper, but I felt it was more than that. He never changed fully but at times I wondered if his beast's temperament lurked in the back of his mind."

"My dad? He never shows any emotion, let alone a wild temper? You must have the wrong man."

"Give me more credit than that!" Eadric declared, laughing at this. "I have tracked every family of the curse that I have discovered over the years, following every persons lineage. I found your dad as I did you, only your dad never changed. Over the years certain lineages have weakened and I believed yours had run its course as the last three generations hadn't changed. Your dad suffered horrendous bursts of rage and I wondered if he would turn eventually if he accidentally triggered the curse, but he never did and after a while he learnt to suppress his temper, rather successfully I might add."

"Yeah," I smirked. "He suppressed everything." I considered the way my father had been through out my life, the way he would just sit there as if we weren't there at all and suddenly I saw those times in a new light, remembering the twitch he would get in the corner of his eye. Now I understood.

"Would you rather the other option? You yourself know the power within you; the beast is capable of great and terrible things.

"So what now?" I asked. "Should I leave? Or is it too late, will you… kill me?"

"No." Eadric replied but there was no humour to his tone. "I will continue to help you whilst humanity still remains within you. Every one of our brothers that I have killed over the years I have believed the human side to be lost, to have been over powered by the beast. You should know that I take no pleasure in it; it is always with a heavy heart that I take another life. I do not take my duty lightly but none the less it is a duty that I must do." Eadric put his hand on my shoulder at this point. "Humanity still reside within your soul but you must listen to your trainers, your dragon is strong, stronger than most. You must be stronger than him. Oh and try to stay away from the mainland." Eadric said walking off down the track that led away from the Abbey.

His words should have comforted me but my conscience wouldn't let it drop. Images of the couple flashed across my mind, I found myself wondering if they had kids, a family. I imagined the headlines in the local and national papers, 'missing' or 'vanished.' I knew that there would remain no trace of them. The dragon was a skilled hunter; he would not have left sloppy remains to implicate my involvement. The couple would have appeared to have just disappeared. I knew now, in this moment, that I would never be able to live with the burden that rested on my shoulders. The overwhelming guilt was too much, first Rebecca, now the unknown couple from the cliff. How could I continue knowing what I had done?

43
1013
Surprise Guests

We had ridden down through the centre of Wessex using the old tattered Roman roads to keep a good turn of speed on our journey. As we travelled the roads had shown us a glimpse of another time when the world had been a very different place. We were aware that the Vikings were also likely to use this route and so I had kept a vigilant eye on the road ahead from above. At the point where the old road narrowed and the roman road turned to a well worn track, our small band followed the trail winding their way through a dense patch of woodland. Over time the trees had grown up either side, all but blocking my view of the track and I momentarily lost sight of the others below the dense foliage. Trojan had been leading the way in horse form whilst Frederick's horse and Walters chariot followed closely behind. I had flown swiftly over the woodland and circled on the other side expecting at any minute to see them emerge from the shadows of the tree line.

But they never appeared.

Another minute passed.

And another.

I gave them one more minute before my patience got the better of me and I flew down to the point where they should have exited. No sign of them. My heart had begun to race. Where could they be? Two men and six horses should not just vanish. I had hoped the track had been blocked by a falling tree and that they were struggling to get past, although the sinking feeling in my heart had suggested otherwise. I shot along the track into the woodland, it felt unnatural to fly under the tree cover but I couldn't sit and wait any longer. The flames that constantly covered my body flared out like a shooting star as I flew through the gloom of the trees singeing the leaves as I passed. I flew around a bend in the track and suddenly the group were there in front of me and chaos had erupted. The horses of

Walters cart had reared up in that moment at something I couldn't see and my sudden appearance had done nothing to soothe them. Walter was enraged; a deep growl reverberated from his chest as he wrestled with something trapped in his huge arms. Whatever it was I did not envy it. Trojan was dancing in fast circles trying to catch a glimpse of something in the tree line, Fredrick's horse had fallen to the ground with a thud as I'd arrived suddenly throwing an eerie light on the scene but Fredrick was nowhere to be seen. Satisfied that whatever he had been searching for posed no imminent threat Trojan turned to Walter, bearing witness to his rage. The roar continued to emanate from Walters throat as his arms wrapped further around the black shape within them, his body jolting as whatever it was that he held thrashed at him, trying to free itself. It was strong, but Walter was stronger, the fact that it still wrestled and had not yet succumbed was testament to its strength. A few more seconds passed and I changed back to my human form with Trojan following suit to fill me in on what had happened.

"They jumped us!" he'd declared once human. "They swung out of the woods. One of them grabbed Frederick and one grabbed Walter, they must have thought me just a horse."

"What are they?" I had asked him.

"Gorillas I think, it was too quick, but there were two of them, Walter has one now. I mean who'd try to attack him?" Trojan had then asked pointing to the huge figure of Walter. We walked to where Walter now held the gorilla, still conscious, but clearly exhausted from his struggle. As I saw the thing clearly I was able to confirm that it was in fact a gorilla, a very large gorilla at that. It must have thought it was strong enough to take Walter on. It was wrong.

"Who are you?" I asked him and I saw the look of surprise in his eyes as I addressed him, he clearly believed that I would assume him simply just a gorilla, but I knew better than that. Gorillas were not native to England and were only heard of through stories, tales of big, human shaped monsters with the strength of a bear. That and the point that animals were not known to organise themselves for simultaneous attacks. I tried again.

"Are you Barda or Lief?" I asked. Trojan looked at me and I knew he had not yet made the connection. As I'd spoken the huge beast in Walter's deadly grip seemed to reach a decision and his body began to shrink back to human size. Walter let him go. The man now fully human once again fell to his knees gasping for breath.

"I am Barda, Lief is my brother. How do you know who we are?" He'd asked gasping between words.

"That is not important, you have ten seconds to get your brother to return our friend unharmed, before Walter here finishes squeezing the rest of the air from your lungs."

Barda seemed to consider this for a moment before taking a deep breath and making an odd noise. The sound came out loud and clear and I realised that he was echoing the sound of the gorilla. A moment later Frederick walked from a nearby bush, dusting himself down, the second gorilla however stayed out of sight.

"You Barda are lucky that Walter here has not already killed you."

"How do you know what I am?" Barda asked.

"I know what you are and who you are because I came here to find you, both of you. I too am a man of the curse, like you and I am assembling an army to fight the impending Viking invasion. I am looking to gather men of the curse to fight back against those that cursed us. I see that you and your brother have had to leave your homes. You live here now? In these woods?"

"Yes, we knew it would not be safe in a town for people like us." He'd replied.

"But yet you have learnt control?"

"Mostly, but we still have a lot to learn before we would risk returning to human dwellings."

"Come with us, we can help you to learn, give you a place to stay without fear of retribution."

"And in return what, we fight for your cause?"

"It is our cause, not mine, they intend to take our country from us and they will leave you no woods to hide in."

"You need to learn to fight first though." Walter added in his deep baritone, laughing deeply at his own joke.

It was at this point that Lief walked from the shadow of the trees, gorilla form at first but morphing as he walked, before standing in front of his brother in full human form.

"I think we should go with them brother." Lief said. "We cannot hide out here forever. The Vikings will be larger in number and we will not be able to steal our living from them. We were lucky this time that these people were indeed not Vikings for Vikings would not have hesitated in cutting your throat brother."

Barda considered this for a moment before replying simply.

"Fine."

"Then I will fetch our horses." And with that we walked clear of the woodland. As soon as we hit the open air I once again took to the skies, my bird blazing like a comet, soaring into the heavens.

44
1013
Broms Trip

We had arrived back at St Michaels on the fifteenth day having encountered little trouble on the return journey that is with the exception of that provided by Barda and Lief. We approached the coast to await the ocean to recede and allow us passage to the large gates set into the outer wall of the Abbey. As the coast had come into view Walter began to curse under his breath and his temper flared suddenly. It was here that I first caught a glimpse of the beast that resided within Walter. We had travelled across the heart of Wessex, the most direct route and Walter had seemed content the entire journey. He had told us that he had little command over his beast but from what I had seen over the past fifteen days he had always appeared in complete control. I had wondered of Frederick and Walters beasts often on the long journey for we had a war looming and I had to know if they would be an asset to our cause but it hadn't been until we had approached the beach that day that we had seen anything of them.

"What's this!?" He had roared. "Nobody mentioned anything about crossing water!"

I had turned after a moment to see Walter had stopped in his tracks, Frederick quickly turning back towards him.

"Walter will not cross water." Frederick had said to me as he returned to where Walter stood. After a moment I had followed.

"Walter, I assure you that we do not have to go by boat, in a short while the land will appear and you may ride your chariot over land to the entrance." I reassured him.

"I will not pass across land that does not promise to be there when I next look." Walter exclaimed.

"It is alright, it is simply the tide, the water rises and falls at consistent points of the day, the land will always return shortly." I had been impressed with Fredericks understanding of the ocean; he was clearly a smart man, although I must confess that I myself had not truly understood what he had meant at the time.

"I will wait here."

"You will see." I said. "The land will rise shortly." Barda and Lief had over heard the conversation and had chosen this point to interject with their own useful addition to the conversation.

"Hah! You're scared of water!" Barda had called out mockingly.

"I fear nothing!" Walter roared. "I will tear you from limb to limb monkey boy!"

At this Barda approached the ocean as it lapped against the shore and stepped into the water before turning to face Walter.

"Come and get me!" he taunted. Walter dismounted and approached Barda whilst maintaining a safe distance from the water itself.

"I can wait." He said threateningly whilst shaking with either anger or fear. I could see that he was about to do something and Lief too must have sensed it for at this point he tried to intercede.

"This is unwise brother, enough is enough."

"Why Lief, he dares not to enter the water! I am perfectly safe." Barda replied jovially.

"Fredrick!" Walter yelled his body shaking. It was at this point that Barda pushed Walter too far for he had cupped his hands and filled them with water before hurling it at Walter where he stood. Walter roared in anger and his body shook violently before suddenly his body transformed, morphing into a large, grey shape. I couldn't tell you in that moment what his beast was but as he changed he continued to roar, only now the sound echoed out of a large lion like jaw but with two huge tusks that had emerged from the top of his mouth and ran almost the full length of his body. The beast was large with a ferocious, angry face; but its body appeared vastly over weight and instead of legs it appeared to have flippers? Barda stood in shock, unsure of what to do next. The beasts roar continued, echoing around the surrounding beach and out across the water before us.

Suddenly a second sound filled the air and we each turned to its source to see the huge gates, the only access to Abbey, as they swung open. The water had not fully retreated but that did not stop the assembly of beasts, now visible in the open doorway, from exiting to begin crossing the barely visible path to where we now stood. At the front of the assembly came Monk in elephant form, a truly magnificent creature. I still remember now how taken back I had been at the sight of him, I had only seen him once before and I had forgotten just how large he was. Following him across the expanse was a raft of beasts, some of which I recognised other that I did not. I did however recognise the large hawk that had shot out from the pack and soared above before swooping down, changing back and landing beside me.

"We heard your approach whilst training," Rowan said, clearly happy to see our safe return as he shook my hand merrily. "I am afraid to say they have all been training hard over the last few days and are glad to have an excuse to roam from the confines of the wall." Rowan continued, turning to look back at the horde of beasts now descending onto the shore around us. I recognised Broms bear among them and Borins panther as it ran swiftly through the shallow water. Terrowin trailed them, charging around frantically with his cape still flapping behind and there were also a few large heard animals and a couple of birds circling above me that I did not recognise.

My mind span suddenly. Walter? In all the commotion I had forgotten about Walter. His beast had no control, I span looking for the attack, for the beast that had appeared before me a moment ago. My eyes came to rest on a large grey mass now lying out cold on the floor. As I watched I saw a small grey scaly looking animal slink away having just unravelled itself from Walter's neck. I watched as it vanished before my eyes. I turned back to Walter to see his chest moving, he was still alive and his form changed back to its human shape. Before I could think anymore of it Monks elephant loomed over me momentarily before shrinking away to reveal Monk.

"Eadric my friend!" He called thrusting out a hand in greeting, "It is good to see you are well."

“As it is you, I see that the other men made it back too.” I stated accepting his hand in welcome.

“Yes they did and with them I hear that we have also gathered some additional fighters. Tybalt informs me that we will have the help of the King’s army aside our own, even if we do not have the King himself on side. They are awaiting the word to march onto London he informs me.”

“Is that so?” I had known that Tybalt had taken a few men with him but I had not known that the King’s troops were preparing to fight too. “How does training go?” I enquired.

“Well.” Monk declared. “It seems that they have taken to their beasts well, although we have had a few surprises along the way.”

“As have I, Barda and Lief here surprised us. I had thought them gone, but with them we now have seventeen beasts and the King’s men to fight back the Vikings. Things are looking up.”

“True and do not forget that the Abbots men will stand with us also, but I think you will find there are eighteen of us, not seventeen.” Monk replied; I thought about this for a moment.

“I count seventeen. There were twenty one men in total. Henry now lies in Chester and Sadon in Swanage. Alric would not join us and Fendrel is Sadons dog. Seventeen.”

“Ah,” The Monk said knowingly as a little smile crossed his face. “Then tonight you shall see, for tonight we will hold a reveal. We must know each others beasts so as to know our allies on the battlcficld.” And with that he walked off, chuckling to himself.

45
1013
The Reveal

We sat together to eat for the first time that night. Drink flowed and quickly the timber framed hall had filled with the deep sound of raucous laughter as the men shared tales of their past. I let the laughter wash over me that evening as it had seemed so long since I had last heard the sound, my mind filling with memories of happier times, times spent with Jolecia and Arthur. The afternoon had turned into evening and as the food settled into the pit of my stomach my eyes roamed about the table. I counted the men around me over and over again but no matter how many times I counted them I still only made seventeen, the eighteenth still eluding me. Sadon the second was cradled between Ulric and Forthwind bundled up in his usual blanket and I wondered, just for a moment, if he was who Monk had referred to. Surely Monk can't have meant the child? He was not even born the day of the curse and a child would surely be obvious if he had been changing as he would know nothing of control. The mystery continued to escape me as I sat talking with Rowan and Brom who filled me in on their own journey to find Hadrian and John. They had made good time on route to Gloucester and Worcester and had found the men with little trouble; however what they had discovered in the process had come as a bit of a surprise. Quickly after tracking each man down Rowan had revealed that both Hadrian and John were fellow men of the sky, like he himself was. This news had not gone down as well with Brom as it had with Rowan, even less so once Rowan had shared his latest plan with him. Apparently Brom had refused Rowans idea point blank and as we had sat at dinner that night he visibly shrunk away at any reminder of the ordeal.

"So what was this plan that struck such fear into the usually brave Brom?" I'd asked curious.

"I'd reasoned that between the four of us three could fly and so it was logical that we would return here in a fraction of the time if we flew." Rowan had answered and so it had come about that with Hadrian and John in agreement and Brom very much not so, that they had created a harness from the available rope and cloth to secure Brom and then, whilst supporting him they had flown back to St Michaels saving days of travel. Unfortunately however it had taken everyday they had saved for Brom to get over the ordeal and he was often heard moping around the place saying things such as 'men weren't meant to fly' and occasionally thanking the ground under his feet. Rowan had been concerned that Brom might never forgive him.

After the seventeen of us had eaten, Monk led us through to the training ground where he'd lived and stood at its centre, awaiting our arrival, was the Abbot.

"Thank you for joining me this evening." He began as we entered the training ground. "Welcome back Eadric." The Abbot said turning to me as I approached the spot where he stood.

"Thank you Abbot, it is good to be back." The Abbot turned to the assembled men now talking to the group as a whole.

"I have called you all here tonight as it is the first time that you, the men of the curse, have been together since the night that this fateful curse was set upon you. The time that you must leave to meet the very foe that inflicted you will soon be upon us and when that time comes it is important that you band together, for only united will you stand a chance against such a violent and blood thirsty enemy. This is why each of you must know each others darker sides and why I have assembled you tonight." The Abbot paused momentarily, letting the idea settle.

"Most of you by now are able to change at will and those of you that aren't; well I am sure that we will be able to assist. One by one please step forwards and declare your beast to your fellow men. Some of you will become mighty warriors and others will be swift, subtle and deadly but know that all of you are equally as important to our cause. In the short time that we have available we must find the best way to realise your beasts potential and so training starts tonight. Eadric, will you start us off?" And with that I stepped forward, turned to face the assembled men and said.

"My name is Eadric and my beast is the Phoenix." And with that I let the beast fly, bursting into flames and launching into the sky. I landed back upon the ground a moment later, the Monk handed me a robe and I rejoined the group as Brom walked to the centre.

"My name is Brom, Brom of the bears." He declared before changing and letting out a tremendous roar into the night sky. Rowan and Trojan followed suit, both revealing their beasts to the group and Monk then did the same. Lief and Barda went next, the brothers both revealing their large gorillas to the group before Hadrian, a man I had not yet met but of whom Rowan assures me was a good man, stepped forward and transformed into a large kite before flying clear from the training ground. Borin too had stepped forward and his Panther broke free before Tybalt entered the centre with Forthwind and Ulric at his sides. I looked on curiously having yet to see the three soldier's beasts clearly. First Ulric had transformed effortlessly into a huge Buffalo that I recalled seeing earlier in the day as he had ran along the beach outside the walls. I assumed that the other beast that had ran with him must be the other two and a moment later my hunch was proven correct as Forthwinds body merged gracefully into a huge Oxen and Tybalt followed suit a moment later revealing a large Bull heading up the truly magnificent trio.

Next up was Terrowin who through shear nerves had already changed before even reaching the centre. A chorus of laughter had then followed as the ram charged around the training ground before vanishing down one of the many alleyways leading out of the arena. Althalos stepped up next which once again grabbed my interest as I had found his company most peculiar in the short time in which we had spent together. He stepped into the centre of the arena and vanished into the dark. The crowd around us gasped and mumbled to each other, each wondering the same as I had, where had he gone? Then suddenly a buzzing sound shot past my face and a small creature flew through the group of us before Althalos suddenly appeared again among the crowd.

"It's a wasp." He said to the men around him, taking in the shocked look on their faces and it was, a larger than normal, all black, vicious looking wasp. Unlike any wasp I had seen before. A moment later, John, another new face, stepped forward and after a bit of trial and error turned into a very large and very ugly Buzzard. Last but not least, Walter and Frederick entered the arena and as I look back even now, I still find their creatures odd. Frederick changed instantly, rolling into a large armoured ball on the floor. Monk gasped, but everyone else had just looked on dumbstruck for none of us had any idea of what it was. Walter knelt down and picked the ball up in one hand holding it out for all to see before suddenly it unrolled itself and slinked up Walters's arm wrapping itself around his neck and sitting there like a scarf momentarily before climbing swiftly down his back and back onto the floor and turning back into Frederick. Silence fell.

"He's a Pangolin!" Monk declared excitedly, "the rarest of creatures. Wonderful." Frederick nodded, clearly surprised that Monk had knowledge of his beast.

"My beast is odd also," Walter said bashfully, it was odd to see a man of his size squirm as he had then. He shut his eyes and with a great effort he eventually managed to turn into the great, grey lump that we had seen briefly earlier. Once again the surrounding fell silent as confusion crossed the faces in the group and once again Monk came to the rescue.

"I never thought I'd see one but he's a walrus."

The walrus quickly returned to the form of Walter and he looked embarrassed. "I am afraid that my beast seems of little use." He said meekly.

"That's because you are on land." The monk said to him. "Your beast is a beast of the sea!"

"Great." Walter had grumbled, dejected by this news. The sound of laughter being restrained could just be heard emanating from somewhere near Barda.

With that Walter joined the main group again and we had reached the end. I mentally recounted the men that had shown, seventeen? I turned to Monk who pointed knowingly to the training ground. I turned to the empty space in front of the group once again. Only now it wasn't empty. Stood at the centre was the Abbot and sat at his feet in the centre of the clearing was the tiny little terrier.

"Eadric." The Abbot called to me as I stood, staring at the strange little dog. "I require your assistance."

I walked out to where the Abbot stood.

"This," the Abbot began, signalling the little dog, "is Fendrel."

As he spoke a chorus of whispers ran through the assembled crowd, the name had been banded about in various conversations and the men knew the name to be on the list of cursed men.

"Eadric, would you help us out by kicking Fendrel." The Abbot said turning to me with a knowing smile. I stood for a moment wondering if I had heard him right before I had turned to Monk who was visibly bouncing with amusement.

"You want me to kick him?" I asked.

"Yes." He answered simply.

"Ok?" The crowd had fallen silent. My eyes panned across each of their faces but their appeared to be little concern, people had cared little for a mangy dog in those days. Finally my eyes had come to rest on Borin for I wondered if he would turn on me if I kicked the dog that had stood so loyally beside him for so long, but he looked unconcerned, he too clearly knew what I did not. I turned again to the mutt that had momentarily paused in his task of scratching himself and now sat looking at me with a slightly bored expression.

I stepped up to the little dog.

And then I kicked it.

"Huh?" I had said as my foot sailed through the air failing to connect with anything at all. I looked down to where the dog had been just in time to see the shape of the little terrier blur as it had moved aside with lightning speed… and then appeared to grow.

A growl emanated from the dog's throat. It began as a low rumble before deepening quickly as the dog grew in size and shape. Its features blurred as they morphed from his canine form into… something more. After a second, clearer features started to form; the image was disconcerting to my eyes as it rapidly shifted shape but before they could adjust a mane had begun to form around the terrier's neck and its teeth began to elongate, framing a large, strong jaw.

All this happened in an instant before the huge lion leapt.

Claws scratched at my body and I felt a damp warmth flood across my midriff as a huge set of teeth sunk into my side.

I was dead before the shock had worn off.

A moment later my phoenix had risen from the ashes of my body and I flew up and away from the still angry, but now somewhat confused, lion and landed across the training ground. A moment later I'd turned back to my human form.

"What the!?" I exclaimed initially. "A bit of warning would have been good!" I had then shouted across to the Abbot a little angrier than I should have. Of course everybody knew I would not die but I had still felt a little disgruntled at being used as bait. I'd looked back to where the Lion was and watched as the huge cat sat down, positioning himself oddly for a cat and began to scratch behind its ear. Slowly, as the cat relaxed, its shape began to shrink back to its previous form and suddenly the terrier was sat where the cat had just been, still scratching his ear.

"It seems that this canine has a feline complex." I said, watching as the mutt got up and meandered away before the Abbot spoke to the crowd again.

"Fendrel will be a great asset to our cause, Borin here assures me that he is a good hunter." As the others whispered of this revelation I thought back to that day in the clearing, the day the curse had been placed. I recalled then that Sadons dog had been there that day but it had never occurred to me that the curse could affect humans and animals alike.

"Is that thing safe?" I heard someone ask from the crowd, I believe it was Terrowin having returned to join the assembly.

"No less than any of you are, however dogs have far less complex emotions than humans, if you kick him he'll attack you, if you don't he won't." The Abbot replied, although this did little to reassure certain members of the group who I was sure had given the little dog a larger berth than usual after that when passing him in the town. Wherever that little dog was from that day onward, others tended not to be.

46
2010
Decision

"Ellie, wait." I called after her as she rounded the corner to the canteen. She didn't slow or even acknowledge my call but I knew she'd heard me, everybody had. Whispered voices drifted to my ears as others made their way into lunch whilst speculating on the reasoning behind the commotion, always eager for some pre-lunch excitement. I ran around the corner after her expecting to see her entering the canteen but it appeared that she'd decided to skip lunch as I saw her enter the mouth of an ally in front of me. I followed, calling after her as I went.

"I just want to talk, let me explain." I said jogging to catch up, but she just kept on walking as quickly as she could. I picked up the pace for the last few feet that now remained between us and grabbed the top of her arm in an attempt to get her attention.

"*Let go of me*!" She yelled. I was so taken aback I let go of her arm and stepped away.

"Sorry." I said as I caught the look in her eye. "I, I just wanted to talk, apologise, explain."

"What is there to explain? I saw what you did!" As she said this I could see the fear in her face, real fear, the fear you see in the eyes of someone who is about to die, the fear I saw in the eyes of the couple last night. I had known she would be upset, afraid, but this? Surely she knows I would never hurt her? I'd never hurt any of the people here, they wanted to help me, they were my friends. But of course I hadn't wanted to hurt the people last night, but that hadn't stopped me.

The realisation hit me in that moment like a dagger to the heart, she should be afraid of me and I was being selfish, putting these people at risk. Snippets of the whispered conversations I had just overheard surfaced in my mind and I saw them now in a new light, they weren't merely curious of the shouting, they were watching me. For a moment I wondered what I was doing here with Ellie after what I had done to Rebecca but I knew the answer. It was this human contact, these emotions that I felt that stopped the beast taking over completely, stopped my mind from becoming lost to the far stronger, more powerful beast inside.

Ellie was shaking now, terrified.

"I'm sorry." I said simply turning away from her. I knew in that moment what I needed to do. I would not put her at risk; I'd go away, take to the air and fly far from here. I needed to be where people weren't, the highest mountains or the lowest valley, away from temptation. I would hide myself from the world.

The others here could gain control of their beasts, their nature was kind and sharing and I could see this in their animal forms, I was not. My beast was arrogant, greedy and proud, I knew now that I would not be able to contain the dragon. He was to compulsive and too strong, he never planned so I never knew in advance of his motives. The beast lived on instinct and cared nothing for the rules that would keep me from harms way. I had to run, I knew this now.

I walked from the alley in which I had terrified Ellie and walked back past the canteen listening to the sound of laughter that echoed from the open windows. A couple of voices stood out among the many and I recognised the familiar chortle of my friend and mentor, Ben, we had not always seen eye to eye but he had always had my back. I wished I could say good bye but he would convince me to stay and I knew I would be weak once again. I walked on with a determined gait to my step, heading up the long track that would lead up to the Abbey.

I knew I would find Eadric up at the Abbey, he was often there discussing some business or another. I did not want to say goodbye but I owed Eadric that much, without him I would be dead already.

47
1013
Winter Training

For two months we had trained working day and night to prepare for the impending battle. Occasionally passing travellers would stop in at the nearby village and we would hear updates of the waves of Vikings already terrorising the land or of the impending battle. The news was never encouraging but we took the tales with a pinch of salt as the travellers tended to talk too much once they'd had a few drinks and the tales would be greatly exaggerated. From what little information we could ascertain we'd deduced that the Vikings would breach our shores early May and so we had prepared to be in London to await their arrival at the end of April. We'd barely had time to settle in at St Michaels as before we had known it February and March had passed us by. Our band of men had learnt control swiftly; able to learn a lot from each other and we're now all, for the most part, able to manage their beasts. However, as I had watched their progress I couldn't shake the sinking feeling of dread that I felt at the knowledge that we were incredibly unprepared for the task ahead. I remembered all too clearly the devastation our foe had caused on our first encounter and I did not relish the opportunity to witness such a thing again. It seemed nevertheless that these feelings were not outwardly shared by my fellow men. They talked typically of heroic deeds and great battles whilst taking bets on who would rack up the highest body count. Their over confidence seemed foolish to me at the time but I see now that this bravado was what held their despair at bay, the despair that I had felt so strongly in those days. Fear is the enemy of any fighter. There is no room for fear or regret on the battlefield; they will only get you killed. This I'd learnt from them for they were braver men than I.

By the end of March most of the men had gained enough control to be able to force their transformations by will and could maintain control under pressure. I hoped that it would be enough but only time would tell. With the help of the Abbots men and facilities we had been able to teach the fighters well, each man had become better equipped in hand to hand combat and weapons training. The Monks had also been able to teach more specific fighting techniques, skills that were specifically tailored to each mans individual beast. Each beast had been pushed and tested to its limits to see just what they were capable of, speed, strength and agility were all trialled before Monk had designed specific fighting techniques to best utilise each beasts assets. Whilst we were training the Abbots smiths had also gotten to work creating metal plate armour to protect the beast's weaknesses. I had watched them train in early April and it made me proud to see just how far each man had come and how each beast had grown, the curse appearing to mature as they honed their skills.

It was a bright spring morning in early April when we had departed St Michaels for what we had believed would be the last time.

The men had stood proudly that morning, their heads held high with pride and anticipation at what the future held. That day marked the beginning of a journey that had been inevitable since the fateful day that we were cursed. After only two months of training we'd set out to end a two and a half year grudge. We would use the curse they had set upon us to ensure that they would never do the same to another soul.

Or so we thought.

48
1013
Plans

We had set off that morning on the first day of what would prove to be a long and arduous journey. Our force worked their way slowly across the country heading towards our intended destination, London. Among our numbers the seventeen men of the curse travelled surrounded by a hundred men from the Abbots guard, the men of the curse travelling horse back and the guards marching behind. The pace was slow and tempers would flare occasionally as the impending battle weighed heavily in all of our minds but gradually we worked our way up the long abandoned Roman roads, heading to London and with it our destiny. We stopped in many of the villages as we passed, drumming up support as we went. Occasionally we would send scouts to outlying villages in search of additional troops and they would return within a few days with whatever men they had managed to recruit. Perhaps the most astonishing of these scouting parties and the one that had lifted the spirits of our rabble quite considerably, was made by Tybalt who had departed our company with Ulric and Forthwind a few days earlier. Ulric had taken Sadons son with him as we had left the Abbey and I had wondered many times of what Ulric had intended to do with the child, as the battlefield was no place for a baby. But my worry had been unfounded for whilst he had seemed reluctant to leave the child with the women in the Abbey the three had returned from their detour to Wareham and the child was no longer among them. What the three had returned with however was what appeared to be the entirety of the Kings guard, maybe two hundred men.

"Will the King not punish your men for going against his will?" I had asked Tybalt upon his return.
"Yes, but I will take the consequences. Each man here follows my command and I will pay the Kings price when the time comes. Still,

if this goes bad I may not need to worry about it." He had replied laughing darkly to himself.

And so it had been, each day passed with the men exhausted and hungry but our numbers had grown daily as more men joined our cause. By the time we had breached the shores of the Thames and followed its winding path into London itself, we had nearly four hundred men marching among us. The number of men would not have looked much by the standards of the great armies of later history, but England in those days was a poor, sparse country with little resources and even fewer men. By comparison our band was as large an army as any of our men had ever seen and the men were in high spirits upon the day that we walked into London.

We did not know how long we would have to wait to face our foe, but had we known then just how little time we had to prepare I believe the mood would have been somewhat more sombre.

The next morning word had spread through London that the first boat had been spotted off the east coast. We had barely made it to London before the Vikings arrival, another day and we would have been too late. The men of the curse had stood around me that morning as we'd discussed battle plans. We had argued many options over the past couple of months but none had filled me with confidence. We knew that the Viking horde would be vast. The last attack saw around a thousand men and we knew this time there would be more; many more.

As we had considered our options they had appeared all but hopeless. Our main advantage seemed to be that we held the element of surprise; they would not be expecting much resistance having seen the failings of the King's army before. Their vast numbers and superior strength however would overpower us quickly in a straight fight. They were fast, powerful and ruthless killers; we would need an edge, something to give us the upper hand.

I had thought for a moment, stood in quiet contemplation while the other men stood around me, also silently racking their brains when suddenly something passed over head and an idea began to form.

"How long?" I had asked Rowan as he landed beside me. Rowan, Hadrian and John had left that morning, as soon as the news had reached them, to see the Vikings for themselves and estimate numbers and a time of arrival.
"Not long, half a day at most and it doesn't look good. There are at least thirty ships."
"How many men per ship?" I had asked trying to keep any sign of concern from my voice.
"About forty." A silence spread through our crowd as each man tried to work out how many warriors that meant. I remember well the look on their faces as they pondered this, mental arithmetic was not generally required a lot in those days and half the men couldn't count past their fingers.
"Twelve hundred." Monk said. The silence that followed was deafening.
"Then our choices are limited." I had said to the assembly in general. "If we wait for them to land we stand no chance, they out number us four to one and are deadly warriors. We must stop them from breaching our shores at all costs."
"I will swim out to meet them." Walter declared, his deep voice sounding clearly from where he sat at the centre of the assembly. Walter had trained hard the last two months and with Monks help had learnt a great deal about his beast. It had transpired that Walters beast, whilst slow and cumbersome on land had turned out to be a graceful, elegant beast in the water and proved to be a most efficient hunter of the seas. The problem had been that Walter had always been, since a young age, terrified of water. This seemed at first to be a cruel twist to the curse that had afflicted Walter, but with Monks help and knowledge Walter had learnt a great deal about the beast that Monk referred to as a Walrus. Slowly Walter had learnt not to fear the water, which was no easy feat, but once he had felt the joy

that his beast felt in the water it had been hard to deny. Walter had still not relished the thought of entering the water whilst human, but he had learnt to trust his beast's natural instincts and is now open, at least to some extent, to compromise. Walter knew what was at stake here and was willing to do what it took.

"I will take the boats from below; they won't know what hit them." He finished.

"We will fly out to meet them, beginning immediately." Rowan added next signalling himself, John and Hadrian. It had seemed that a natural hierarchy was forming among these three; they had become good friends during training and seemed to fly in sync together. Rowan had always flown at the front of the formation with the other two flanking him, in those days this seemed of little consequence but it struck me many centuries later that fighter pilots adopted a similar protective flight pattern, something that had come naturally to them.

"And I will too." Althalos added. At the time I had thought that Althalos may have been better served fighting in his human form, his wasp was tiny and it was hard to see what use he would be against the Vikings, but I had let this thought go unsaid for he may prove useful yet.

"Good. We will meet them from the water and the air; I too will fly out to meet them before they enter the mouth of the river. The rest of you take the armies up river away from London, you will form the second stage of our attack. Your best chance will be to hit them at the point where the boats pack together as they pass through the narrow section of the river. You need to stop them from docking the boats." With that people begun to cheer around me inspiring confidence and rousing the beasts within as they prepared for what may be their last stand. Given the gravity of the situation at hand I'd felt it appropriate to say something so I held my head high and spoke clearly over the noise.

"The time is upon us, our moment has come. This is your opportunity to fight for all that these men have put you through. Fight to revenge the curse you now carry and for the lives that you've lost. Fight until every last ounce of strength has left your body or every one of your foe is dead. Save those that you love here on Earth and to avenge those that await you in heaven. Go now and may God be with you all." And with that Rowan, John, Hadrian, Althalos and I all leapt from the ground, transformed in mid air and took to the skies.

49
1013
The Vikings are Coming

We flew up and away from London. As I had looked back I recall seeing the huge grey figure of the Walrus drop into the Thames. I had known we would be at the target before Walter but he was fast and would not have been far behind us as we soared across the mainland and out over the channel. As we flew I took the lead. The other three instinctively falling in behind me, following in my slip stream whilst retaining a careful distance. They weren't fire proof after all. Althalos had vanished but I knew he would not be far from us, he had a way of always turning up when least expected.

As we passed the east coast of England a dark cloud had seemed to be forming just over the horizon. At first my eyes couldn't make out what was ahead of us, it looked as if a storm was brewing up from the sea, despite the warm, calm weather. The dark, ominous cloud drew closer as we flew onward and after a minute my eyes began to take in more detail of the huge black mass that closed in.

It wasn't a storm or at least not of the weather kind. As my eyes adjusted I began to make out shapes in the distance. What had appeared at first to be a large black cloud on the horizon was in fact a large collection of smaller objects closely bunched together. There had to be at least thirty of them. Boats, as my eyes picked up further detail it became clear that it was a large armada of wooden, Viking longboats; all travelling in a tight pack towards the English coast. Each boat must have easily contained forty men, each rowing hard with huge powerful strokes, pushing the boats with incredible speed towards the mainland. It was a truly terrifying sight to behold; each man was dirty and sweaty from the exhaustive rowing with huge muscles bulging from their arms as they pushed ever onwards. As they drew closer to their destination they appeared to become more and more enthused; rather than tiring they merely grew more vigorous with the taste for blood fresh on their lips. Shouting, chanting and the sound of drums began to echo up to where we were now circling above the first of their boats, looking for a weak spot, a point of attack. The task looked impossible, how could we stop such an imposing force? Just the four of us? If we stopped ten of their men the other thirty on the boat would continue onwards unperturbed.

At that moment Althalos appeared buzzing around between us. It appeared he had grabbed a ride on the back Hadrian's kite, knowing the distance of the journey here was beyond his ability. For the first time as I hovered over the Viking ships far below, I took in the sight of Althalos's wasp. It was clearly no ordinary wasp. It was the size of a small bird and there were no yellow stripes around his body. The wasp of Althalos looked like an everyday wasp's big brother. It was vicious looking, even for a wasp, with sharp, angular features that gave him an armoured appearance. His body was entirely black with a huge sting protruding from his rear end, exceptionally large by contrast to his body. I also noticed an added extra that looked to be a small ceramic container with a sort of shallow cork in its end that hung from the wasps mid section, no doubt something that Monk had conjured up. Monk was known for dabbling in medicines, remedies and poisons and as such the thought of what might be in that little ceramic jar sent chills down my spine.

The Wasp turned mid air and our eyes met, whilst I was unsure on his plan, his look told me all I needed to know. It was time. And with that he promptly drove that long needle like stinger of his into the cork before swiftly retracting it again. I saw a tiny drip fall from the end of his stinger moments before he took off towards one of the ships below. A second later I darted after him; he was surprisingly quick over short distances and had made it to the boat before I was even halfway. As I descended I watched on as one by one each Viking down the port side of the ship jumped from their seat, every one feeling a slight sting to the neck. There was a moment of confusion as they each turned to the one behind them questioningly before the strangest thing happened. Suddenly and completely unbeknownst to the rowing Vikings on the starboard side, each of the men on the port side collapsed inexplicably over their oars, dead.

Whatever was in that jar of Monks was lethal. The Vikings on the starboard side, focussed on the job at hand, gave another huge push driving the boat on. Without a following surge from the opposing side and the boat no longer balanced, the prevailing stroke powered the craft forward simultaneously plunging the port bow down to meet the water. The men on board fell from their seats, one or two being flung overboard, splashing into the water before the boat swung back upright. The longboat flailed wildly momentarily righting itself before swinging back the opposing way. The boat was out of control, flinging the crew side to side before crashing spectacularly into a second boat that had the misfortune of being beside them, cracking its hull.

Pandemonium ensued. The other vessels behind these two longboats found themselves having to take drastic action to avoid further collision whilst trying in vain to determine where the attack had come from. A couple of the boats, unable to turn in time, smashed into the aft of the wrecks before them, throwing the Vikings into disarray. I myself was so surprised that I almost hit the deck of the swinging boat and had to pull out of my dive to avoid being knocked from the air. The little wasp had made a big impact. Abruptly shouting began from a nearby ship diverting my attention as I knew that I had been spotted. I turned away from the craft I had almost hit to see a Viking preparing to hurl a long spear with a viciously sharpened iron head directly at me. Before he could throw however the huge hawk of Rowan had swooped down gracefully with lethal speed, tearing the man from the deck. The Viking flew clear off his feet before finding himself hurtling towards the neighbouring boat. He hit the adjacent crafts hull with a sickening crack.

I took back to the skies to regain my bearings before hurtling towards another boat below me. I flew straight through the deck into the store below, circling the inside of the craft, setting it aflame in the process; the supplies of food, bedding and cloth igniting easily. I shot from one boat to another, darting in and out, setting ablaze their mast, sail, stock and the Vikings themselves; anything that would burn. After approximately ten minutes I rose once again into the tranquillity of the sky far above the fleet and watched John and Hadrian as they soared over the armada dropping huge bits of debris, or at times the odd Viking, that they had torn from a damaged ship. At first I had thought their attacks to be random but after a minute I noticed a pattern emerge and saw their true intent. It seemed the debris was in fact hitting its intended target every time. By dropping the heavy bits of ship from a good height, straight through the centre of the ship the impact was enough to crack the hull. The sea would then do the rest of the work as the pressure of the water forced the crack to open further and a spring of water would shoot from it. After a minute the spring would grow with intensity, filling the boat with water before inevitably sinking.

My attention was suddenly drawn by another loud boom that echoed up to where I was and as I turned to the source of the noise I saw the ship at the very front of the armada begin to sink, nose first. A second later a large grey shape shot out of the water, transforming to human form before landing on the deck of the lead boat as it sank. As Walter stood facing the now enraged Vikings the air filled with the deep thundering sound of laughter. I flew down to where Walter had begun to throw the Vikings aside as the boat tipped upwards, sending each man toppling towards where he now stood. The boat sank before I got there, taking the Vikings and Walter with it. I wondered briefly if Walter had gotten off in time but a moment later another huge crash echoed up into the air as the walrus punched a second hole into another boat, unseen deep beneath the water.

I veered to the left, heading towards another boat opting to soar straight through the seated Vikings as they rowed. I flew as close as I could to each man setting fire to them as I passed. I caught the first couple off guard but now the others were aware of my presence. As I passed each man he lunged for me, these Vikings clearly held no fear of the flames that covered my body and I had barely got passed the last man as he swung a huge oar at me, missing by barely the thickness of the timber. I shot through the horde of ships, looking for a point to attack, we had sunk roughly ten of their ships but already the mainland of England loomed. It dawned on me that we would not be able to stop as many as we had hoped and we had now lost the element of surprise. As my body skimmed the water swerving between the vast amount of vessels my mind raced, there had to be a way to increase the efficiency of our attack… but the train of thought became lost as the sight before me took the wind from under my wings. There, towards the back of this vast convoy of ships, three longboats were roped together with a temporary platform straddling them. Stood upon this large stage, amongst a series of cages and crates was a man I hadn't seen for two years. Not since the day he had killed my wife, my son and me.

Tilsted.

50
2010
Family History

I entered the Abbots main chambers, a series of rooms all segregated to allow the Abbot to go about his work undisturbed. This part of the Abbey was usually off limits but the guard had let me pass after conferring with the Abbot directly. I entered the Abbots personal library walking between rows upon rows of books that lined both walls, leading to a large desk at the centre of the room. Eadric and the Abbot were stood at the desk pouring over a pile of old scrolls that had been strewn across the desk.

"Hello James." The Abbot called to me as I approached the desk.
"Hello sir."
"What may I do for you this fine afternoon?" He continued so merrily that I wondered if Eadric had even told him of my actions, but I knew that everyone would know by now and the Abbot had eyes and ears everywhere.
"I came to say good bye." I said trying to keep any emotion from my voice. Eadric turned to me as I spoke, a brief look of surprise crossed his face but he quickly composed himself.
"Well that is a shame." The Abbot continued, "And you were progressing so well." I couldn't tell if he meant this or if it was sarcastic given recent events, so I didn't reply. It was Eadric who spoke next.
"I do not think that is wise James, you still have a lot to learn."
"I will not cause you any trouble, I plan to go somewhere remote, you will not hear from me again I assure you."
"That is not necessary, control can be learnt. It will take time."
"No. I will not risk hurting anymore people."
"You are not the only one that has suffered with their curse; we all have our crosses to bear. You must stand strong in the face of yours."

"I do not see others around here eating people." I replied, emotion waning heavily in my tone. With this Eadric turned back to the desk and shuffled a few scrolls out of his way, pulling a very old scroll towards him and unrolling it across the desk.

"You still have a lot to see, maybe by knowing of your past you may be better equipped to face the future. This James is your family tree."

Curiosity got the better of me and I approached the desk, looking over Eadric's arm at the italic script on the page in front of him. Sure enough hundreds of names branched out from the left of the scroll, working across the page. Various notes were scribbled above or below many of the names; words such as 'unaffected' and in some cases an animal would be mentioned.

"This is *my* family tree?" I asked him taken aback by this ancient document.

"Yes. I have followed your family for many years, documenting each generation at birth and following each of their progress over the years that passed."

"Why my family?"

"Not just yours, all of the families that descended from the men of the curse. I have meticulously documented each birth and death, a record must be kept."

"But how? There are hundreds of people here alone." I took in the rest of the scrolls that spread across the table, there had to be at least forty of them.

"Over the years the Abbots have been generous enough to help me on my quest. The church too knows the importance of keeping our kind hidden from the world."

"But why? Why not just let them know of our existence?"

"Simple. If we did we would not be allowed to live, or those of us that were would be caged and would never see the light of day again. We once roamed freely across the world but as the human species became stronger with more powerful weaponry and more advanced surveillance systems, we were forced to hide our true nature; but you know this. Tales occasionally escape of our kind but they are quickly dismissed. People believe that there are no mysteries left in the world which makes them quick to find the ordinary in anything extraordinary."

"Who's this?" I asked, pointing to the first name on the list. The word 'Hydra' was written under it. "And what's a Hydra?"

"That's Tilsted. He was a huge Viking from the eleventh century that was cursed along with myself. Tilsted's inner nature was conflicted; he suffered a multi personality disorder with no comprehension of right and wrong. As such he was a monster before thc curse was ever set. His beast also reflected this; it was bigger than anything I had ever seen."

I didn't know what to say to this. The sudden knowledge that I had descended from some ancient Viking psychopath was a lot to process and he too was a monster like me. In fact he was the first.

"So what is a Hydra?" I asked again.

"A breed of dragon, a huge elemental dragon, but unlike you he had four heads and a vast body. Each head represented a specific element. If our beast represents our true nature then Tilsted was an enigma, dragons normally contain the characteristic of only one element, but Tilsted carried all four. He had some issues." Eadric said grinning.

"Elemental dragons? Characteristics? What does that all mean?"

"Dragons are very strange beasts that live closely within their natural environment. They generally fall into one of four categories, Earth, Wind, Fire and Water and take on the characteristics of that element. The early dragons would all reflect one of the four. Earth dragons had tough, rock like hides than were completely impenetrable from attack. Water dragons could breathe underwater and inhale huge volumes of water that they would then expel from their chests, washing away their enemies." Eadric paused momentarily as if reliving an old memory before continuing.

"As you can see most of your family in later generation did not change, the curse that runs in your veins is… temperamental. Your recent ancestors rarely transformed and when they did it rarely had the ferocity that it used to. The curse is strong in your veins though."

"What sort of dragon am I?"

"Only you can answer that, it will show itself when your beast fully develops, which is why you must stay. We can help you when that time comes."

"Fully develop? I thought I had!"

"No, you must notice that every time you change you beast is a little bigger. It can take anything between a few weeks to six month to fully develop ones beast, the more you exercise him the quicker the transition will be."

This was all news to me; it was easy to forget that this whole thing was bigger than me, that the curse had been around for centuries. Seeing history stretched out in front of me like this took me by surprise but I had made up my mind, I would leave, now and I would deal with my beast on my own.

"Thank you Eadric for all you have done, but I must leave." And with that I turned to walk from the large library. I felt my beast stir smugly as I walked away, the elemental dragon information was news to him too and it caught his interest.

"I'm sorry too." Eadric called after me as I walked away. "Sorry I didn't act sooner. I should have warned you of your curse before, before you killed that girl."

51
1013
Final Battle

I had shot down to where Tilsted stood. I had hoped to get a jump on him before he had seen me, to strike while I'd had the opportunity. But Tilsted was quicker than I had anticipated. A split second before I could strike he had turned, shield in hand and deflected my assault, slamming me to the deck of the large boat. The flames of my phoenix had extinguished as my body returned to my human form before I'd stood to face the man that had haunted my dreams for so long. I held this man responsible for all the pain and suffering I had felt and I would not stop hunting him until I saw the life leave his body. I'd pushed up from the deck on which I had landed and turned to face him.

"So here we are again Tilsted, I have dreamed of this day for some time." I had said standing tall in the presence of my enemy. I remember watching as he turned to me, stared intently into my face, looking for a spark of recognition. Whilst I had thought of nothing but him for two years he had barely given me a second thought, he had not even recognized my face. Tilsted and his men killed my family, killed me and to them it had all been in a days work. I was just one face in a thousand to him and the thought of this caused bile to rise from the pit of my stomach and made me hate him even more. A fact that I hadn't even thought was possible before that moment. As he took in my face I saw a flicker realisation dawn in his eyes before he finally spoke in very broken English.

"Uh. I kill you already?" He'd asked before laughing deeply, his laugh carried an evil undertone that spoke directly to my hatred for him.

"Clearly, you failed." I replied, preparing to fight. He was considerably bigger than me but I held no fear, I welcomed death if at last it finally came.

"Then I try again." He'd said grinning. Tilsted held a huge hammer in one hand and a solid wooden shield, now scorched from where he'd hit me with it, in the other. I'd run at him in my human form, no longer able to stand so close and not attack the man that had killed my point of being. The only thing on this earth that had made my life worth living was gone because of this monster.

I remember the satisfaction I felt as I had hit him as hard as my human form was able. I caught him across the jaw, forcing Tilsted to step back but he had taken the blow well, better than I had hoped. I turned once again sending a blow into his stomach with my other hand, nearly breaking it in the process. I knew I had to stay close, keep tucked in and out of reach of the huge hammer he wielded, knowing that it would crush my skull in a single blow. I did not fear death for I would inevitably only return, but I did not want this man to have the pleasure of killing me for a second time. So I hit him again. A strike to the ribs, a knee in his side, blow after blow connected but it did little to slow him and after a moment I felt my ribs shake as he dropped the wooden shield before driving his fist heavily into my side. A burst of pain erupted within my face as an elbow followed, hitting so hard my vision blurred momentarily. Knocked of balance I stumbled then my breath caught in my throat as his hand closed tightly around my neck. I'd struggled, grasping at his arm as he held me out in front of him and then, before I knew it, the hammer in his other hand had come around in a slow but unstoppable arc. The vast weight of the stone sledge hammer caught me in the side at the same time that he let my body drop from his hand. As the hammer connected I'd heard my ribs crack before my body had been thrown across the deck, slamming against the large cages at the edge of the makeshift raft. My body slumped to the ground and a searing pain flooded through me. I lay there for a second watching as Tilsted crossed the distance between us when suddenly I'd felt something warm and damp breeze across my neck.

I turned where I lay, fighting the desire to keep my eyes fixed on Tilsted as he stalked towards me. As my head turned my eyes took in the cage behind me and its contents. The sight turned my blood cold.

Who would do such a thing? I had turned to face Tilsted once again and watched his grin widen as he approached.

"You think were only one?" He said, a noise emanated from his throat that was half laugh and half growl.

"You're a monster!" I had yelled struggling to form a coherent sentence as my teeth gritted in pain. The shock had hit me like a train, my mind reeling at what I'd seen and I knew I had to get out of there.

"Yes. I am monster." He replied.

And then, when I thought further shock impossible, he stopped where he stood, threw his head back and I watched in horror as his body began to grow.

I had scrabbled to my feet in that moment, teeth gritted as pain shot from my ribs and I fought the urge to pass out. I took one last look at the sight in the cage behind me before turning to see the row of equally sized cages that lined the boat around me. A split second later I leapt into the air, burst into flames and was gone. I'd had to warn the others, they had no idea what they were up against.

The Vikings entered the mouth of the Thames, clearly planning to follow the river into London as we had anticipated; as they had done before. I had known the others would be waiting for them but the game had changed. The memory now seemed hazy; adrenaline had coursed through my veins giving the recollection of that moment a dream like quality. I remember the fear that struck me all too well though as I had flown up into the air away from Tilsted, his monsters and whatever his beast was. I'd seen Rowan and the others also still in combat and as I passed each one flew up to meet me, following me back inland. It wasn't long until I could see our army gathering on the low lying land at the point where the river narrowed, giving us a strategical advantage. I landed quickly where I could see Brom and Trojan discussing tactics, changing in the process. The others following suit soon after.

"What brings you back so quickly?" Trojan asked. "Are they upon us already?"

"Yes they are moving rapidly, but that is not why I returned." I said as the others landed gathering around us. "I bring grave news, I found Tilsted, their chieftain. I tried to kill him, but he changed, he too is cursed and has control. I could not let you go into battle without knowing of this."

"Surely though he is only one beast?" Brom asked. "I will take him out myself."

"While it is true he is only one beast, he is unlike any beast I have ever seen. I did not get a good look at him but I can however tell you that he is bigger than any of us, bigger even than Monk." This took them by surprise. "And he is also not alone." I finished.

"What do you mean by not alone?" Trojan asked. I could sense his impatience as he willed me to get to the point.

"His boat is full of cages, at least fifteen of them."

"And what is in these cages?"

"I'm not entirely sure. They may once have been men of the curse, but they are no longer man or beast. These were hellish creatures, repugnant atrocities, minions of the devil himself. They seemed to be in mid change, part animal and part man. Some of them were still changing, flicking one to the other uncontrollably. Others appeared stuck halfway. I saw one half wolf; a wolfs muzzle protruded from half a human head, one clawed hand and his back arched over so he stood on all fours with a mouth full of huge teeth."

"What could cause such a thing?" Brom asked.

"I think they were men of the curse, Vikings, infected like us; but now they are demons born from the hell Tilsted has created for them. Maybe Tilsted was experimenting, pushing them to their limits, seeing what triggers the change. I imagine he tortured them, forcing them to change until they went mad and their minds merged. Unable to distinguish the man from the beast their bodies followed suit, a physical representation of their minds. The ones I saw showed no human traits, caged up like monsters. It was all I could do not to vomit there and then." I had finished.

"So what do we do from here?" Rowan asked.

"We fight still." Trojan said. "Even more reason to stop this mad man."

I considered this for a moment before answering. "Yes we fight, but I will take Tilsted alone and I want each and every caged demon dead. These monstrosities can't be saved; end their misery for them." I paused to let this sink in before continuing. "If this goes wrong, don't get taken alive, I could not bear to think of any more of our brothers facing that fate." They all looked solemn for a moment before retaking their positions.

A minute later the first boat came into view.

52
2010
Knowledge

"You knew?" I asked, turning to face them again. "And you could have warned me?"

"I knew you were cursed but your family hadn't changed for many generations. I believed that the curse had run its course within your bloodline." Eadric replied calmly as if it was of little importance.

"But it hadn't!" My voice was beginning to rise as I spoke, the dragon stirring inside.

"I didn't expect you to change; you could have lived your life without ever knowing of the curse, carried on oblivious to this whole world."

"But I did change and now Rebecca is dead, you could have prevented it! You could have helped me! Told me before! You could have stopped me!" I saw it all now; I don't know how I had missed it before. Eadric had known of Rebecca, he knew of the curse, of my family, of course he could have prevented this from happening. Images of Rebecca flooded my mind once again; I had not had an onslaught for a week or so and had almost forgotten the pain that the images brought with them. Now the pain was tenfold, unbearable. It was as if the break had given my mind time to heal and now the wound was being torn open, the images once again pounding the inside of my eyelids. He could have prevented it? The dragon roared and my mind span. A nauseous, dizzy sensation hit me as I felt myself sway where I stood. The beast took this opportunity to strike out, to take control and I felt the all too familiar feeling as the beast tore from my mind and out through my body, my arms and back twisting and tearing as he fought to take form. My mind didn't fight back; I was too lost with the consequence of Eadric's words. What if he had helped me? In that moment I hated him and blamed him, it was his fault; everything came down to that first night, my eighteenth birthday. That day my life had changed forever, the day my normal life had ended; the day normal me died.

I wanted to kill him.

My dragon felt the same.

The Abbot dived for cover just in time to avoid the huge teeth of the dragon as he darted from where I had just stood. Eadric looked up at me and instantly burst into flames, rising from where he himself had stood just moments before my dragons jaws tore through the desk. Scrolls and paper scattered everywhere, the Abbot quickly trying to extinguish the ends of those scrolls that had been nearest Eadrics flames. The Phoenix circled the library above me, the dragon following his movement with a practiced eye just waiting for the moment to strike. The library was big, but my dragon had grown immensely and I could feel the edges of the book shelves pressing against the tips of my wings.

The beast leapt suddenly; a single, powerful beat of my wings surged the beast forward, snapping at the phoenix as it circled passed. I felt the intense heat as it warmed my dragons hide after narrowly missing. I awaited the burn to intensify, but it never came. The dragon seemed to know this as if he now knew something I didn't, something instinctual, like the knowledge that our skin was fire resistant. The dragon turned mid flight to give chase to the phoenix, taking out the nearest bookshelf in the process. Books rained down around me as I felt the dragon panning the room, searching for Eadric once again. The phoenix shot from nowhere, suddenly hitting my beast square in the chest, pushing the dragon back into the book case and setting fire to several volumes in the process. The dragon roared. I was not harmed, the dragon was considerably bigger than Eadric's phoenix and a lot stronger but he had taken me by surprise and now the dragon was enraged. He was not used to being challenged.

My mind was full of anguish, so much so that I had no control of the beast as he charged around the Abbots library, smashing everything in sight. The guards had heard the commotion and came running. The first two stood dumb struck, just starring at the huge dragon tearing through the vast library but the next few that followed were better prepared. The more experienced guards were no strangers to large beasts breaking loose around the Abbey and after a moment a couple of them entered with bulky weapons that looked to me like some variation on a bazooka.

They took aim and fired.

Two huge bundles of rope shot from the cannons, extending outward as they propelled towards me and before I knew it two large nets were looming down upon me. I felt the dragon's confusion but it was only fleeting before a decision was reached. The beast drew in a deep breath filling his lungs with air before a split second later, just as the nets closed in, the dragon let out an almighty roar. Air flooding up through my body from my lungs, I heard the deep, guttural roar as it resounded through my vast throat and out through my monstrous jaw and passed my razor sharp teeth. Only this time it wasn't just air that shot out before me as the roar was quickly stifled by a huge ball of flame that erupted from my throat. I could feel the intense heat as it extended out before me, incinerating the nets as they closed in around me. The ball of fire was projected forward with terrifying speed, swiftly engulfed the guards before me.

Screams rang out around the library as people fled, many now doused in flames. The Abbot had vanished but Eadric, now back in human form, was stood watching me from the other side of the library. Our eyes locked for a moment, the rage and hatred in my blood had clouded my mind but a fraction of my human conscious still registered the look in his eyes and for a brief moment it threw me. I'd expected anger, hatred or the steely determination of a man ready to fight to the death. But what I saw was worse; sympathy, sorrow, remorse.

The dragon launched a huge burst of flame towards Eadric, but he didn't move, didn't flinch; he just let the flames engulf him. The dragon's anger flared at this display of contempt for the beast's fire whilst all I could do was watch on as Eadrics skin burned, his body turning black and falling away under the intense heat. He didn't recoil or scream out, not once. The dragon beat our wings, raising us from the floor before launching upwards, crashing through the vaulted ceiling above as roof beams and tiles rained to the floor around me. I looked back to see Eadric's phoenix rising from the ashes behind me but he didn't give chase, he rose into the sky instead and just watched as I flew away.

53
1013
They're Here

The boats had begun to fill the Thames as they'd filtered their way down the winding river. Rowan and John had taken Monk and Barda and crossed the river, awaiting our signal on the far side of the Thames. Our army filed along the riverbank obscured by the surrounding tree line, awaiting the moment to attack. The silence was palpable; the only sound a light rustle in the trees as the wind blew up from the river. Very soon the silence would be broken by the sound of battle but for now the land was at peace, completely unaware of the devastation that was about to ensue.

A minute later the distant sound of drums reached our ears followed closely by the Viking war cries that announced their arrival, confident enough in their victory that they gave little regard to maintaining an inconspicuous approach. We watched on silently as the longboats drew nearer, they would be expecting us now after our earlier onslaught so the timing had to be right. They travelled onwards as we waited silently, patiently, each minute felt like an hour as they closed the distance that separated us. We crouched, ready to attack, listening only to the rhythmic thumping of our hearts pounding in our chests. As they approached their boats were gradually forced to pack closer and closer together as the river narrowed, winding its way onwards towards London.

"Ready?" I asked Lief, stood at my side in his human form.
"As I will ever be." He'd replied.
"Then on my word."

Time slowed in that blissful yet eerie moment of calm that had settled upon us. My heart and mind had been buzzing as the gravity of the situation dawned and the adrenaline coursed through my blood. After what had felt like an eternity the front line of boats finally levelled with the spot at which our men had taken cover within the tree line. They were so close that I could see the determined look in the eyes of the Viking warriors as they anticipated the next assault, hungry for more bloodshed. I lingered for another minute, awaiting the front line of boats to reach the optimum location to best execute our plan.

"It's time." I'd said, turning to Lief before starting out at a run towards the Viking longboats. I ran as quick as my human legs would allow, striding rapidly across the distance that separated us from these vicious Viking savages. Shouts had risen up from the Vikings as they'd first caught sight of me and when the time came I burst into flame before taking to the air.

I flew onwards, maintaining my trajectory, heading directly towards the savages. I felt a perverse joy at that point as the waiting was over and the moment had arrived, a joy that was further amplified by the surprised look on their faces. I had waited for this moment for so long, this was my time.

As I ran Lief had followed closely behind me, keeping pace every step of the way. In the instant I had changed, he too had taken the form of his large gorilla, trailing behind him a long length of rope. A split second later our army descended from the tree cover, charging toward the Vikings with every weapon they had been able to muster drawn and ready for combat. The better equipped and better trained men from the Kings guard then launched a ferocious hailstorm of arrows that was quickly followed by a second and then a third onslaught sent directly into the now packed armada. Whilst arrows rained down over their heads the frontline reached the banks of the Thames to meet the first wave of Vikings with swords, hammers, cudgels and hatchets drawn. Prepared to fight or die trying. As I had hoped their rush had distracted the attention of the Vikings from Lief and I as we continued our own charge.

The world around us exploded with the sound of a thousand men as they entered battle. Metal screeched, swords clashed and shields rang out under the strain before the screams of dying men surfaced from the cacophony of sound. Hell had come to the Earth that day.

At the same moment that Lief had charged Barda too had set off, leading from the other side of the river with Rowan flying at his side. A split second before we hit the edge of the river, Lief leapt, hurtling towards the front end of the first longboat, dragging the length of rope with him. Barda mirrored him perfectly on the opposite bank, landing with an almighty thud onto the front of the first boat. Rowan and I shot through the centre of the front line of ships, throwing the Vikings into chaos as we hurtled through the middle of them. Lief and Barda flung themselves from one boat to the next putting their beasts strong arms and powerful forms to full use. They swung their way across the river, each aiming to reach the furthest ship from their start point, having crossed in the middle. Upon reaching the opposite side to which they had begun they proceeded to attach the rope that had trailed behind them to the prow whilst Rowan and I ducked and dived, keeping the Vikings from impeding them as they passed. After seeing Lief tie the end of the rope over the stern of the final boat I soared clear, returning to the river bank, Rowan also doing the same. The second I landed Trojan, with the end of the rope harnessed around his massive chest, began to charge away from the Viking longboats heading back inland. Rowan having landed on the opposite shore had signalled Monk, who in turn took off, the elephant crashing through the tree line as if the trees were mere reeds on a river bed.

The effect was not instant. I had turned back into my human form and could see the confusion on the faces of the Vikings still looking to the skies for us. A split second before the effects took hold I saw a Viking, clearly a little quicker than the others, as he turned to where I now stood. His eyes caught mine then he noticed the rope. I could see his mind whirr as his eyes tracked along its length to where the rope had been secured to the stern of the longboat on the far side of the river. The Viking turned to the others and began to shout, but he was just a moment too late.

The ropes length ran out snapping tight.

The two boats at either side of the river suddenly jerked sideways, the rope tearing them from the water thanks to the colossal strength of both Trojan and Monk. The Vikings were in disarray as the boats were torn from the water and dragged across the neighbouring ships, smashing their way through the tightly packed rows. The effect was inconceivable, devastating, far worse than I could have imagined. The boats now being towed across the width of the river smashed into each of the other boats in its path, shattering the masts, ripping the sterns clean off, obliterating them leaving a trail of destruction. The Vikings had stood no chance; they were either flung from their boats or killed by the impact. Those left flailed desperately as they tried to avoid the debris that rained down around them. The second row of boats still being propelled by their own momentum had nowhere to go and no way of stopping, crashing into the wreckage before them and damming up the entire of the Thames River.

It didn't take the Vikings long however to regained their composure. The longboats came to a halt and further swarms of the colossal savages had begun to leap down from their boats, charging out of the water to fight along side their brothers on the banks of the Thames. The sound of battle heightened as further men joined the brawl and yelled out loudly in both anger and pain. Beasts roared, swords and shields clashed vociferously and fear filled the air as death stalked the bank of the Thames that day. The scene was horrific. The Vikings fought like savages, tearing through our men, slashing and hacking at anything that moved. The English fought well in return however. The King's men having learnt from the previous encounter and trained tirelessly held their ground against the ferocious onslaught, fighting tactically, looking out for each other and working as a team. I circled around looking for my next target when suddenly, from the corner of my eye, I saw Brom being flown through the air in human form by Rowans huge hawk. As Rowan let Brom go his body transformed mid flight and the huge bear landed in the midst of a group of Vikings that had been trying to clamber clear of one of the boats, right in the thick of the action. Brom instantly began tearing at the Vikings, ripping them limb from limb, moving swiftly across the longboat leaving no man standing. He too owed a debt to these men that he fully intended on repaying.

As I took in the scene I swooped once again attacking another Viking before hurtling over the deck of the nearest longboat, burning its contents as I went. I hadn't seen Althalos since the first assault but I knew he was around as every now and then I caught a glimpse of a Viking that would suddenly drop dead inexplicably. I glimpsed Borin as he tore through a group of Vikings slashing at one, then another, fighting them back from the banks of the Thames. Fendrel the terrier was even fighting alongside Borin, always at his side, before suddenly bursting into the Lion that I had once had the misfortune of meeting. The two of them were savage, fighting back the horde whilst always instinctively covering each others movement. They tore swiftly through the Vikings that clambered from the water, slashed to shreds before ever reaching the land. The water had turned red as the bodies piled up against the shore.

Whilst all this was happening Monk had returned and charged into the shallow water at the edge of the Thames. Monk was wearing huge sheets of armour that had been beaten to the shape of his elephant's body, a terrifying sight as he charged one of the large boats that had just docked in the shallow waters. The huge elephant hit the longboat with an almighty crash, the wood it had been built from splitting like twigs as he drove forward. The force of the impact pushed the boat clear out of the water, sending it crashing down onto a second boat, the Vikings falling from the ship as it went.

The savages were now pouring out of their boats quicker than we could hold them back. They swarmed the banks like locus, too many of them to stop. Trojan suddenly charged from nowhere leading the herd of horses we had travelled to London with, running them towards the horde of Vikings that swarmed the banks of the Thames. Ulric, Tybalt and Forthwind had stampeded along behind the horses, each man in his beast form and each dragging a huge tree behind them. The horses scattered the Vikings, sending them running clear of the pack before the buffalo, ox and bull literally ploughed through the Vikings as they fled, crushing them with the huge trees that they dragged behind them.

For every one of them we killed however, two more breached the shore as the remaining Vikings worked their way across the graveyard of ships that now dammed the Thames. I took back to the skies, diving once again through the vast pack of Vikings, burning men as I passed. Barda and Lief were in the thick of it, crushing skulls as they savagely worked their way from one Viking to another, each of them towering over their foe ten times stronger than any one of them. Borin and Fendrel were also fighting heroically and I could see Trojan and the others circling for a second run. As I'd surveyed the scene I noticed that Walter had also reappeared, working his way through the Vikings in human form with an evil smile on his face as his vast human form was proving formidable. It was then as I scanned my surroundings that I finally found what I had been searching for. Tilsteds ship had arrived amongst the longboat graveyard with him stood in human form at its centre, surveying the carnage around him. I knew in that moment what I had to do for I couldn't let him get any closer to shore. His beast would be devastating on land and so I flew out to meet him.

54
2010
Crossing the Line

I flew onwards for some time. The sun was still up and I made no attempt to conceal myself as I soared across the country side. Occasionally I would hear the sound of metal hitting metal echoing up as I passed. I'd glance down from time to time and watch dispassionately as the cars far below hit each other, their drivers attention distracted by the sight of something that they couldn't possibly have seen. The dragon and I rose and fell on the wind, revelling in the freedom of flight. He was happy to be out; I could feel the joy flow through his body and it was hard not to share in the happiness. I let the feeling engulf my mind, masking the fear and despair that my human mind was feeling.

I stopped watching the landscape as it flashed by below me and sank to the back of the beasts head, letting the dragon take complete control. I knew I should stop him, he was revealing our kind to the world, flaunting the secret that Eadric had hidden for a millennia. I told myself that I should regain control, tame the beast, but I couldn't and I knew it. Not only was the dragon stronger than I could ever be, but I knew that deep down a part of me didn't want to stop him. My heart was broken, crushed by this new world in which I lived. My old, simple life was over. I had committed the worst crime of all, I had played God, taken life and the numbers were beginning to stack up. I wanted desperately to forget the things I'd done. I could no longer face the human world with the knowledge of my crimes as they followed me, forever lurking in the shadows. The human world was controlled by rules, laws; people were subjugated, oppressed. They feared society's rules and the consequences to breaking them and this fear was used to control them. The dragon didn't want to hide from the world and didn't care for societies rules, too proud to live in the shadows. I on the other hand craved obscurity like an addict did their fix, I wanted the world to swallow me whole but the dragon wanted to show them our power. Perhaps he was right, he certainly saw things with a simplistic clarity that I craved to share; to be so certain and unflinching in my actions, to know what I wanted and to take it with no regards for the consequences. The world should know the truth, it was what it deserved, what I deserve. Our kind would no longer hide from the world; the truth will set us free.

My eyes focused again, I felt the intense heat bellowing up from my lungs and I watched as an old cottage burned below me whilst I soared away from the scene; the dragon content, happy with his game and the knowledge now that he is a dragon of fire. I too felt joy at the sight of the flames and I wondered whose thoughts they really were. I knew my human form would not revel in such things, but the beast cared nothing for human life or for the destruction of someone else's property. The dragon cared for nothing but his own needs and he would do as he pleased from now on. I knew that the dragon was out now, fully matured and stronger than my human form could ever have dreamed. The dragon grinned inwardly as images of my human body, my old human life, flashed across my mind. He pitied the weak, callow boy that I was. I could feel him grin knowing as well as I did that he was now in charge and that things would be different from now on. We would show them all, show the world our new found strength, no longer a slave to society and their rules. As these thoughts floated into my mind I knew they weren't my own but they carried with them a strength of character that I had never know in my human form. Confident, resolute, they made me feel strong as if the world was mine for the taking and nobody would be able to stop me. I felt my mind surrender to the thoughts, to the feeling of strength that flowed through this magnificent beast, how could I not join him? What else could I do? My human life was over, murder and death smeared my name and I would be locked away and left to rot, never to see the light of day again. But my second life could begin now, a life full of power, I would no longer cower in fear.

No; they will fear me.

I passed over the land quickly, flying eastward across the country. The land below rapidly became more populated as I flew inland and before long chaos was erupting below me as the motorways ground to a halt. People had begun getting out of their cars to watch as I passed, just stood staring, openly gawping. Their jaws literally hanging open as their brains were unable to process what their eyes were telling them. Every now and then I would dive down to burn a building or a car, just to watch the occupants flee. The adrenaline that coursed through my veins was like a drug and I felt my mind swell with the rush of power that came from people running in fear. It felt good to no longer be oppressed, scared and panicking from the repercussions of life. It was just me now and the world below that would fall at my feet.

I threw another ferocious burst of flame at a car and watched as the roof burned bright red and the paint rapidly peeled before the steel roof melted entirely just as the driver fell from the moving car. I could hear screams ringing out as I passed but I cared nothing for them, my human mind would have felt their pain, worried for their well being and tried to help them; but my beasts couldn't have cared less. We just moved on to the next thing that would sate his desire for destruction, for revenge.

Before I knew it London came into view and with it a whole new playground. I flew low over the buildings on the outskirts of London, my destination its centre. The town would be heaving with early evening traffic and my presence I knew would cause a commotion. I swooped through the streets, occasionally clipping the edge of a building with my claws, tearing at the ancient ornamentation that decorated the roofs of London. Debris rained down on the rush hour traffic as I passed; horns blared, angry shouts echoed around me before quickly falling silent as my huge body passed by. The traffic came to a stand still, London grounding to a halt. Pedestrians stood and stared at me as I passed, briefcases fell from hands as people stopped dead, shocked at the sight of me. The usual bustle and hustle disappeared as London fell uncharacteristically silent, no one sure what was going on or what they should be doing about it. Camera flashes exploded around me, but I paid them little attention, the media would have a field day with this. Just as the thought formed itself in my mind a helicopter passed over head, CAPITAL NEWS written across its side. I watched the chopper for a moment before beating my wings, blowing a car aside in the process and rising to meet the helicopter. As my head levelled with the pilot, equal in size to the choppers cockpit, I saw the fear in the crews eyes. I guessed that when the call had come in that a dragon was loose in the city, the news crew where sceptical. They weren't now. My heightened dragon senses were incredibly acute. At first I smelt just the diesel fumes from the choppers engine but as my mind focused I began to separate the different scents. Car fumes, oil, smog from far below initially and as my mind focused further I was able to distinguish individual odours; the smell of sweat and urine confirming the fear that the chopper crews eyes had done little to hide. The pilot frozen in fright and not daring to move a muscle just let the chopper idle before me. The fear that I evoked only further fuelled my resolve, this was what I deserved, power; people should fear me. I rose away from the chopper avoiding the blades above it. Killing them would be counterproductive to my cause, I wanted them to broadcast my image across the world so I reasoned that the least I could do was give them something to see.

I dropped from a couple of hundred feet above London, swooping down across Piccadilly. I grabbed a double-decker bus within my talons as I passed; crushing its roof in the process before hurling it into the huge TV screens that surrounded Piccadilly Circus. Screams rang out as people fled the hypnotic trance that I had first induced. The wonder and surprise that I had invoked within the crowd's minds now snapped as the realisation that a dragon was dealing out death in their city. They ran, fleeing for all their lives were worth.

I tore the statue of Eros from its plinth at the centre of Piccadilly before letting it fall through the roof of a car now abandoned in the road before the air around me exploded as five jets shot by overhead. The air force had arrived. I suspect they won't be able to attack me in London; missiles would cause too much collateral damage and their guns would do nothing. I'd deal with them shortly. The news chopper now hovered some distance away and I could see the camera crew filming me from the side door. I perched on the plinth that Eros had, until now, stood and let a huge jet of flame loose over the road below me, engulfing the surrounding scene. Cars exploded as their fuel tanks ignited, hurling wreckage into the surrounding shop fronts. I let the flames die away and surveyed the carnage that surrounded me. I knew that I should not be enjoying this, lives had been taken, property destroyed, but for the first time in weeks I felt good; brave, powerful, in charge of the situation. I felt like a God among men. Nothing could stop me, I was just too strong.

As I took in the scene my heightened eye sight caught a flash of something pass by, far overhead. This time it was not the air force; it looked like a comet, a tail of flame following behind it.

It seems that my tutor has arrived.

I watched as the comet corrected its course, turning back towards my location before vanishing behind an upturned bus. The creature moved with more elegance than any creature I had ever seen, the perfectly controlled movements finessed over hundreds of years of practice. A moment later and Eadric, having returned to his human form, walked from behind the bus to stand before me. He studied my face carefully, as if trying to find something, a spark of recognition maybe? He was searching for the soul inside of me but he would no longer find it. The cold, dead sensation that now sat where the warmth of my heart once resided, tells me that.

My heart is dead and I will not rest now until Eadric is also.

"You didn't have to do this, we could have helped you." Eadric called up to where I perched. I had nothing to say to this and couldn't have replied even if I'd wanted to. I simply watched him as a hawk would its prey, waiting for its moment.

"You have undone years of work, the humans will know now that there is more to this world than they had thought. They will hunt us now, they will search for further dragons and they will not stop there." Eadric said and for the first time I head an undertone of anger in his voice. "They will question everything that they thought to be myth, they will wonder what else is out there and that will lead them to our door. You have condemned us all to a life of fear; we will be hunted for many years to come." Eadric stood stock still and just stared at me, waiting for some sort of response. I heard his words but cared nothing for what he had said; he hid his true nature as if ashamed of the strength that resided within. I had done him a favour, even if he didn't see it. I took a deep breath and shot a burst of flame at him, I knew, as I had seen already, that it would not kill him, but it felt good to do it anyway. This time Eadric did not wait to die. I watched as the phoenix burst forth and rose into the air before me slowly, with a very deliberate meaning. This I knew was it; I had left him no choice.

He moved fast, the burning form of the phoenix flying straight as an arrow and equally as lethal. I growled; a deep, menacing roar as my anger flared. Now I would kill him. I took to the skies moments before he struck, soaring upwards with a single beat of my wings. Power filled my mind as I felt the strength that surged through my body, I would crush this bird, flames or no flames. Fire burst from my lungs once again as I took my anger out on the nearest building, the dragons temper was swift and violent. My mind, now indistinguishable from the beasts, felt every bit of that anger, funnelling it into the fight. The phoenix circled for another strike. I did not know for certain the effects his flames would have on my body. My dragon skin was scaly and thick and resistant to my own fiery breath, so I assume it would oppose all forms of fire. But I'd been wrong before. I let him close in, luring him towards me before I lashed out with my tail to strike him from the air. He was quick, quicker than I had given him credit for. He ducked under my tail before swooping upwards, grazing by me in the process. I was right; his fire had little effect on my skin. I turned as he passed, snapping at his wing but he was quick and I was unprepared. I would get him next pass. We flew higher over London, chasing then fleeing as each got the upper hand. It became a game of cat and mouse, only we were both the cat. Fire engulfed the city below as I tried in vain to burn an already flaming phoenix. I knew that I had to find an edge, something that would kill someone that won't die; but how do you stop an immortal? I didn't know the answer but I would endeavour to find out.

We flew through the great city of London rapidly moving in and out of buildings, each of us waiting for the moment to strike, both of us searching for a weak spot, a chink in the others armour. We rapidly discovered that we were both of the same ilk, creature of fire both offensively and defensively, both of our attacks ineffectual upon the other. We were more evenly matched than either of us had known; this fight would be won by the head, not by shear force. We circled Big Ben and the houses of parliament before shooting down along the river staying low above the water. Eadric led the way whilst I snapped at his tail trying desperately to close my jaw across his back. He was faster than I had thought always one step ahead of me, just out of reach. Eadric increased his pace and appeared to burn brighter than before, the heat radiating from him so intensely that the world around him shimmered as a mirage did in a desert. I was so entranced by this that I fleetingly lost focus. It was at this moment that Eadric dropped lower still, hitting the water and I felt the steam strike me, engulfing my head as I flew right through it. The steam filled my nostrils and seared my lungs; the burn flooded my internal organs, a deeply painful sensation that grew rapidly inside me working its way through my body as I breathed. My skin and throat may be fire proof but my lungs are not, I roared out in anger but it only further spread the burn. I thought quickly as I lost control and fell from air, hitting the water of the Thames. The water felt good, cooling my lungs as huge gulps of it flooded in, but the ordeal wasn't over yet. My lungs recovered from the steam only to then fill with water, my dragon floundering in the water, unable to swim, wings beating uselessly against the surface incapable of getting any lift.

I was done for.

After all I had been through, it would end like this? This ferocious, proud creature would drown in the Thames like so many other weaker animals must have done before me. This wasn't how it was supposed to go surely.

After a moment I managed to right the beast, turning in the water and spreading my wings flat for ballast. With my composure regained I breathed in deep, head once again above water and filled my lungs with air. Once ready I lifted my great wings from the water and beat down twice in rapid succession, once to clear the water and a second time to launch myself into the sky. Clear. I beat again to make sure and a second later I once again soared into the sky, free from the grip of the Thames. I recovered Just in time to feel the phoenix slam into my back, trying to force me back down into the water, but I had my strength back now and it greatly outweighed his. I turned to face the bird but he had vanished, retaining the element of surprise. This wasn't working, he was quicker and more agile than me but I just needed to hold out a little longer, the tables would soon turn in my favour. I looked across to the setting sun disappearing now over the horizon. Soon the land would fall into darkness and the phoenix will light up the sky as if it were New Years Eve. My beast's eye sight was second to none and I knew the darkness would bring me the advantage, for now I just had to hold out.

We had exchanged blows for what felt like forever. The sun worked its way slowly across the sky as the evening withdrew and night descended at last. Eadric and I had chased each other through the city of London each trying in vain to kill the other. The city of London was looking worse for ware as a result and the British army had arrived and set up borders around its outskirts, evacuating the centre. I had hardly noticed the arrival of the army, too preoccupied with Eadric's relentless onslaught. My body tired as the evening drew in; Eadric had caught me more times than I cared to remember as the pain in my body reminded me constantly but from what I could tell no serious damage had occurred. The night fell not a moment too soon and as the darkness engulfed us Eadric lost the element of surprise, the flames of his beast clearly visible in the dark. My night vision was excellent and I found myself able to lose Eadric now; a quick burst of flame would momentarily impair his vision just long enough for me to lose him. I lurked in the shadow of a large tower block; it was easy to vanish in the night time gloom of London's vast metropolis. The air force had returned and now that central London had been evacuated their attacks began increasing in ferocity with every pass. I would have enjoyed toying with the feeble jets if it were not for Eadric's constant attacks; he was relentless, trying to wear me down. I had underestimated Eadric assuming his bird to be elegant but weak. He had been doing this for sometime though and I could only imagine the beasts he had faced over his long history.

A jet burst through the dark night sky launching a missile at the point where I slunk in the shadows. A trail of smoke billowed out behind it as the missile closed in on my location. A short burst of flame ignited it mid air and only the shockwave from the explosion hit me with little effect. I took to the skies in anger and tore the wings from the jet as it passed, its cockpit now free falling before impacting one of the many generic high rise blocks and bursting into flames. As I watched the jet burn a second burst of flame caught the corner of my eye as Eadric shot passed some distance away, tailed by three fighters. I would use this disruption to my advantage, the air force creating the distraction that I'd craved. I ducked away, circling around London keeping to the shadows. London was unusually dark with the absence of people. No lights lit up the windows in a city that rarely slept, no advertising boards flashing away or headlamps on the roads. The street lamps had come on as they would always have done but their eerie orange glow that bathed the city only accentuated the gloom, adding depth to the shadows. Clouds had formed in the night sky, obscuring the stars behind a blanket across the heavens. I watched Eadric elegantly carve his way across the sky above me, searching whilst clearly trying not to take any unnecessary human life. He cared too much for those that would hunt him and that would see him dead. It would prove to be his down fall. I could only imagine the confusion that would be moving through the humans minds now, dragons and flaming birds would be fairly difficult to explain away. I rose into the air, aiming for the cloud cover above. Four more jets found me in the process but they were easily dealt with as my body was engulfed in clouds. I stopped suddenly, lurking and waited for them to pass before lashing out with my huge talons at the first two planes. They never saw what hit them, their wings violently torn off, broken. The third clipped the side of the now stalled second plane, spiralling out of control before the forth was engulfed in a ball of flame that extended from my lungs; the heat incinerating the jet and its pilot.

After quickly disposing of the jets I turned my attention back to the real target, Eadric. I circled around to intercept his path, keeping to the cover of the clouds. I watched as he too used the clouds to lose one jet after another but he was bombarded with jets now, his flames giving his location away easily. Soon he will have to land and take human form again but that would then risk further exposure, giving away his human form too. The humans had only seen our beasts so far; they did not yet know that we were humans too or of the curse that ails us.

I circled turning into Eadrics flight path, carefully closing in on his location, watching as an eagle would its prey. As the seconds ticked by I closed the gap, he'd not seen me yet, I knew it. This was too easy.

I could hear bullets sizzling through the air as the jets tracked Eadric's path, tracer bullets missing him by millimetres. I had seen Eadric die in human form many times and he would always turn to flame but I had no idea what happened if he died in this form. I hoped that I was about to find out. I tracked him closely now, flying above the cloud cover, completely oblivious to him or the jets that followed. I dived suddenly from my position, opening my huge jaws, ready to bite. Eadric dropped lower still, dodging the bullets but this made little difference. Closer and closer I flew, I could feel the heat of the phoenix as he came within reach…

I felt my jaws close over his back, folding his wings in with them. I felt the warmth in my mouth, my throat was fire proof but my lungs were not. I could feel the heat searing them as I inhaled, but I cared not. I had caught my prey. I clenched my jaw down and felt the bones in Eadric's wings break between my teeth. I heard the bird squawk and felt the thrill of the chase and the joy of the prize. I could taste him in my mouth as his warm blood ran down my throat.

I roared in pain as something exploded into my back, crashing sharply into the point between my wings. I craned my neck to see one of the jets that had been tailing Eadric had flown straight into my back. The jet felt like a freight train had run into my spine and I roared in pain and anger. Eadric fell from my grasp, the body of his phoenix now barely aflame as he fell like a stone and vanished from sight into the concrete jungle below. I don't know if he's dead yet but the pain in my back was my priority now. I turned awkwardly in the air as more jets opened fire; tracer bullets ricocheted from my hardened skin before suddenly explosions filled the air around me. The army had moved in launching anti aircraft missiles and as I turned to regain the advantage, a missile caught me off guard, knocking the air from my lungs as I caught the brunt of the explosion. I let out a burst of flame but it was weak, I was weak, the shell in my chest hindering my beast. I roared again in anger as further tanks became visible below, the army continuing to file in. More shells exploded around me and I could see further smoke trails winding their way up. The fight was over, I was out numbered. I had lost Eadric and the army's assault was becoming troublesome. The memory of the taste of Eadric's blood filled my mind and I grinned inwardly, I had done enough for now. The world around me filled with noise as the entirety of the army and the air force concentrated their weaponry upon me. I mustered every bit of strength in my body and pushed myself upwards, into the clouds once again and flew with all my might southwards, away from the capital.

The air force gave chase. I flew as fast as I was able in my wounded condition, smashing any plane that dared get too close with my powerful tail and sending them hurtling towards the ground. Within minutes I was out over open water, before crossing the channel to France and beyond. Once out of British airspace the jets turned tail, unable to follow without provoking their neighbours. I flew onwards with no destination in mind, I needed shelter, a place to rest and recoup. I would return soon to ensure that Eadric's legacy is lost. I will reveal them all, we will take our rightful place within this world, I would see to it.

The dragon flew onwards crossing Europe to an unknown destination. It would not be the last the world would see of me.

55
1013
Tilsted

I shot straight at Tilsted, grazing his face in the process. He had seen me coming and to my surprise it only widened his grin further as he had stepped aside a fraction of a second before I'd hit him. I turned for another strike but as I did I saw him approach the cages and release the demons that resided within. The savage monsters had leapt from their cages and for a moment I thought they would kill Tilsted for me. But animals, as I knew myself, could sense a stronger hunter and knew when they had met their match. One look at Tilsted was all it took for the savage, ferocious, caged demons to turn and flee, relieved to be clear of the cage and keen to distance themselves from the evil of their captor. As I approached the platform on which Tilsted stood I saw the monsters run, leaping across the longboats, heading for the armies that clashed on the shores. The smell of death and blood had no doubt wet their appetite as their new found freedom exhilarated their minds. These creatures would be devastating but I'd had no time to warn the others. The abominations were flying, some of them literally, across the distance now and I would not make it there before them. I would have to hope that the others would see their approach.

I flew with all my might towards Tilsted, my anger charging my body and forcing my flames to burn hotter than ever before, turning white as I flew. The huge Viking stood ready, anticipating my advance. Still clutching the hammer and shield he swung the latter out to connect with my side a split second before I could hit him, deflecting me away again, the shield bursting into flame as he did. I turned once again as he tossed what remained of the shield aside before hurling the colossal sledge hammer at me. I ducked as the vast stone weight flew by then charged at him once again; this time he had nothing to deflect me with. As I closed in on him, his body began to shake, his form beginning to grow. I had not hung around to see his beast clearly upon the last encounter but there was no avoiding it this time. His form increased at an alarming rate, his skin growing scales as his body blew out into a huge chest. His hands and feet became claws as his back arched forward momentarily throwing him to the ground. I watched on unsure now and slowing my approach as two huge wings burst from his back. As they unfurled the tips of his wings cleared each side of the platform on which he'd stood, his sudden weight increase illustrated as the boat sank further into the water. Suddenly my blood ran cold as I saw his face, contorted in agony, shaking violently before his head began to tear itself apart. Something had to have gone wrong, he couldn't possible survive this but no sooner had the thought entered my mind it had been pushed aside as I watched his features twist in agony. Tilsted face ripped into four distinct sections splitting down the centre and across the middle, his nose being pulled four ways until the skin gave way with a horrific tearing sound. Next each of the four sections elongated forming four long necks each with its own distinct head. Each of the heads morphed, a muzzle forming from the front complete with a set of vicious, needle sharp teeth and a pair of horrifying yellow eyes that held nothing but death in their depths.

I knew he was a dragon of some sort. I had heard tales of such creatures as a child but no one that I knew had ever seen one and I had never heard of any beast with more than one head. Later I would come to know this four headed dragon as a hydra but at the time I had not heard of such a creature.

I pulled up quickly but I was too late as the first head swung at me, his teeth barely missing my wing. I ducked to the right, avoiding the second head before flying straight at the creature's chest. A second later I pulled up, circling one of the creature's long necks before shooting up into the sky, a huge dragons head biting at my tail as I went. How do you kill a dragon? I'd wondered to myself as I flew clear of his reach but my question was cut short as a sinking sensation hit my gut. I had turned to observe my enemy, to take stock of the situation but as I'd watched the huge beast below me beat its wings and with one almighty thump it had taken to the skies, heading straight for me.

I flew faster than I had ever done before. The knowledge that I couldn't die had done nothing to ebb the flow of fear that flooded my veins at the sight of the huge dragon that tore after me. I was fast, but I couldn't keep him from my tail. It seemed that everywhere I turned a set of huge teeth awaited me. Suddenly a burst of flame shot by and I looked back to see that it was being emitted from one of the dragons four heads! A moment later a blast of ice water narrowly missed my right side as a second of the heads joined in. This was not something I had expected or known was possible but then this was the first dragon I had ever seen. I glanced at each head as it snapped at me, trying to take a bite and I began to see differences in each of them. The one that shot ice had a bluish tint to its scales and another appeared to be covered in rock. One of the four heads looked enraged with a dark burnt tinge to its outer skin then the fourth was the oddest of them all because it looked as if it was made purely of smoke. Light shone through its form giving the appearance that it was going to blow away at any moment. Many years later I had discovered that dragons were elemental creatures but at the time my only thoughts were of avoiding whatever these heads threw at me.

I ducked left as he barely missed me, before swooping to the right only to encounter another of his heads. I tried in vain to escape his clutches but regardless of what I tried he appeared to gain on me with every second. I couldn't outrun him that much was rapidly dawning on me; I needed a plan and quick. I soared upwards before turning swiftly back upon myself hoping to out manoeuvre his huge bulk, but I only ever gained a second that was then instantly lost with a single beat of his huge wings. I looked around desperately; I needed something, anything…

And there it was. The main battle was still raging savagely but the King's men appeared to be gaining an advantage pushing the Vikings back towards the river. The men of the curse had left the main battle gathering in an adjacent clearing and Brom was signalling me to approach. At this point I'd had no idea what, if anything, they had planned but it was the only option available and so I took it. Suddenly a burst of flame engulfed me, it had no affect on my already flaming body but it still came as a shock. I circled in a long arc, ensuring that I didn't close the gap between me and the dragon, before shooting towards the ground and skimming just a few meters above it. I flew in and out of the tree line trying to slow the dragon down. I could hear the crashing of trees behind me but I gained very little advantage as he simply tore the trees roots from the ground as if they were mere weeds.

I could see the armies still battling ferociously before me. The Vikings gradually being forced back into the graveyard of ships at the rivers edge. It struck me as odd at the time that the Vikings horde did not appear to be as vast as we had first envisaged. Stories had talked of Viking hordes three or four thousand men strong, but this one was not much over one thousand, similar in size to the last time we clashed. They still vastly outnumbered our army but with our new tactical approach it looked now as if all may not have been lost. The thought was quickly pushed from my mind as the tree to the right of me burst into flames, the dragon gained on me still further. I could see my brothers just beyond the battlefield so I'd shot over the Viking horde, showering them with flames as I went. The dragon, seemingly unconcerned by their presence, also continued to discharge both flame and ice over vast quantities of both Vikings and the Kings men indiscriminately. Suddenly I flew over my brother's location, looking for any sign of what they were planning and then Walter, in human form, caught my eye.

Walter was stood just to the right in front of the tree line, holding what looked like the rolled up form of Fredrick's pangolin in his right hand. I had seen the pangolin do this before. It was a defence mechanism that allowed him to curl up into a perfectly spherical ball, leaving only the armoured outer shell visible and therefore shielding him from attack. A split second later a huge burst of ice froze the ground before them as the dragon approached. Brom, now in bear form, ran clear to where I could see others gathered just inside the tree line, waiting. What were they up to? I was so perplexed by this that I almost forgot about the huge dragon chasing me. I quickly turned a sharp left before circling back to see what was about to unfold. Suddenly, moments before the dragon passed them, Walter hurled the pangolin as hard as he could, straight at the left of the two central heads of the huge dragon. I couldn't believe what I was seeing; it was surely a death sentence for Frederick. He stood no chance against the dragon and if the dragon didn't kill him then surely the fall would. But what happened took my breath away. The dragon had also seen Frederick as he flew through the air and turned towards this strange little creature, tiny by comparison, as it headed directly for him. As I'd watched from a distance, holding my breath with anticipation, I could see that something was trailing behind the pangolin; a rope? Leif's rope that had been used to take down the first ships was now attached to the little pangolin as he flew through the air curled up into a tight ball. The dragon's central head snapped at the pangolin as he approached and for a split second I thought Frederick was done for… but then I saw the pangolin spiral down the dragon's neck. Frederick must have uncoiled mid flight, avoiding the dragons attack and scrambled onto the dragons head as he'd lunged for him. I could see confusion cross its stony face as he wondered where the little thing had gone. A second later Frederick changed, morphing back into his human form, then held on tightly as he'd proceeded to tie the rope firmly around one of the dragon's necks. Tilsted tried to shake him free but Fredrick did not wait around. No sooner was the rope attached he'd stood and run down the dragon's back and leapt into the air changing once again just in time for the huge buzzard of John to catch him in flight. I was astounded; I had never seen anything so brave. I could list a million things that could have gone wrong but yet they'd pulled it off. But what next? Monk? Trojan? Together they wouldn't be strong enough to bring the dragon down, let alone single handed. He would just rip them from the ground before undoubtedly killing them. They had clearly thought of this though as suddenly the rope went tight and I could see from my elevated position that the rope led through the trees and was tied to a large, ancient oak tree in the distance. The huge tree groaned but held firm as the dragon, caught off guard, was wrenched back by its tethered neck. The beast lost all momentum or ability to fly as its neck was dragged beneath him and his body flipped over in the air. The dragon's wings, now useless upside down, meant its huge body had only one direction to go. A second later the ground shook for miles around as the heavy weight of the dragon crashed down to Earth.

My brothers and I swarmed, not wanting to give the monster a moment to recover. Each man charged to the point at which the dragon landed, Broms huge bear ran in attacking the blue tinted head, his claws glinting in the evening sun. Walter, in human form, ran to join him landing a blow to the dragons jaw as hard as if a mountain had hit it. He laid punch after punch into its eye socket, giving it no time to regain its composure whilst Brom sunk his teeth into the dragon's throat waiting for the head to fall limp to the ground. The buffalo, bull and ox rammed into the dragon's side one by one, the sound of its ribs cracking rang out as they did so. Lief had joined the fray slamming a huge boulder against the rock dragon's skull, trying with all his might to cave the beasts head in. Simultaneously Barda had tried the same trick with the smoke dragon but to his surprise the rock passed straight through its misty profile burying itself deep in the ground below. Before Barda could act the dragon retaliated, its form solidifying as it sunk its teeth deep into Bardas leg. The gorilla yelled in pain before proceeding to hit the dragons head with his huge fists. This time they connected, once, twice but as he swung the third time the head turned back to smoke releasing Bardas leg and allowing him to stagger free. I swooped into action, landing and taking human form quickly, running forward to face the colossal dragon…

But I was too late.

Trojan had reached the fourth head before I'd been able to, charging bravely in to attack. The dragons head was thrashing out wildly, snapping at anything that moved. The erratic nature of the attack caught Trojan off guard. He knew his mistake the moment he made it. He had run straight into the beasts grasp. Our eyes met in that moment and we both knew what came next. I ran forward but my legs felt slow and heavy, exhausted from the chase. I tried with all my heart to reach him but the dragon was too fast and Trojan knew it. As I watched in horror the dragon's huge jaws closed in on Trojans equine form.

Time slowed.

The dragon's lips snarled, baring its razor sharp teeth. Trojans head turned towards the threat unable to do anything. The jaws reached him before I could. I could see every sinewy muscle in the dragons mouth as his jaw flexed wide. Every fowl bit of saliva as it dripped hungrily from his teeth. I remember it all so vividly, I was too late. All I could do was watch helplessly. I yelled once again for what good it would do, stumbling forwards before seeing something else that I will never forget. Terrowin's ram charged across my vision. I had not seen him since we'd arrived and thought he had run, choosing to leave rather than fight this impossible battle. But I had never been so wrong. Over the years I have often thought back to this moment with shame in my gut at how badly I had misjudged this brave little mans nature. The valiant ram hit Trojan in the side at full speed, knocking the horse clear of the jaws a split second before they snapped shut, sealing Terrowin's fate instead. Trojan got swiftly to his feet now back in human form and began to hit the dragons head with everything he could, but there was nothing he could do. I fell to the ground before them, despair hitting me hard at the sight of Terrowin's cloak, now dangling from the dragon's clenched teeth. The dragon appeared to grin, if that were even possible, as I knelt before him my body drained of all energy. Monk charged in from nowhere, smashing his huge armour plated beast into the side of the dragons head. The beast now down and broken from the onslaught could take no more and this final blow knocked the dragon into unconsciousness. I staggered up and watched the form of the dragon shrink back down to once again reveal the human form of Tilsted lying broken on the ground. I took a sword from Trojans hand as I approached. Standing over Tilsteds naked body I drove the sword deep into his torso, piercing his heart before forcing the sword through the back of his ribs with a sickening crack and driving it into the ground below him, skewering him to the floor.

As I stood again the air was eerily quiet, the realization dawned upon me that the fighting had all but stopped and silence had filled the air once again. Only this time it was not the silence of emptiness but the noise of many people not making a sound. As I turned to take in the people around me I saw that the Kings guard and the Abbott's men had overpowered the Vikings, the last few were surrounded their bodies beaten and now their spirit crushed at the sight of colossal form of their chieftain defeated. Both the few remaining Vikings and our own men simply stared at where I now stood over Tilsteds dead human body.
I seized the moment whilst I could, conjuring up every last bit of strength in my body before I spoke with as much authority as I could muster. Shouting was not required, my voice travelled easily across the silence that had fallen.

"Today you fought for your land, for your families, for your freedom and today you were victorious." I said as cheers rose up from the men that surrounded me. As I spoke again I directed my attention straight to the few remaining Vikings now under armed guard. "You few are free to go as long as you leave this land and never return. Tell your kinsmen of what you have seen here today and let it be a warning to any others that may decide to come." As if on queue the beasts that were surrounding me all roared in unison, driving the message home. The few remaining Vikings turned and fled, boarding the nearest sea worthy vessel. Others would no doubt try again under someone else's rule but for now we were victorious, we watched as they ran from the shores of the Thames leaving England under British rule once again.

Or so we thought.

56
1013
No Rest for the Wicked

We had watched on as the Vikings fled our shores. Again a suspicion that something was not right prodded the back of my mind but I pushed it away indifferently. Our own army had dispersed quickly after the battle, many of the men carrying out their fallen comrades with grim expression. They might have won the battle but it was at a great personal loss and as the adrenaline wore off they realised they had little to celebrate. The brothers of the curse gathered later that day with news and reports from the activities since.

Rowan, John and Hadrian had followed the Vikings retreat and ensured that they had in fact left. Tybalt, Ulric and Forthwind had seen to the Kings men, burying the dead within the earth that they had fallen before preparing to lead the remaining soldiers back to Corfe Castle to face the wrath of the King. Tybalt would see that the men faced no punishment themselves but his own fate was in the hands of the King now. I'd thanked the three of them for all that they had done, I was forever indebted to them for their bravery and would not forget the fact.

Barda had patched up his leg before he and Lief had joined Frederick and Walter. They set out to capture or kill the demons that Tilsted had created, those men of the curse that had been pushed beyond the realms of sanity and set free during the battle by Tilsted himself. As fighters they had been extremely effective but they were so crazed within their own mind they were unable to determine a side and simply tore through whoever was before them. Many had died in battle but many had also escaped, fleeing once out of their cages and never looking back. Barda, Lief, Frederick and Walter set out that same day to follow their tracks, promising to hunt each one down and put an end to the cruelty that is their life. A friendship had formed among these four, a bond as strong as blood, a bond of brother hood and I knew that I would see them again. I too would continue to hunt the men of the curse; I would not stand by and let them run loose across our great land.

Those of us that remained buried Terrowin, a brave man that gave his life to save Trojans, before we too set off. We headed back to St Michaels to report to the Abbot the events of the day before we would rest and see what the future held next. We would continue to defend our land from any and all invading forces that might try to take it from us and as none of us had homes to return to so we had formed a sort of family together, outcasts as we were.

Two weeks later we passed by Corfe Castle on our return to St Michaels a day or so behind Tybalt and his men. I left our band behind to go alone to the Castle to find out for myself the consequence of Tybalt's treason but I had not expected what I found when I arrived. The people of Corfe were no longer in residence, the village burned to the ground. Many of the villagers had fled to the woods where they now hid, living on their wits. I had been told how two weeks previous, on the day that we had faced the Vikings in London, Sweyn the Formidable had arrived with a second, considerably larger, horde of Vikings. They had travelled around the channel and had taken Corfe Castle from under our noses, the Kings army greatly depleted to fund our cause had left the Castle all but defenceless and it had been an easy victory for the Vikings. The King had been exiled to France and Sweyn now resided upon the throne. My heart sunk with the realisation that we had been outsmarted, out fought and that our efforts had all been in vain. Sweyn had won out in the end regardless. Suddenly it became clear why the Vikings numbers had been smaller than we'd envisaged, they were just a decoy. While we fought them their greater force took the Kings Castle from under our nose in its greatly weakened state. The country was now under the rule of the Vikings and the King's army had fled, Tybalt Ulric and Forthwind among them.

With a dizzying head I returned to the awaiting men with which I travelled, taking with me the grave news from Corfe. Our victory had been ripped from beneath our feet, the country torn from our grasp and our sacrifice meaningless.

57
2010
Eadric

The first thing I saw was the sinister night sky above me shrouded by dark clouds that seemed to swirl menacingly over head. I tried to move my arm but it was non responsive, my fingers not answering either, no matter how hard I willed them. My other arm felt numb but the fingers moved upon request but my spine hurt badly and I wondered at first if it was broken. London was deserted now bar the sound of tanks rumbling by. It sounded as if the army was retreating as the rumbling slowly faded into the distance. I heard no further gunfire around me so I can only assume that James has gone and that my opportunity to stop him is lost. I had rarely before fought a creature that was impervious to flames. He was my toughest challenge yet and as with so many before him the prospect of what I had to do weighed heavily upon my mind. For now though I would need to mend. I had never before been beaten in my beasts form and now I see that I do not recover as I did in my human form. My phoenix would usually return my human form unscathed, returning it to the place at which it had frozen in time so many years before. But this time it brought the injuries sustained as a phoenix with it. My body screamed in pain as I mentally checked each limb, determining what was and wasn't broken. I had searched for many years for the secrets to unlocking my eternal life, could I finally have found it? Would dying in my beasts form mean I never returned? I would think about this, for finally I could see the light, a glimmer of hope that I might once again see the family that I still yearned for after all these years. My wife with whom I had born a son, both of which were brutally taken from me. The hope that I would see them again at last filled my heart with joy but first I had to stop what I had started. I should have finished James the day of his eighteenth birthday. I had known of his legacy, his violent family history and that the curse that ran in his veins was darker than most. A certain style of violence flowed in his family's blood that corrupted the beasts and now it was clear to me that control was not an option. I had known this all along but I had hoped he was different, prayed that he would not follow the footsteps of his descendants before him, but I was wrong. I will finish it now once and for all for James is the last in his line, no longer will the dragon's blood haunt this world, I would see to it. And then I would see my family again. The face of my son filled my mind as I fell back into unconsciousness lying broken on this non-descript London back street. I dreamt of seeing my family again.

58
1030
Descendants

Many years later I had stood with Tybalt and the Abbot within St Michaels. Tybalt had visited me to bring news that would prove to be of great interest but would also prove equally devastating. It had seemed that they had travelled the country living off the land and staying hidden from the Viking reign before returning to Corfe Castle many years later. The news of which he had brought me today was of the child that Ulric had rescued so many years earlier. It appears that the son of Sadon had travelled with them, learning as they went and he had proved to be a great fighter, growing into a strong young man. He had known of the beasts and of his father's fate as Ulric had been honest with the boy as he grew. It was on his eighteenth birthday however that the curse had hit him too.

Sadons son, now also known as Sadon, having taken his fathers name, was the first son of a cursed man to reach adulthood. We had not known or even suspected that the curse was hereditary at this point so this was grave news. I had thought that the curse would die out within our lifetime; that the death of us would mean the end of the nightmare. This was the first day that I had discovered that our journey was only the beginning, that the curse would haunt our families too. This was not news that would be welcomed by the others. Many I know had children of their own by that point that would, it seemed, share their father's fate. Who knew how many of the others had had children already, the Viking men that had turned? The enormity of the task ahead hit me, the weight of the world resting upon me and I knew what I had to do.

I would find the others, each and every one. I would help those that could be helped and kill those that couldn't. I would follow the lives of every descendent and ensure that the curse dies out with them. We could not spread this disease any further than it had already gone.

The bloodline of the cursed men must be stopped. I would see that it is so.

Character List

11th Century		21st Century	
Alric	Chicken	Eadric	Phoenix
Ulric	Buffalo	James	Dragon
Tybalt	Bull	Ben	Bear
Forthwind	Oxen	Ellie	Eagle
Sadon	Lynx	Brad	Shark
Terrowin	Ram	Aaron	Rhinoceros
Eadric	Phoenix		
Brom	Bear		
Rowan	Hawk		
Borin	Panther		
Althalos	Black Wasp		
Hadrian	Kite		
John	Buzzard		
Henry	Wolf		
Frederick	Pangolin		
Walter	Walrus		
Leofrick/Trojan	Horse		
Lief	Gorilla		
Barda	Gorilla		
Thomas	Elephant		
Sadon II	?		
Fendrel/Terrier	Lion		
Tilsted	Hydra		

www.eadric.co.uk